Bestest.
Ramadan.
Ever.

Medeia Sharif

Bestest.
Ramadan.
Ever.

flux ™
Woodbury, Minnesota

First Edition
First Printing, 2011

Book design by Steffani Sawyer
Cover design by Adrienne Zimiga
Cover images © 2011
        girl: iStockphoto.com/Ashwin Kharidehal Abhirama
        boy: Imagerymajestic/Alamy
        keys: iStockphoto.com/Uyen Le
        cupcake: iStockphoto.com/Ruth Black
        swirls: iStockphoto.com/Jamie Farrant

Flux, an imprint of Llewellyn Worldwide Ltd.

Library of Congress Cataloging-in-Publication Data
Sharif, Medeia.
  Bestest Ramadan ever / Medeia Sharif.—1st ed.
    p. cm.
  Summary: Not allowed to eat from sunrise to sunset during Ramadan and forbidden to date, fifteen-year-old Almira finds that temptation comes in many forms during the Muslim holy month, as she longs to feel like a typical American girl.
  ISBN 978-0-7387-2323-5
  [1. Ramadan—Fiction. 2. Muslims—Fiction. 3. Middle Eastern Americans—Fiction. 4. Self-perception—Fiction. 5. Dating (Social customs)—Fiction.] I. Title.
  PZ7.S52975Be 2011
  [Fic]—dc22
                           2011004256

Flux
Llewellyn Worldwide Ltd.
2143 Wooddale Drive
Woodbury, MN 55125-2989
www.fluxnow.com

Printed in the United States of America

Acknowledgments

Bestest. Ramadan. Ever. wouldn't have been published without the support of many people ...

My agent Marlene Stringer took a chance on me. There aren't enough words to thank her for what she's done to launch my writing career.

I had the pleasure of working with acquisitions editor Brian Farrey and production editor Sandy Sullivan—their keen editorial eye not only made this book blossom, but I've grown as a writer under their care. Publicists Marissa Pederson and Steven Pomije also reached out to me, making this debut author feel at home. I'm fortunate to have the Flux team by my side.

The SCBWI Aventura Group has done wonders for my writing. They welcomed me with open arms and large doses of encouragement. Thank you Dr. Stacy B. Davids, Angela Padron, Ellen Slane, Jennifer Hill, Marjetta Geerling, Norma Davids, Pascale Mackey, Steven dos Santos, and Ty Shiver.

1

Mom has said that I could lose a few. I've never thought it was possible. My first diet was five years ago, when I was ten. I daintily ate crackers and cheese with a glass of juice for every meal, so proud of myself that I ate so little by the end of each day. Then it became too hard and I ate like a pig again. I tried to cut out carbs last year, but rice and bread were too yummy to give up. I don't want to eat a burger without a sesame-seed bun. No way. And life without pizza. Is that even possible? Might as well ask me to cut off a limb.

I don't like what I see in the mirror. My hair is frizzy from the Florida heat. My shirt is baggy to hide my potbelly, which grows after large meals. I was minding my own business at the mall one day, waiting in a long line to buy some jeans, and an older woman asked me if I was pregnant. Gasp. At fifteen? And do I really look that fat and bloated? On a bad day, on a high-carb day, maybe I do look like I'm carrying a bun or two in the oven. I'm not overweight, just at the high end of normal on the height/weight chart. Sometimes I console myself that it's called big-boned, not fat.

I'm starving, but I can't eat lunch since it's the first day of Ramadan. Ramadan is the month God revealed the Koran to Muhammad, so we purify ourselves physically and spiritually by fasting. My family is halfway religious—we do most things, not everything, Islamic. Let's just say holiness has tapered off through the generations. My grandparents follow Islam to the tee, my parents are pretty religious (they pray frequently, but not every day), and I'm sort of religious. I pray once in a while, and I've been to a mosque only twice in my life, but I still feel I should do this. I don't want to be the only one in my family not fasting, which was the case in previous Ramadans.

I'm fifteen years old and I vow that this will be my first successful month of fasting. No cheating. No Oreo cookies eaten in my bedroom away from prying eyes. No sipping water from the water fountains at school. No snacks when my friends offer me any. I shalt not eat or drink from sunrise to sunset. Day = no food. Night = all you can eat.

Last year I tried to fast, but it didn't last. On the first

day, I cheated. I remember that day; it was a Saturday and my grandparents were visiting. I went to my room, had a few chocolate wafers, and came back to the living room. Grandpa was watching *Dr. 90210* with the rest of my family, and he looked up at me. "Almira, are those crumbs around your mouth?" he asked. The shame rained down hard on me. Grandpa shook his head and lectured me on the importance of religion.

My parents looked upset, but then they told me it was all right and I could try the next day, but I didn't. It's taken me a year to get the gumption to tackle Ramadan again. Can I last a whole month without eating during sunlight hours? That task is my own personal Mount Everest.

"Almira, come here this minute!" my mom yells from the living room.

I push my glasses up my nose and rush to my mom, who is less than genial when she is fasting. Fasting makes her kind of mean. My stomach growls with hunger, so I know why Mom is such a monster during Ramadan— hunger makes me nervous and testy as well. I frown and stomp toward her voice. I listen to her tell me how slovenly I am because I left my wet umbrella on top of a pair of suede shoes, her shoes to be exact. I look at the high-heeled pumps and see that they're mottled and funky looking. Yup, I did a boo-boo. She looks so mad that I want to tell her to eat a cookie to calm down, because cookies have always soothed me. But there can be no cookie breaks on account of the fasting. Peanut butter cookies and macadamia nut cookies swim in my head as Mom lectures me on how suede and water don't go together. Duh, I already know that. Now eat a cookie.

• • •

When I hear a crash outside, I know that my grandfather is here. He always hits something in or around our driveway when he comes to visit us. I'm waiting for the day when he'll crash through the picture window of our living room, but so far he only targets garbage cans, mailboxes, and pillars.

I rush outside past my grandfather's tanklike car. Old people are attracted to planet-sized cars because they seem so safe. Dad may get flattened in his sports car, but Grandpa will survive any driving mishap. Grandpa knocked down the garbage can, so I straighten it out. At least it's empty since the sanitation truck had visited this morning.

"*Marhaba!*" Grandpa hollers.

"Hi," I say. I don't speak a word of Arabic, even though Grandpa tries to teach me simple phrases. I'm bad at foreign languages, but I speak *un poco español*.

"*Azizi*, let me look at you," Grandpa says as he exits his car. He's short and skinny with white hair and a white bushy beard. When I was little I used to call him "Santa," but he told me to stop calling him that since Santa is an infidel. An infidel is someone who doesn't believe in God, or anyone who's not Muslim. Grandpa calls anyone he doesn't like an infidel.

My grandmother emerges from the other side of the

car wearing a huge dress that swallows her and a scarf wrapped around her head. She started wearing a scarf a year ago. According to her, she's getting old, nearing death (she's only fifty-nine), and aims to go to heaven. So basically she's telling God, "Love me because I'm covering my head in one-hundred-degree weather." Prior to her religious fervor, she looked like a typical Miami mama in makeup and high heels.

"I can't believe you drive like that," Grandma says.

"Then you drive, if you don't like my driving!" Grandpa thunders.

"You know I can't drive," Grandma says.

"Feh!"

Older-generation Muslim women don't seem to know how to drive, Grandma included. I'm so happy that Mom knows how to drive, as if it's something, a badge of honor. Women in Saudi Arabia aren't allowed to drive. That sucks. I'm glad that I don't live there.

"I'm just saying watch where you're going!" Grandma bellows as she walks toward our front door.

"Do I ever get into any accidents?" Grandpa says, facing her head-on as if he's about to charge at her.

Mom winces whenever Grandpa yells, which is all the time. Mom and Grandpa have this uncomfortable in-lawship, with either silence or hints of an argument bubbling between them. I look at Mom and her shoulders are hunched over the stove. She shoots an askance look of annoyance toward us.

"Eh." Grandma waves her hand in the air dismissively and then turns her attention to me. "Almira, you've lost weight."

I give her an embarrassed smile as she rakes her eyes up and down my body. I hate being reminded that I'm hefty. I've fasted for four days straight and feel lighter. Indeed, I lost two pounds. It's probably just water weight rather than fat, but it's something.

Mom continues to cook. The smell of shish kebabs makes me salivate. I haven't eaten in ten-and-a-half hours. That is, like, forever. The sun rose at about seven this morning. At least it's November and the days are short.

On the news, a mug shot of some guy accused of money laundering flashes on the screen. "Infidel!" Grandpa screeches.

"Calm down!" Grandma tells him.

"Don't tell me to calm down. This is a sick world and it breaks my heart."

Grandpa's a bit of a drama king. He winces, puts one hand on his chest, and flings an arm in the air as he watches television. Yes, okay, I get it; his heart bleeds for the sins of this world. With his accent—Asiatic, but less choppy than an Indian one—he is one eccentric grandpapa.

A sigh issues from Grandma's lips and she adjusts her scarf. Mom raises an eyebrow and asks, "Will you be dining with us tomorrow, too?"

"No, Asma!" Grandpa says. "I have plans."

"Great."

"We're going to go out with friends, but my son did say he wanted to break fast as a family."

"Well, it's hard to please everyone, but I'm sure your friends will appreciate your company," Mom says. She talks in a stilted, non-Mom way when she's around Grandpa. She also looks relieved that she won't have to entertain the in-laws tomorrow. I sit with them, wriggling in an armchair, wondering when the tension in the air will dissipate.

Dad comes in. He's a dentist with his own practice. He totally looks like a cosmetic dentist. He has jet-black hair that is moussed into inertia (it won't budge) and teeth as white as chalk. All day long he bleaches teeth, slaps on veneers, and makes smiles look pretty. I refrain from smiling at him. I smiled this morning and he asked me if I'd flossed. It's hard to live with someone who inspects my teeth on a daily basis.

All of us migrate to the dining table, which faces the golf course behind our house. Dad stares at the setting sun. I stare. Grandma and Grandpa glare at the sun. Die, sun. Die.

"You've lost weight," Dad says.

I feel myself blushing.

"Keep it up," Dad says, flashing me his million-dollar smile. Has anyone spent a million dollars on a smile? I'm sure some of his patients did. Dad has shown me some before-and-after pictures, and some of his patients had truly heinous teeth. Overbites the size of canyons. Chipped teeth that looked like old china cups. Teeth as yellow as butter, which makes me momentarily turn my stomach against butter, which would taste great on a baguette right now.

"You look great," Grandma says.

I flare my nostrils in anger. *You were a fat cow and now you're less of a fat cow.* That's the way I interpret these compliments.

Grandpa pinches my arm—cowlike, I'm being manhandled as if I'm livestock—and grunts in approval. "Did you have any snacks today?" he asks.

Why do some people have to remind others of their faults and weaknesses? It seems so overly critical. It's a new Ramadan but Grandpa is trying to rehash the last ... chocolate wafer crumbs stuck on my Bonne Bell lip balm. "No, I haven't cheated," I say in an even voice.

"All right, all right."

Setting the awkwardness aside, I close my eyes and inhale the food. Mom sets a large tray of meat and vegetables in the middle of the table. The juice from the beef runs in rivulets around the cherry tomatoes. The red peppers are slightly black around the edges.

The sky is a rainbow of red, orange, and purple where the sun is a mere sliver on the horizon.

Next, Mom puts a plate of pita bread next to the shish kebabs. They're imperfectly round, white, and tan. They sure look like they can soak up the broth running out of the beef.

The sun is no longer visible, but the pretty rainbow colors of refracting light are still there.

Mom fills our glasses with icy water. I haven't had anything to drink since before sunrise.

Dad puckers his lips as if he's kissing the air. Grandpa twitches his mouth like a squirrel eating an invisible nut.

I'm going to faint if I don't get a bite of this delicious food soon.

The pretty colors are gone. The sun vanishes. The sky is dark. What happens next is not a sight I'm proud of.

We all simultaneously lunge for the food. My shish kebab stick gets stuck on top of Dad's and we each yank hard to disengage them. We don't speak to each other as we operate on pure animal instinct. The bread disappears quickly. I take a slice of bread and fill it with beef, peppers, and cherry tomatoes. I bite into the sandwich, barely chewing, transforming into an eating machine. I gulp the chunky meat as if I'm a wild animal chewing on raw deer in the Serengeti. We all belong on National Geographic.

I drink my water in one gulp and Grandpa reaches for the pitcher before I can. No one offers to refill my glass. We all work independently. This is how we break fast in the Abdul household. I burp loudly and don't bother apologizing.

2

My mom is hot, which is hard because I'm not. I'm average, whereas my mom looks like some toned superbabe that men stare at with lust and women with jealousy. At home she always wears exercise clothes, like tank tops, shorts, and leotards. And when she goes out, she dresses to the nines, with strappy sandals and designer clothes. Too ridiculously hot. This situation reminds me of the music video for "Stacy's Mom," except my mom doesn't dance on stripper poles, not as far as I know. And she can't steal my boyfriend's attention because I don't have a boyfriend. And if I did have a boyfriend, I hope he wouldn't lay eyes on her because then he might fall in love with her.

Before I leave for school, Mom is doing yoga from one of her many exercise DVDs. Her skin is golden, her black hair is in a ponytail, and she wears a leotard. She doesn't have any cellulite and her stomach is concave. How annoying. I pinch my belly and the fat rolls on my hips. I look like a hippo compared to her. For years Mom asked me to exercise with her, but I kept resisting and she stopped asking. Her hotness will not be passed on to the next generation.

I eat breakfast, leftovers from last night, as I look at the dark sky through the kitchen window. The same thought comes to my head every morning that I'm fasting: why am I fasting? I look at a tapestry on the wall that has Arabic calligraphy on it, probably something saying how *Allah* is great—*Allahu Akbar*—and other stuff like that. I start to think about my afterlife and if all the righteous stuff I do will get me into heaven. Grandpa always tells me that there's an angel on my right shoulder writing down everything good I do and one on my left shoulder taking notes of all the bad things. Sometimes I feel that I'm doing bad things by writing love letters to Robert Pattinson (which I never send out) and daydreaming of having a boyfriend in the near future.

I chew absentmindedly as I think about all of this heavy metaphysical stuff. Mom is standing on her head, and she peers at me while I eat like a maniac. Perish the thought that I'm still chewing once the sun tickles the horizon.

"Don't eat everything in the Tupperware," she advises. "I want some, too. Show some consideration."

I look at her upside-down face. Her thin legs are pointed toward the ceiling. I wonder how she does that, but she's a limber skinny minnie. Whenever I stand on my head, my skull hurts and my legs wobble.

"Yes, Mother," I say, putting the lid over the Tupperware, leaving some shish kebab for her.

"You look really good today."

I smile. I don't get many compliments from her. The fasting makes me feel leaner, and my size-eight jeans are loose on me. Yay for weight loss.

As I wait for Mom to get the car out of the garage to drive me to school, I see the dreadful sun rise. Now I can't eat the Tootsie Rolls I keep in my bookbag for light snacking. Never before have I felt such animosity toward the sun, giver of heat, keeper of life. But I'm determined to fast and prove my religiosity.

While we drive, I look at all the kids walking to school with their bookbags and trendy clothes. I'm the only Muslim in my school. It's weird, but at the same time cool. Since we live in the middle of Miami-Dade, most of my classmates are Hispanic. I blend in, with my dark hair and brown eyes, but at the same time I'm different. Dad is Syrian and Mom is Iranian. Grandpa once told me that he forgave my mother for being Iranian, as if it's a sin not to be Syrian. I was like, okay Grandpa, forgive someone for something they can't control! My mom didn't choose her nationality. But I didn't really say all of that to him, since he scares me.

I meet with my bestest friend Lisa Gomez in front of school. We've known each other since kindergarten. We're exact opposites. I'm brainy and love to read, while she's in love with celebrities and only reads magazines. She's tall and skinny, while I'm short (five foot three) and on the heavy side. We have the same round brown eyes and curly hair, though, and sometimes our friends joke that we're sisters.

There's twenty minutes left until the bell rings, so we hang out on a bench by the school entrance watching buses and parents drop off students. Lisa has some squiggly black marks on her upper arm that she made with a Bic pen. She's totally obsessed with Angelina Jolie and literally wants to be her.

She catches me looking at her messy tribal armband, which must have gotten smeared when she dressed this morning. "I can't wait until I turn eighteen," she says. "I'll be in a tattoo parlor on that birthday."

I sigh, because I've heard all of this before. "You shouldn't get a tattoo because you might regret it," I say. "Can you imagine being an old lady with tattoos all over your wrinkled skin?"

"There's always laser surgery. Aren't you getting any tattoos?"

"No. Mom said it's against our religion."

"Oh, that's terrible," Lisa says with genuine sadness in her voice. She pulls a magazine out of her bookbag and shows me the cover story about Angelina's latest adoption.

"She's going to run her own school the way she's going," I say.

Lisa brushes her curls out of her face. "I'm sure this will be her last kid."

"Uh-huh."

"Ohmigosh, look at him."

"Who?" I say.

This awesome guy with deep-set eyes, brown hair falling around his face, and broad shoulders walks past us. It's Peter Hurley from our biology class. Lisa's been drooling over him recently and I think he's cute, too. He's quiet and keeps to himself. He isn't loud and obnoxious like the popular boys.

"He's like Brad Pitt," Lisa dreamily says.

I don't see the resemblance, but Lisa likes to humor herself by comparing everyone to a celebrity. I look like Penelope Cruz, with an added twenty pounds and glasses, and Lisa is Jennifer Lopez (during her Selena days, not when she became blond and bronzed after becoming superfamous).

"He's hot," I say.

"Yeah."

"Let's sit next to him in lab today."

"That's a good idea, Almira."

The bell rings and we get up to go inside. As we walk, I lick my finger and use it to swipe at the Bic tattoo below Lisa's sleeve. I rub a good chunk off.

"Almira!" she screeches.

I step away from her to get to my locker, which happens to be next to Peter's, and I get a good look at his Greek god profile—he resembles the gorgeous statues from the world civ textbook that I've taken a liking to, even though it's sort of sick to lust over a hunk of carved marble.

• • •

Mr. Gregory is my biology teacher. He used to be a Hollywood actor but somehow ended up teaching science at Coral Gables Preparatory. He's hot, for an older guy. Lately I'm thinking that most guys are hot. It must be my hormones. I imagine all these wriggling bubbles of hormones flowing through my blood, swooshing through my body in swift rage. They're microscopic, but they pack a punch.

While watching *Twilight*, I saw Mr. Gregory in a cafeteria scene. He was an extra in that film, and he's young enough to pull off being a high school student, but he denied it when many of us saw the movie last week on cable. So my teacher is sort of famous and had the honor of working with Robert Pattinson, who's immensely talented and extremely hot.

Mr. Gregory flashes a smile my way. He has brown hair combed back with gel and a fit body under his suit.

But his canines are yellowish. The birth of a coffee stain, as my dad would say.

We have to do a lab exercise. Eww, dissecting a frog. Lisa gives me a meaningful look and then darts her eyes toward Peter, who is seated a few feet from me. We planned on doing lab with him, so I go in for the ambush.

"Hi, Peter," I say, sidling up to him.

"Uh, err, hi," he says, looking confused.

"You want to be my lab partner?"

"Yeah, okay." He's awkward for someone who's good-looking, but he seems like a loner. I know he's on the chess club, so he's an intellectual. He also carries a sketch-pad around for art class, and I hear that he's really good at drawing. I also know his hotness grows incrementally by five percent a month, because last year he was slightly heavier and had more pimples, and when he returned to school this August, he had clear skin and a defined waist-line. Some people are like that: they're okay looking, and all of a sudden you notice they're hot. I wonder when I'm going to blossom, if I ever am destined to. Soon, I hope.

"Hi, Peter, can I join you?" Lisa says.

"Uh, yeah, okay."

Peter isn't much of a talker, but that's fine. I'm sat-isfied by looking at his wavy brown hair and jade green eyes. Sometimes someone doesn't have to talk, because it's enough to just admire the person. When I go to bed at night I leave the television on mute, like an animated night-light, and it's great looking at Eric Bana or Jake

Gyllenhaal while I doze off. There's no need for them to speak. Look handsome for me. Thanks.

Lab groups consist of two or three people, so this is our trio. Lisa glows and squeezes my arm. Then we both watch with horror as Peter leaves our station and returns with a metal tray that has a brownish blob on it.

I hold my hand to my mouth and Lisa looks pale. Peter hands us latex gloves and when his hand touches mine, I feel nothing. This romantic moment of skin colliding is ruined by the dead frog in front of us. I think of my Kermit stuffed animal that's propped up against the lamp on my nightstand. Dead Kermie.

Peter wields a scalpel and follows the directions in our lab guide. When Mr. Gregory walks by, he admonishes Lisa and me on our lack of participation. "Ladies, you need to give a helping hand."

I gingerly pull at one of the frog's legs as Peter cuts into the abdomen. I'm touching the leg of a dead frog. Eww. I really want to vomit. The formaldehyde stench gets to me and the sight of torn froggy corpses doesn't help my nausea either. Lisa doesn't look as bothered. She's participating the easy way by playing nurse and handing Peter a pair of surgical scissors. She leans in, pretending to be interested in the frog, but really she's staring at Peter's profile. She gets so close to him that she places her cheek on his shoulder.

Is it normal to hate my best friend? Yes, because this is the first time that either one of us is dealing with Peter and she's throwing herself at him. Plus, she showed interest in him first and now I want his attention, too.

"Do you need help?" I ask.

"I'm okay," he says.

A quiet, dignified boy. How regal. I sigh. I wonder what it'll be like to have a boyfriend. Dad and Grandpa both say I'm not allowed to date. They tell me over and over again that if I ever want to be with somebody, they'll find a husband for me. Grandpa once mentioned that he knew many boys my age or a little older who would be perfect for me, but his style is old-fashioned. Arranged marriages are so last century.

Peter discards the frog. Poor frog. He died for our lab and he's crudely thrown in the garbage. At least I'm no longer gagging, on the verge of throwing up, at the sight of the carcass. We have to do the questions at the end of the lab and Lisa continues to hover over Peter. They're head to head, laughing at something, but I can't hear their conversation. Students are clanging their metal trays and scalpels, talking amongst each other. I feel left out. When I scoot my stool closer to Peter, I hear him talk about intestines. Lisa smiles at him as if she's listening to a comic act.

"It's like our intestines are the same as a frog's," Peter says. "Did you see how the frog's intestines were all curled up like ours?"

"We have nothing in common with frogs," Lisa says, giggling.

"Of course we do. We have similar anatomy."

"No, we don't."

Lisa can be really stupid. The whole point of biology is to learn that we're related to animals and have the foundation of the cell. It's about evolution stuff and how we all came from the sea. So my best friend is a man stealer *and* a dummy.

I can smell his balsam shampoo—he even smells good. I want him to turn his head to look at me, but he's still leaning toward Lisa.

"So, like, how did they kill that frog?" Lisa asks.

"Probably drowned him," Peter says, shrugging his shoulders.

I emit a loud, hysterical laugh, forcing the humor out of me. *Notice me, Peter.* Peter raises his eyebrows. I can be such a dope. Why do I have to act like an idiot in front of him? Now he must think I'm a nutcase with a horrible, unsexy, high-pitched laugh. I touch my hair and it's frizzy since it's a muggy day. My face is oily because I didn't have time to blot it before getting to class. How am I ever going to get a boyfriend when I'm such a mess?

"Ohhhhhhhh!" Lisa says. "I get it, like, frogs are manphibians."

"Amphibians," I correct her.

"Ohhhhhhhhh!"

"So you can't drown them," I say.

"It was a joke," Peter says.

"Ohhhh," Lisa says. "So they strangle them instead?"

"Why don't we stop by the library later to find out," Peter says.

Now they have a library date? This is the first time Lisa has talked to Peter and now he's all over her, educating her about frogs and offering to show her our library's reference website. I laugh again and neither one of them turns to look at me. I have to try harder to get him to notice me, even if that means pissing Lisa off.

• • •

Mom picks Lisa and me up from school. Sometimes I walk, but if Mom's available she drives by. It's nice to have a ride, especially on rainy or sweltering days, but things can get uncomfortable. Boys stare at her. Mom's gorgeous with her hair down and full makeup; sometimes her tanned shoulders are left bare by a tank top. And the boys look and look. It's a hard blow on my self-esteem that my mom gets more attention than me.

Lisa and I get in the back seat of her blue Mercedes. Mom has the radio tuned to the '80s pop station and she's singing to Madonna's "Dress You Up." She's crooning with her eyes closed.

Traffic after school is terrible, with the seniors driving out of the student parking lot from one side, teachers leaving from an adjacent lot, and buses coming from the other direction. We're at a standstill behind dozens of automobiles. Some football players stand to the side of the parking lot. One of them, a husky giant, catches sight of my mom and blows a kiss her way, which she doesn't notice since her eyes are still shut.

"Mother," I whisper.

"Hmmm," she says.

"Mother!"

"I love vintage Madonna."

"Mom!"

She hears the urgency in my voice above the radio's volume. She stops, knowing I'm embarrassed. She just gave a juicy show to the jocks and they all saw me—now they know Almira's mom is an *American Idol* wannabe who sings off-key. At least she isn't singing to "Like a Virgin."

Mom shimmies her shoulders to some Aerosmith tune. "Your mom's so cool," Lisa says to me.

Then you can go ahead and have her, I feel like saying. Lisa has a normal mom. Her mom has short hair and glasses and practices podiatry. She barely says a word to me whenever I visit, so there's no room for embarrassment with Lisa, unless it's embarrassing to have a mom who cures feet all day. Feet are gross, unless they're fresh from a pedicure, and I can't imagine touching them for a living.

We drive by Peter, who happens to be walking home. He looks up when he sees our car. His eyes become glued on my mom.

"Do you see how he's looking at me?" Lisa asks.

Um, no, he's like totally checking out my mom! A burst of rage explodes inside of me. I want Peter to notice me like that! I look at Mom, whose eyes are on the road. She doesn't even notice Peter's attention. That's completely ungrateful of her. If he ever looks at me like that, I'll feel like I've died and gone to heaven.

Peter crosses the street, his head turning as he walks so that he can continue to look at Mom. He's going to morph into the girl in *The Exorcist*, but he can't swivel his head in a three-hundred-and-sixty-degree angle, so he turns away. I don't feel relieved, because now I know I'm the only female in the world he won't pay any attention to. He admires Lisa, the other girls at school, and now my mom. Everyone but me will be graced by his attention. I close my eyes and silently pray that he was looking at me instead. I'm right behind Mom in the back seat. But it really did seem like he was focusing on her. Why would he look at me like that?

Lisa's house is at the beginning of our block and Mom drops her off. Then we make it to our house. It isn't until I'm inside the kitchen that I realize how empty my stomach is. During lunch I had studied in the library, away from the temptations in the cafeteria. I watch Mom prepare chicken for sundown. But I'm really not that hungry to begin with. I'm too flustered about Peter, and trying to hatch a plan to get him to notice me.

3

Sifting through my folder tonight, I see that Parent Night is coming soon. Traditionally, students go to Parent Night all dressed up and afterwards they find a hangout. Last year it was so fun. I got a manicure, had my hair straightened, and wore a little red dress. While my parents did the boring task of talking to my teachers, I gossiped and texted. When the conferences were over, my friends and I went to a Chinese buffet, which cut into my curfew, but Dad kindly didn't rip into me when I came home at midnight.

I give the flyer to my parents, hoping that they'll go again this year even though they embarrass me. I'm at the age when everything they say or do irks me. Dad clipped his nails in the bathroom this morning and I could hear the snip-snip of shorn fingernails through the door. How uncouth. And a week ago, the living room curtains were wide open and some boy from school stood on the sidewalk watching my mom do contortions to an exercise video. They don't see that their behavior is uncool.

Sometimes I feel that I don't fit in. Years ago, during a sleepover at a friend's house, some girl I barely knew asked questions about my ethnicity. I was wearing pink nail polish and she asked me, "Your parents allow you to wear nail polish?" As if Muslim girls can't wear something harmless like nail polish. Those ignorant comments only come once in a while, because my real friends know that I do fit in. People who know very little about me think my mom will come to school wearing a veil or sari, and they're wowed by how hot she is (the only time her hotness makes me look good). Or they think Dad will have a long terrorist beard and bland clothes, but he always comes to school in a suit, looking all suave and charming. I don't mind if my classmates see my parents, but it's best that they don't. Like most people my age, I pretend that my home life and my school life are on different planes of existence.

"Dad, are you going to Parent Night?" I ask during our nightly snack. It's late, and we eat as much as possible during the night hours.

He neatly rips the meat off a chicken bone with his precise teeth. As a dentist, he sees his teeth as fine instruments, like meat cleavers to a butcher or cuticle scissors for a manicurist. "Yes," he says.

Mom walks in, wearing her usual tank top and shorts—which she wears all day long, unlike normal moms who wear sweatsuits, housedresses, and robes. She perks up her ears when she hears my question. "Of course we're going, Almira," she says.

"Woo hoo! Can you just drop me off, though? I get good grades. You don't need to stick with me or talk to all my teachers. I just want to go to dinner with my friends after the meetings."

"We want to see all your teachers."

"Their pictures are on the school website!"

"Stop whining, Almira," Dad says.

I pout, feeling put out, as if my emotions don't matter. I guess I'll just suffer through things the way I normally do.

"My father called today," Dad says.

"Yeah," I mumble through a mouthful of chicken.

"He's going to give you driving lessons starting this weekend."

My jaw would be dropping, but I'm still chewing. A few months ago I had an argument with my parents about how I'd be sixteen soon and that I wanted my driver's license. They had taken me seriously, so Dad gave me some lessons. Driving is terrifying. And now with Grandpa as a teacher! In his tanklike car. Will I live to experience my sixteenth birthday?

"Isn't it best that you continue to teach her?" Mom says.

Thank you, Mom, I think. *You overexercise and sing in a crummy voice, but thank you for defending me.*

"My father insists," Dad says. "Almira has had a learner's permit for nearly a year, and I don't have time to finish teaching her."

"Dad, with six lessons already, I know how to drive," I say. "But I'm out of practice."

"I don't have time to give you more lessons," Dad says.

"He's a really bad driver," Mom says.

"He's just old, that's all. His faculties are with him."

"What faculties are those?" Mom asks.

Dad presses his lips together, and I don't want to be around during one of their fights. I hope to never have in-laws. I want a drop-dead-gorgeous husband who's extremely wealthy and has parents who live across the world in some exotic country. I'd only have to see my in-laws during holidays, and maybe not even then because they'd live in the middle of a jungle and I could always use the excuse that I didn't get immunized for my trip or that the water makes me sick. But then they could visit me. I'll worry about that when I get older, but in the present I know that Mom and Grandpa don't like each other.

I go to my room. Through my door I can hear Mom and Dad hissing at each other, refusing to raise their voices so that they won't emotionally scar me. I call Lisa's home phone to bounce my worries off her (her cell is always low on minutes). Her line is busy, which means that she's online. She has dial-up, which is prehistoric. That's like using VHS when there's DVD and TiVo.

My DSL box blinks at me when I get on the Internet to use Instant Messenger. Lisa is on her computer, as I predicted. I start typing.

AlmiraRules: hey

GorgeLisa: hi

AlmiraRules: my parents are definitely going to parent night, so i hope we'll see each other there

GorgeLisa: my parents are coming too. It's until 8. so late

AlmiraRules: No! that means I have to fast longer, past the sun setting!!!!

GorgeLisa: at least u get to eat. a real fast means no food at all.

AlmiraRules: it's not easy

GorgeLisa: i know. do you think peter will be at parent night

AlmiraRules: i hope so, I want to see him there

GorgeLisa: what do you mean?

AlmiraRules: i mean i know you like him, so of course i want him to be there for you

GorgeLisa: thanks, because he's important to me

AlmiraRules: ok, anyway grandpa is going to give me driving lessons since I haven't had a lesson in a while, then my learner's permit can become a license when i turn 16

GorgeLisa: no, don't let him, he's practically blind

AlmiraRules: say nice things about me at my funeral

GorgeLisa: i'm sure you'll live. his car will flatten anything that you hit.

AlmiraRules: yeah, right

GorgeLisa: ur parents are really going to let you drive with him?

AlmiraRules: yeah, they care about my welfare and whether or not I have a pulse. just watch my accident on the evening news. your best friend will be famous.

GorgeLisa: don't be so pessimistic. anyway, isn't Peter a q-t? i hope he likes me

AlmiraRules: yeah

GorgeLisa: I need help with my social studies homework

AlmiraRules: the newspaper research assignment

GorgeLisa: where is the boston chronicle published?

AlmiraRules: where do u think?

GorgeLisa: don't know

AlmiraRules: BOSTON

GorgeLisa: thanks, you're the bestest

AlmiraRules: night

GorgeLisa: bye

Lisa and I are in the same honors classes, but sometimes she acts like she can't think properly. She also likes Peter, just when I start to think that I like him, too. I eat a slice of cake before going to bed. I'll wake up extremely early to have breakfast with my parents, to fill up before the daylight hours of starvation.

I'll feel hungry in other ways, too. Like how can I get Peter to notice me? How can I get my parents to lay off me? How can I get Grandpa to drop the idea of giving me driving lessons? I want so much, but don't know how to get things going my way. I stare at my computer. I have a Jake Gyllenhaal desktop, and it transitions to a Robert Pattinson screensaver. I kiss my fingers and then place them on my screen. Maybe I'll take a picture of Peter with my cell phone so that I can have a new desktop image to adore. Grandpa doesn't know squat about technology, so he never checks my computer. He doesn't want me to know anything about boys, yet I have a whole PC file of hunks that he doesn't know how to get his hands on. And I want to add Peter to the collection.

· · ·

My family is really strict about banning boys from my life. A boy, who was nothing more than a friend, once walked home with Lisa and me. Dad happened to drive by while we were walking, and when I got home he gave me the third degree. Who was that boy? Why was he with me? How long have I known him? Was he interested in me? Did he inappropriately touch me? Who were his parents? Did he ask me out? And Grandpa is always ripping posters off my wall. He tore off Brandon Flowers because he thought he was a classmate I had fallen in love with. I can only wish that Brandon went to my school.

They act like boys are poison. I suppose that some of them are toxic. For example, Kevin Federline ruined Britney Spears. She'll never return to her former glory after knowing him. So some boys can destroy girls, I'm well aware of that, but others are okay. Sometimes I feel weird thinking about boys, because it seems wrong for a Muslim girl to be lusting after them. But isn't that what typical teenage girls do? Am I allowed to be typical?

Roberto Aguilar once asked me out, in the first month of ninth grade, but I declined. He was funny and sweet, but he had small, crooked corn-teeth that bothered me (also, what would Dad think?) and a cast on his foot from a football accident. His dry, hairy, grotesque toes peeked out from the end of his cast. I regret turning him down, because now he wears clear braces and no longer has the cast. His feet also improved, because I saw him in flip-flops at the mall the other day and his toes looked normal. He's totally hot, and I blew the beginnings of a relationship by being shallow. I wonder what a relationship with him would be like. Am I supposed to sneak around with him, or tell my parents that he's a friend? I don't think my parents will even accept me having a male friend.

Another guy I sort of fell in love with was Buff12, who IM'ed me one day (by accident, he said; my ID was similar to his friend's) and we emailed each other for a month. Then he became honest and said that instead of being an eighteen-year-old soccer player from Brazil with a buff body, he was really an unemployed thirty-year-old actor who was out of shape. Pedo alert. I put him on my ignore list and didn't think of him again.

I want a boyfriend. I'm ready for one, even if my family isn't. I'm determined to have one. I close my eyes and think about all the boys at school until my mind settles on Peter. Mmmmmmmmmm.

My stomach roars like a lion, which halts my romantic thoughts. It now feels like my belly is separate from the rest of me, like I have a dog inside of me that needs to be walked, fed, and bathed. Down, boy. I eat breakfast to silence the beast.

I walk to school, because I don't feel like listening to my mom sing again. Lisa walks alongside me. She's wearing a pink sweater-dress that clings to her skinny body. Her arms are slender, with knobby elbows. I look at my own arms, which are on the plump side. Mom assures me that bracelets look good on me because of the fat on my arms, as if I'm supposed to take that as a compliment. *No, you're not a ravishing beauty, but you can always be a hand model.* Wow.

At least I'm losing weight. I pat my stomach, which is less poochy than normal. My pants are even sagging on me. I adjust my glasses. I have contact lenses, which I really want to wear everyday, but they make my eyes red and itchy. I don't have too many pimples, so my skin is good. I wonder if I could ever be considered hot, but the idea seems laughable to me.

We stand by the front entrance and try to spot Peter. I'm sweeping my eyes over the crowd, as is Lisa. Maybe that explains the way she's dressed. She even wears makeup, which she usually doesn't have on, and she applied it wrong. Two thick stripes of pink blush look out of place on her round cheeks.

While we're on the lookout for Peter, a silver monolith comes into view. It's gigantic. The sun shines on the massive vehicle as it moves toward us. Dewdrops glint off of it like diamonds. It's a Hummer. I've seen many of them, but it's still odd to see such huge vehicles on the street. Why does anyone need such a huge car? Dad says that it's to show off. I'd be afraid to drive one of them. I'm still afraid to drive any sort of car.

The Hummer stops in front of us. My eyes try to penetrate the tinted windows, but all I see is a reflection of me and my classmates. The door opens and I see one tan leg, followed by another. A beautiful face follows, and then a tiny waist emerges as the girl unfolds herself out of the vehicle. Boys whistle. I see Peter stop in his tracks to stare. Lisa tenses up next to me, her muscles taut. I wonder who this person is, with her silky brown hair, flawless skin, and a modelesque physique.

The girl smirks, looking coyly at her admirers.

"Who is that?" Lisa asks.

"I don't know," I say. "She must be new."

The girl has long, thick, Catherine-Zeta-Jones-type hair and bottomless brown eyes. We watch her go inside the building, and we see her again in first-period English. Our teacher, Ms. Odige, introduces her. "This is Shakira Malik. Shakira, tell everyone a little about yourself."

Shakira stands up, her beige dress flowing around her toned legs. "I'm Shakira, and I just moved down here from Orlando," she says. Her voice is sexy and husky, a grown woman's voice.

Malik? I wonder if she's Middle Eastern. I hope she is, because then I won't be the only Muslim in the school. It isn't like I'm lonely or anything, but to know someone else who shares my culture seems comfortable to me, the same way many of my classmates speak Spanish to each other all the time. I want to be around someone who shares that with me. I look at her short dress and become skeptical on her possible Muslimness. Muslim girls aren't supposed to dress like that (even though many Muslims wouldn't like the way I dress). Maybe Malik is Eastern European. But then she has that first name, Shakira, which is definitely Arabic. It's the coolest name, the same as one of my favorite pop singers.

Shakira barely pays attention to anything going on in class. While the teacher talks, she continues to give coy looks to boys. Mike winks at her and she grins at him over her shoulder. Luis can't pry his eyes off of her. Shakira's eyes skim his athletic body in a predatory way.

There are grumblings from girls about her. Girls can

be petty and vicious when it comes to competing with each other on looks and attention. Surprisingly, the pretty, popular girls don't seem to take to her, even though Shakira seems to be their type. "What a man-eater," Lisa whispers in my ear.

I can't agree more, but I want to know more about her. Where are her parents from, and is she fasting like I am? I see her hand in an assignment to Ms. Odige, and she has large, bubbly handwriting. She also puts hearts above her i's. Even her penmanship is awesome. I look at my sloppy handwriting. Sometimes I can't read what I've written down. Some people are just perfect, and I'm not one of them. There is this whole secret club of perfect, cool people. I'm in high school, so I can tell. There are the higher ups, the riffraff, and the people in the middle. I'm considered a middleton, which isn't horrible, but of course I wonder what it feels like to be on top.

4

"What's this?" Grandpa asks me, pointing to his nose.

"*Anf,*" I say.

"And this?" He points at his chin.

"*Thaqn.*"

"What about this?" His teeth.

"*Asnaan.*"

Grandpa has played this body-part game with me since I was a child. He wants me to know Arabic, but it really never sticks. I know words and phrases, but can't string a sentence together. It doesn't bother me, because I'm in America, after all. It only feels important to know

English. My parents took me to France last summer and I didn't bother with *oui* or *merci*. I tried to talk to everyone in English. *Parlez-vous Anglais?* I'm a typical American expecting others to conform to my ways.

We're sitting at the dining table late at night. Grandpa lives fifteen minutes away, so he drops by often. Sometimes he makes surprise visits and his excuse is that he's going to Walgreens. So whenever he needs Gas-X or Listerine, he drops by. I know these visits make Mom uncomfortable, but he is Grandpa. I always make myself available to him. He's a retired car salesman—he's not a great driver, yet he was a stellar salesman during his heyday—and it sometimes seems like I'm his hobby. Instead of playing golf like other retirees, he comes over to bother Mom and teach me what he thinks are important life lessons. He taught me that infidels should never be trusted, women must be dutiful wives, I should read the Koran everyday (which I don't), and other things that I don't really understand. I once asked him who made God and he told me that I couldn't ask that question. But I did ask that question. And I really want to know.

"I wish you had Muslim friends," Grandpa says.

"There aren't many Muslims around here," I say.

"There aren't any at your school?"

"There's this new girl, but I'm not sure what she is. Her last name is Malik."

"Does she cover herself?" he asks.

"No, she doesn't cover her head," I say. "In fact, yesterday her dress was pretty short."

"She dresses like a prostitute? She can't be Muslim."

"Maybe not."

Grandpa pats my hand. "You're such a good girl. I hope you'll be a doctor someday."

"I don't want to open anyone up," I say.

"Not all doctors open things up."

"But you have to dissect stuff in college to become a doctor," I say. I don't want to tear apart frogs for eight years straight. That's gross. And it doesn't stop at frogs either. There are cats, human corpses, all sorts of dead things. Dad told me all about it.

"You only have to dissect for a little bit."

"Yeah, right."

"And after you become a doctor, I'll help you find a husband."

I become deadly silent after that. Dad saves me by walking in and talking to Grandpa about cars—are Audis any good and should he get one the next time he buys a car? I rush to my room and sit at my computer to IM Lisa and my other friend, Maria.

AlmiraRules: grandpa is going to find a husband for me!

MamiMaria: that's messed up

GorgeLisa: that's crazy!

MamiMaria: you're not even legal yet

AlmiraRules: he'll do it when i'm older. he'll arrange a marriage with some ugly guy i don't love

MamiMaria: maybe he'll be rich

AlmiraRules: i don't care

MamiMaria: girl, if he's rich you can't turn him down

GorgeLisa: money doesn't matter! run away if you have to

AlmiraRules: maybe i will

GorgeLisa: he could be super ugly

MamiMaria: but rich

GorgeLisa: why can't you just tell your parents that you want a boyfriend and that you don't need their help?

AlmiraRules: you don't get it! they won't get it! my parents didn't date

MamiMaria: WHAT?

AlmiraRules: that's right, grandpa knew her parents and he introduced her to my father and they were chaperoned ... they weren't allowed to be alone

MamiMaria: that's messed up

AlmiraRules: that's just how it is with them!

GorgeLisa: you'll figure something out, maybe have a secret boyfriend or slowly tell them the truth

AlmiraRules: i don't think so. Anyway, the thing is i really like

GorgeLisa: what do you like?

MamiMaria: who do you like??? what boy do you have a crush on?

At this point my fingers become frozen. I can't reveal that I want Peter. Not to Lisa. That would hurt her. She'd think I'm a manipulative, backstabbing best friend who's lusting after her conquest, wanting him to be my conquest. It's like I'm playing an invisible game of chess, making moves, trying to knock down Lisa and get to Peter. Oh … I don't want to feel these things for my best friend's love interest. Guilt slams me down and my spirits fall.

> *AlmiraRules:* i like the idea of doing whatever i want
> *MamiMaria:* i hear ya
> *GorgeLisa:* night everyone
> *MamiMaria:* see you tomorrow and i'll bring you a cookie
> *AlmiraRules:* don't tempt me when I'm fasting!
> *MamiMaria:* ur favorite, chocolate chip

I smile. Peanut butter cookies are really my favorite. I log off and go to the kitchen to have one before I go to bed. Grandpa is not there, thank God. No more hearing about having Muslim friends and a Muslim husband that he'll handpick for me.

· · ·

The next day I skulk around Peter, watching him drink at water fountains and retrieve books from his locker. He carries a horror paperback that he reads when he finishes his work early and he grips his sketchpad tightly. He's achingly handsome, movie star handsome, Robert Pattinson hand-some. Other girls look at him, and I want to tear their eyes out. How dare they look at him! *Calm down*, I keep telling myself. Don't go crazy over him, but I'm crazy in love. Lisa brushes up against him in the hallway between classes and something goes *ping* in my heart. Jealousy, anger, longing.

And of course hunger.

Maria waves a chocolate Twizzler under my nose before lunch. Her limp curls are in a ponytail and her large hoop earrings sway as she dances in front of me. She bites into the Twizzler, and I want that chocolaty goodness for myself. "Some friend you are," I huff.

"Don't be mad, boo," she says. "It's only fooooooo-oooood."

"Yeah, food that I can't eat." *And a boy who doesn't look the least bit interested in me*, I think, as I see Peter walk past me without giving me a second look.

During lunch I go to the library. My friends want me to sit in the cafeteria with them, but I tell them I can't. If I see fries and smell the aroma of meatloaf, I'll just die. My mouth already salivates all day long whenever I see my classmates snacking on candy in between classes. Stacks of books on symmetrically lined shelves will distract my mind from food. I convince myself of this. Archeology, mathematics, astronomy, music. *Be interested in classy stuff*, I urge myself. Forget food.

I go to the fiction section to see if there are any romance books I haven't read, and Shakira is there. She has a Stephen King book (good choice) open in her hands. I've read almost every Stephen King book out there. He's classic. My parents read him, which was how I got into reading him. Now I see this pretty girl Shakira interested in him.

For a moment I stand there dumbstruck. I've wanted to talk to her ever since she introduced herself in English class, but when the opportunity arises, I don't know what to say. Shakira frowns. Of course she would, since I'm staring at her like some psychopath. I approach her.

"Hi," I say.

"Hi," she whispers, in the silence of the library.

"You like Stephen King?"

"Yes."

"I do, too. I have all his books."

"That's nice."

"You don't like the lunch selection?"

"I'm fasting."

"Me too."

She looks at me less severely. She's taller than me, and I feel short and squat compared to her. She has at least five inches on me. I have to look up at her, whereas most of my friends are at eye level. Her hair is smooth and wavy, while mine is curly and frizzy. Her eyes are deep brown and rimmed with liner and mascara. How can a teenager be sultry, and why can't I be sultry as well?

"I'm starving," she says.

"So am I, but at least we get to pig out when the sun sets," I say.

"The last hour before sunset feels like forever."

"That's so true."

"I'm Lebanese," she says.

Grandpa was wrong. She isn't an American prostitute.

"I'm Syrian and Persian," I say.

"I thought you'd be something like that."

"So, I have a bunch of Stephen King hardcovers at home."

"I do too," she whispers. "I buy them used since I want the hardcovers."

"Yeah, paperbacks don't last that long … "

The two of us are getting along, but then Peter walks by. Shakira's eyes light up at the sight of him. "Hi, Almira," he whispers to me. He gives Shakira a lingering look before he walks out of the library. Why can't he look at me like that? I'm just a lab partner to him.

"Is that your boyfriend?" Shakira asks.

"No," I say.

"Didn't think so."

She says it with an edge to her voice. Tears burn behind my eyes. What does she mean? Am I ugly? Am I not boyfriend-worthy? What was I thinking, trying to talk to some tall, skinny, *America's Next Top Model* look-alike?

"You don't seem his type," she says, digging the knife in deeper.

"And you are?" I say. I feel stupid insinuating that she's

interested in him, but I want to get a word in, and that's something I once heard a friend say in retaliation to someone. *And you are? Yeah, you. Who do you think you are?* So I have my say, as small as it is, then I turn around and walk away from her look of boredom.

I was wrong to think that beautiful Shakira, of the gazelle legs and high cheekbones, would want to talk to me. There are boundaries that can't be crossed in high school. My friends are all in the middle of the social hierarchy, neither popular princesses nor invisible nerds. A jock will never ask me out, and I won't go to a school dance with a science nerd (but I won't be mean about it). That's the difference: kids in the middle are not as cruel as those in the highest rank.

I slowly breathe in and out. I blame myself for trying to talk to her. I should have known better than to talk to Shakira. Just because we're Muslim and fasting doesn't mean that we're instant friends.

5

"You should have told her to drop dead," Lisa says.

"Don't let anybody talk to you that way," Maria says.

"You're not ugly, and any boy would be lucky to have you," Jillian says.

I must look really upset after lunch when I blurt my exchange with Shakira to my friends. They instantly come to my defense and bolster my self-esteem. But I don't believe their kind words, as I'm boyfriendless and will probably be so for the rest of my life.

What an ugly situation I've just experienced. To be starving and then told that Peter will never go for me ... from the lips of someone I now view as an archenemy. I've never had an archenemy before—I thought they only existed in comic books or macho movies—but Shakira is definitely my foe. I panic at the thought of being uncomfortable every day of my life. I've also never been bullied before—in the past I've experienced light teasing, but nothing close to harassment. Am I going to dread every school day, at the prospect of seeing Shakira in classrooms and hallways? Am I going to be like the nerdy girls who wash their hands in a rush to get out of the girls' bathroom because they don't want to be seen by anyone? And a new girl is making me feel this way! I want to tell Shakira the school is my turf more than it is hers. Wretched new girl.

"She makes me so mad," Lisa says, squeezing her eyes shut.

"Can we just forget about it?" I say. I'm still upset, but I'll get over it.

We go to science class. I see Shakira sitting in the back. Her eyes meet mine and I quickly look away. I wish I hadn't. She's just arrived, while I have a solid foundation within the school. She should be looking away from me.

Peter has his sketchpad open and he's gliding his pencil over it. I know he takes art, which I won't dare sign up for since I can only draw stick figures. I walk up to him so that I can inspect what he's drawing, but he closes his pad shut. What he's working on is left a mystery.

"Oh, hi," he says.

"Hi," I say, sitting on the stool next to him. My dark

mood is lifted by gazing at his handsomeness. On a scale of one to ten on handsomenosity, he's a ten.

We look at each other silently. I nervously twist the spigots of the Bunsen burners. They're inactive, since Mr. Gregory teaches biology not chemistry. What should I say next? I have to say something, because he isn't a big talker.

"You like science?" I ask. What a lame question. I'm so uncool.

"Not really."

"I bet art is your favorite class."

"Yes, it is. How did you know?" He sounds impressed by my psychic abilities.

"Just a guess."

Peter pulls his bangs off of his face. What pretty green eyes he has. He smiles. Such good, strong teeth, albeit his two front teeth are long and rabbity. Why do I have to be so teeth-conscious just because my dad's a dentist?

"I'm trying to find a really good picture of a knight and a maiden," he says. "My art teacher gave us a medieval project to do, and the first step is finding a model or source of inspiration."

"Maybe I can help you look for it," I say.

"Would you?"

"Of course."

Lisa comes over. *Go away,* I think. *Just … go … away.*

"I made this drawing last night," Lisa says. She reaches into her bookbag and pulls out a wrinkled paper darkened with graphite. Her picture is of a fugly man with small eyes and big teeth.

"Who's that?" I ask, my voice raised in disgust.

Lisa glares at me. "It's Robert Pattinson," she says.

"Don't even joke about that!"

"I'm just kidding, Almira. It's my older brother."

"That looks nothing like him," I say.

Lisa puckers her mouth angrily. Peter clears his throat and says, "That's really nice."

"Really?" Lisa says, her face brightening up.

"Um, yeah, it's a really good portrait."

Lie! The picture is super gross. It's covered in eraser marks, there are no ears, and the hair is scraggly. Lisa's older brother is a hot college guy and the picture doesn't resemble him in any way. Lisa puts the picture away and I'm relieved that she's no longer embarrassing herself in front of Peter, who's a real artist.

"You're coming to Parent Night?" Lisa says, a large grin on her face.

"Yeah," Peter says.

"Do you want to come with some of us afterwards for pizza?" she asks.

"I'd like that."

She just asked him out, sort of. A bunch of our friends are going to a pizza place after Parent Night, but I'm not sure if I'm going. I've been breaking fast with my parents ever since Ramadan started, but now I feel that I have to go to this pizza shindig to spy on Lisa and Peter. Even if our friends are surrounding them, it's still a date. Lisa is going to go out with my crush. That's unbearable. I have to be there to supervise and see what Lisa is up to.

"We'll have fun," I say.

Lisa gives me a sharp look, which quickly disappears. I'm Almira, her fun-loving, smart, goofy friend. She doesn't see me as competition.

Parent Night is a week away. I have to figure out what to wear. My hair needs to be straightened. I have to get a mani and pedi. My clothes are getting bigger on me, so I have to cinch my dresses with belts or buy a new ensemble for that night.

Mr. Gregory gives us a lecture on cell life, and then we have some book work to do. I'll hand in my work early, before Lisa can ask me for it. I hate it when she wants to see my work, so that she can change her wrong answers and copy off me. I work for myself, not for anyone else. Anyway, she's after Peter, which isn't cool. Now I have a grudge against her, even though I love her.

"Here you go," I tell Mr. Gregory, who's standing at his lectern.

"Almira, you're always a model student," he says, putting my work on his desk.

"I try."

"You seemed upset after lunch," he says. "Is anything wrong?"

I look at his handsome face, which is frowning in worry. He's one of the few teachers who asks about my emotional well-being, but I'm not going to regale him with girly gossip. If I have a beef with Shakira, I'm sure he isn't going to be interested in it. If I'm after the same guy that my best friend is, it's not like he can help me in any way. I turn around and see Shakira hovering over some boy. Man-eater. That's what she is.

"Nothing's wrong," I say. "I'm just hungry."

"I've never met someone celebrating Ramadan. You're the first, and I see that you have great willpower. I don't think it's something I could do."

"Thanks."

I go back to my seat. As soon as I sit down, Lisa leans across Peter and asks me, "Can we see your paper?"

"I turned it in," I say.

"Shoot," she says, wrinkling her face. "We're stuck on a question."

I shrug my shoulders. I feel rotten and I'm not sure why, since Peter isn't mine.

"Oh, by the way, Peter told me about the knight and maiden picture he's looking for," Lisa says. "I told him my mom has an old art book that has a picture like that. I just have to find it." She smiles big, as if she's won an award, even though neither one of us has found a picture for him yet. Which one of us can help him first on his project? I need to start looking right away for a suitable picture, so that I can receive due credit. *Almira, thank you so much for finding this old painting of a knight and maiden*, I imagine him saying. *You really care about me. I care about you, too.*

At the end of the day, I see a new Bic tattoo on Lisa's wrist. She shows it to me, grinning like a Cheshire cat. *Peter*, it says, in misshapen calligraphy. The font is close to Angelina Jolie's Billy Bob tattoo, the one she had lasered off to ink the coordinates of her children's birth places. I don't want Peter to be her Brad Pitt. I want him to be my Brad. We won't be Brangelina, but Petmira.

• • •

A few nights later, we have shrimp for dinner. My family eats it as if we're in a competitive eating contest. No chewing. Just scarfing it down. I'll never invite my friends over on a night that we break fast. It would be too mortifying. *Oh my God, Becky, the Abduls eat like savages. They don't even know how to swallow.* I just know people will say that. But it's understandable since we're so hungry. When it's not Ramadan, our etiquette is normal and high-class, I swear.

I'm minding my own business, watching late-night news, when Dad sees me laughing at a story about a cat who's nursing a puppy. It's cute and makes me giggle.

"Almira, have you been brushing the back of your teeth?" he asks.

"Yes, Dad," I say. Always about the teeth. Can't he leave me alone? He cleans my teeth twice a year like clockwork. He should only bug me about my teeth during those visits.

"You haven't been flossing."

I don't want to tell him that I floss when I feel like it, which isn't much at all. I'm tired before going to bed and skip that task most of the time. And in the morning I'm in a rush to go to school. Our house is like a dentist's office with a plethora of dental supplies. We have enough floss, prescription toothpaste, and electric toothbrushes to last a decade, but that doesn't mean I'm a fanatic like he is.

"Bite down for me," he says.

I sigh. I turn toward him and bite down, my lips pulled back so that he can see my wonderful teeth.

He tsks-tsks. "You're bottom teeth have always been crowded, but they're slightly crooked."

"What?" I say.

"Look in the mirror."

I go to the bathroom. I don't believe his words. My teeth have always been good. I received compliments my whole life on the straightness of my teeth. Leaning forward, the bottom of my shirt becomes drenched by the water pooling around the sink from the last person who washed his or her hands there. I stare at my bottom teeth. Dad is right. They're slightly crooked, some teeth shooting at eighty-five degrees rather than at a perfect ninety degrees. It doesn't look noticeable when I smile, and my teeth still look better than 99.9 percent of the population, but they're flawed. I'm a freak. Every three seconds I run my index fingers over my lower teeth, feeling the ridges of teeth that stick out the slightest bit when they aren't supposed to. I want a perfect oval outline, but I'm feeling crags as if my teeth are broken piano keys going in different directions.

I stomp back toward the living room. It isn't bad enough that I wear glasses, am fat, and don't have a boyfriend. Now I have to have defective teeth on top of all of that! The world seems inordinately cruel. Can't I have a relaxing Friday night without having to dwell on yet another problem?

"Why me?" I ask him.

"You might need braces. We'll see."

"No!"

"I don't do orthodontia, but I'll make an appointment with my friend," Dad says.

"No!"

"We need to nip this in the bud. You don't want to have crooked teeth for the rest of your life. And we'll get x-rays. Maybe your wisdom teeth are coming in and are adding to the crowding effect."

Dad is right. I have to nip this in the bud. I go to my room and look into a hand mirror. Looking so closely at my teeth, I'm noticing a bunch of imperfections. A chipped incisor. A small crater on a canine tooth. Yellowish molars. I call Lisa, but her phone's busy. I go online and she's there.

AlmiraRules: i'm going to the orthodontist soon.
GorgeLisa: get out
AlmiraRules: my bottom teeth are messed up
GorgeLisa: you have beautiful teeth

AlmiraRules: i thought i did too, but dad is a dentist and he can't have a daughter with ugly teeth, so i'm going to get checked next week.

GorgeLisa: get the clear braces so you don't look like a metal mouth

AlmiraRules: of course

GorgeLisa: me and peter talked so much during science, we really bonded

AlmiraRules: that's nice

GorgeLisa: i think he likes me

AlmiraRules: great

GorgeLisa: and this girl who sat behind us told me that he was sketching a girl in his pad before class. i hope it was me he was drawing.

AlmiraRules: that's really romantic

GorgeLisa: i know. he's quiet, but he's not boring when you get to know him

AlmiraRules: grandpa is going to give me a driving lesson tomorrow, so i'm going to bed now

GorgeLisa: be safe

AlmiraRules: thanks, but if you don't see me monday ...

GorgeLisa: don't talk that way

AlmiraRules: i want to go to a real driving school

GorgeLisa: this is what you're stuck with. night

AlmiraRules: night

I spend an extra half hour on the net researching braces. There's the regular metal type, the ones that go behind the teeth, the clear brackets, Invisalign. I know that any of them will be painful, since my teeth will be forced to shift around. For the first time in my teenage existence, I'm overwhelmed. I lead a charmed life, living in a nice home and attending the poshest public school in the county. There's been little drama in my life until this point. I'm fasting for the first time, have my first serious crush, am learning how to drive, and now I'm going to get braces. What will Peter think about my braces? He'll hate them. Who wants a girl with braces? How am I ever going to receive my first kiss now? This Ramadan is proving to be very hectic. I wonder what the rest of the month has in store for me.

When my drowsiness gets so bad that I can't ignore it anymore, I go to bed. When my head hits the pillow, I realize that I never searched for the knight and maiden picture for Peter's art project. I want to go to Google Images to see if I can find a really nice picture. Dad had ambushed me with his (now mine) obsession with perfect teeth, and I totally forgot about the future love of my life. I haven't asked Lisa yet, but I bet she already dug out her mom's art book and will have the picture ready for Peter the next time we see him. I feel the burn of jealousy in my heart right before I enter a dream state.

6

I wake up at five to eat breakfast. My parents are rubbing their eyes and I'm yawning. I remember how normal Saturdays transpired. I'd wake up late and have brunch, but now I have to wake up early to fill myself up. Mom makes hardboiled eggs, toast, and sliced tomatoes. I liberally sprinkle the eggs with salt and pepper. I eat slowly, nervous about my upcoming driving lesson. Then I pace around the house, exploring the sunken living room, cozy family room, and airy dining room. I inspect ballerina figurines and snow globes as if I've never seen them before. Not knowing what to do with myself, I revisit old territory ... my own home.

My feet lead me to the master bedroom. Mom washes up for prayer, dons her praying clothes (headscarf, gown, and socks, the most clothes I've ever seen her wear), and prays *Fajr*, the early morning prayer. She stands on her praying mat, which is laid down in a corner of her bedroom. She bends down, places her forehead on the floor, and murmurs all the prayers in Arabic. I don't know what she's saying. I learned the prayers by rote when I was a kid, and then forgot them. Mom prays a few times a week (not the five times a day required) and I usually don't see her in the act, so it feels like a treat to watch her pray this morning.

"I prayed for your safety at the end of it," Mom says, kissing me on the forehead after she's done.

I look at her face, which seems so old-world when it's surrounded by a cotton puff of fabric. She then unwinds the scarf from her head and her dark hair tumbles down. Now I recognize her.

"I think I'll be okay," I say.

"Not with that man."

"Why don't you two ever get along?"

"You have to ask that?" she says, rolling her eyes.

I shouldn't have asked, because I know the way things are between Mom and Grandpa. Feeling too old for cartoons, I watch *The Brady Bunch* on TV Land. There's something comforting about really old TV shows—the innocence, the simplicity. Mom sits watching with me, wearing a leotard, and then she goes to the family room to do her stretching.

I hear a crash outside and slowly get up. Grandpa crashed into our mailbox. It's bent but not totally out of the ground. This is the fifth time he's hit our mailbox. Dad never gets mad at him, but Mom's frustrated at having such an inept father-in-law. "Can you park his car for him?" Mom has asked Dad many times over. But Dad thinks Grandpa needs to feel independent and confident about doing things on his own.

"*Azizi*," Grandpa says, kissing me on both cheeks.

Grandma comes in with her billows of Shalimar perfume and a floral headscarf. She sits on the sofa, immobile as she watches the morning news. This is her cue for sending us off, just me and Grandpa. Holy crap.

"I've never caused an accident," Grandpa says in his raspy voice. "You're in good hands. I'm not like the infidels around me ... people in Miami don't know how to drive."

Yeah, he's never caused an accident. He only knocks things down and doesn't know how to park. It's true that Miami drivers are very random, making inappropriate U-turns and doing other crazy things, but I'd rather be with any other Miami driver than him. I'm willing to have a taxi driver teach me how to drive, even though around where I live, the taxi drivers aren't too far off from Grandpa's level of poor visual acuity and atrocious reflexes.

I tremble as I walk outside and get into his gigantic

car. The inside smells of a pine air-freshener hanging off the rearview mirror, and Grandpa's aftershave. A necklace with a charm that has *Allah*'s name in stylized Arabic swings from the rearview mirror also. May *Allah* protect me in this endeavor, I silently pray. Mom looks through the living room window. She looks pained that I'm going to this lesson with a maniacal driver. Why oh why couldn't Dad have finished his lessons with me? Now I'm stuck with someone who's not only lethal, but who talks and talks and has a mind stuck in the 1950s.

Grandpa glides down the driveway, and someone has to brake sharply behind us since he pulled out too fast. I close my eyes and open them to see that we're heading off to a major street that isn't so busy since it's early in the morning. I see dark skid marks on the road. That sight makes me more nervous, because it looks like a car made several crazy swerves before stopping, possibly from a car accident or wet road conditions. I hope to never cause skid marks like that.

A girl is walking on the sidewalk wearing a cute little pink dress. "She's dressed like a prostitute," Grandpa says.

I feel insulted. I have the exact same dress. I wore it to school several times since last year, but never around Grandpa. It hits mid-thigh. For shame. I don't have a pimp and I'm not an entrepreneur, so there goes his prostitute theory.

"I'm so glad you don't dress like that. You're so clean."

My nerves are effervescing. I don't know if I should

laugh or yell at him to be quiet. We have a polite conversation during the rest of our journey, even though I poke and prod him a little bit.

"So, Grandpa, these American prostitutes seem to upset you," I say.

"They don't know how to dress," he says. "Then they go out and people can't help but look." His face is so sour that he could compete with a bag of lemons.

"This is a free country. I know you don't like it, but they can dress like prostitutes if they want to. So how come you and Grandma came here?"

"Because it's a free country. I loved Syria, but you know it has problems."

Yeah, like war and bombs. I don't really worry about that stuff—not once have I ever thought that a grenade would land in my backyard. Mom talks about what her parents escaped in Iran—they didn't stick around for the Iranian Revolution and the Iran-Iraq War—and Dad shakes his head anytime the news comes on about bombings in the Middle East. We're all lucky to be in America, land of the free. And not only can women dress the way they want, but Grandpa has the freedom to call these women every name in the book. Of course he has only one word for them: prostitutes.

"You say that there are no other Muslims at your school," Grandpa says.

"There's some new girl, Shakira, who I told you about," I say halfheartedly.

"Ew! So she is Muslim. Maybe I met her parents at the mosque."

"She just moved from Orlando."

"Are you friends with her?" he asks.

"No, she's not friend material," I say.

"You should be friends with her."

"I'm not going to be her friend just because she's Muslim, Grandpa. There are other reasons to be somebody's friend, you know."

"All right, all right."

Grandpa takes me to a shopping plaza that's empty since all the stores open up at nine on Saturday. We have an hour to kill until any of these restaurants, dry cleaners, and office supply stores unlock their doors.

"You're going to do exactly what I tell you to," Grandpa says.

I swallow a lump in my throat. "Okay," I agree.

"Get out and switch places with me."

We do just that. I'm in the driver's seat and place both hands on the steering wheel, which feels foreign in my hands. I might as well have a snake in my grasp. It has been months since Dad took me for a driving lesson. The lack of practice and experience makes me nervous behind the wheel.

"Look at the gears," Grandpa says. "R is for reverse, D is for drive, P is for park ... "

Now he's talking to me like I'm an idiot. I already know this stuff.

"Press on the brake pedal now," he orders.

The car is in park, so I do what he says.

"Press on it hard!"

"I am."

"Now gently press on the gas."

The engine revs up.

I change the gear to Drive. I'm driving. I look at the speedometer and see that I'm going ten miles an hour.

"Stop!" Grandpa says.

I press on the gas by accident and shoot forward a few feet, but then I find the brake pedal to the left.

"Turn the corner!"

The parking lot of the shopping plaza is turning into an L, so I have to turn right. I slow down and do as he says. It feels so cool to be back behind the wheel. Grandpa might be a horrible driver, but he's a pretty good teacher. Sure he's impatient and yells a lot, but I can tolerate that.

A light bulb forms on top of my head. I never took pictures of myself behind the wheel during Dad's lessons. Why not take one now?

"Grandpa, can you take a picture of me with my cell phone so that I can show all my friends?" I ask.

"What do you mean?" he asks. "People can take pictures with their phones?"

I demonstrate by taking a picture of the store in front of us. He frowns as he wraps his mind around what I'm showing him. "You just watch the screen and press the button in the middle," I instruct.

"Fine," he grunts. I give him my pink BlackBerry Pearl and he gets out of the car, steps a few feet away, and holds up my phone. The window is down and I smile a large, braces-free smile. I might as well smile as much as possible before I have a mouth full of metal, ceramic, or plastic.

He snaps my picture. My hand caresses the steering wheel as if I own the car and I'm mistress of the roads. And then something happens. The car starts rolling forward.

"Grandpa!" I scream.

"Use the brakes!" he says, running after me in slow motion.

My foot finds the gas instead and I keep going forward. I want to cry. There's another L in front of me and I make another right turn, and then I calm down enough to find the brake pedal. I slam on it, not with a light foot this time.

"Park the car!" Grandpa yells.

With jellylike fingers I park the car. I get out and we switch places. He seems less angry now that he's in the driver's seat. I look at the picture he took. I look so cute. My face is slimmed down, my smile is bright, and my hair is pretty since it's not a humid day. Maybe I should show the picture to Peter. Will he even care or will he proclaim how cute I am? My heart hammers manically thinking about him. My stomach growls, trying to compete with my daydreams of Peter. Peter. Hunger. Peter. Hunger. Peter wins, because instead of daydreaming about lavish meals and heaping platefuls of food, I think about the bow of his lips, the golden strands in his hair where the sun has bleached it, the smooth lines of his neck, and his green eyes that have a touch of brown on the outer rims.

I'll definitely show the picture to everyone at school, since not everyone my age knows how to drive yet. Maybe Dad will give me my own car, and then I'll get to park it in the student parking lot. I want a Mercedes. The least I can get is a cute little VW Beetle.

7

When I get back home, Grandma and my parents are watching *Dr. 90210*. Some lady just had a fresh boob job and all her girly bits are blurred out. I think Dad would jump at the opportunity of having his own cosmetic dentistry show. I can just imagine it—with his thick, dark hair swept to the side, maybe highlights (like the ones Dr. Rey has), and a new suit everyday. Then the cameras would come into our house. Mom is the pretty, thin wife. I'm the winsome only child.

"He filled out those pancakes," Grandma comments. It always seems weird when she talks about modern things, because with her head covered she looks like an immigrant fresh off of an airplane. But Grandma curses—dropping F bombs occasionally—and even nudges me when cute guys pass by us, provided that Grandpa isn't around with his constant disapproval of *Amriki* behavior. Go Grandma.

"Good job," Mom says.

"He's an excellent doctor," Dad says.

"Why are you watching this show?" Grandpa asks, frowning. "What is this? That woman looks naked."

"Her wickedness is covered," Grandma says.

"Change the channel. Almira can't see such things."

I cross my arms, angry that Grandpa thinks I'm some little kid who can't watch *Dr. 90210*. It isn't pornographic at all. All the nasty body parts that Grandpa wants to shield me from are pixilated into blurriness. He's such a censor nazi. When I was a kid, if Grandpa stayed over at our house, he'd never let me watch horror movies. He wouldn't let me see *The Sixth Sense* or *Poltergeist*. He says infidels will corrupt my mind. He's never let me have any fun.

"Almira will drive just as good as I do!" Grandpa thunders during the commercials.

Oh God, I don't want to drive the way he does at all, but I smile anyway. I show my parents the picture of me behind the wheel and Dad grabs my phone to email the picture to himself, so that he can print it out for memories. I feel so proud of myself, so grown up.

Lisa calls and she wants to go to the mall. I say sure. I'm all hyped up after my successful driving lesson.

Maria is a junior, with her own car, so she drives us.

She has a convertible, and we feel very sophisticated with the top down and the wind blowing through our hair. Maria doesn't have much movement in her own hair, since it's in a ponytail slicked back tightly with gel.

The only unpleasant thing that happens during the drive is when some gross truck drivers honk their horns and holler at us. We can't hear what they're saying, but I know it isn't anything good. Maria extends her middle finger at them. Lisa and I look at each other and then do the same.

The rest of the time we're checking out guys. Miami has great-looking guys. I haven't traveled too extensively, but I feel that I might be in the best-looking city in the world, which means that I have to work hard to match the status quo. I pat my stomach. Yes, it's still decreasing.

"He looks like a senior I know," Maria says when a guy with very broad, muscular shoulders drives by us.

"That guy looks like Orlando Bloom!" Lisa yells in my ear.

We turn to look. Maria gets distracted and comes too close to the car in front of her. "Watch out!" I yell.

We get to the mall all in one piece. First we go into a beauty supply store and Lisa buys something called *Fierce Pout* that promises bee-stung lips. "I'm going to look like Angelina Jolie with this," she says.

Maria and I roll our eyes. I purchase clear lip-gloss and Maria buys several lip liners and eyeliners. Sometimes Maria puts on a thick swipe of eyeliner as if she's Amy

Winehouse. Lisa loves makeup and wears it occasionally, while I only wear it sometimes. At least none of us looks scary, like the woman who keeps pressing us about a free makeover. She looks gruesome with frosted blonde hair, bubble gum pink lipstick, and purple eye shadow.

"I'll make you look beautiful," she says. "You won't regret it."

The three of us giggle and go next door to buy clothes. I pick out some shirts that better suit my slimmer physique. I wonder what will happen after Ramadan ends. Will I gain the five pounds that I've managed to lose? I'm thinking about exercising with Mom so that the weight won't come back on. It seems like a horrible prospect, waking up early or staying up late to exercise, spending time with my hot mom who will make me do all sorts of impossible contortions to match her awesome body.

Lisa picks out a blue satin dress from a rack. "Do you think Peter will like me in this?" she asks.

I can feel the skin droop off of my face as I frown. I force myself to smile weakly, so that I won't give away my true feelings. "I don't think so," I say. "The fabric is too shiny."

"Yeah, you're right."

I pick an irresistible lavender dress for Parent Night and try it on. "You're smokin'," Maria says.

"Thanks," I say.

"That dress is great for your coloring," Lisa says.

There's a mirror attached to the outside of the dressing

area. My flip-flops are off and I'm walking around barefoot, twirling around. I look slender in the dress. Even my legs aren't as canklelike as usual. I like what Ramadan is doing to my body. What a shallow sentiment, since it's such a holy month, but I'm fifteen years old and I forgive myself for thinking this.

As I'm admiring myself, someone floats into my vision. Sultry eyes and lots of thick hair swim behind my reflection in the mirror.

"Shakira," Lisa whispers to us.

We all turn around. It's her. She's wearing a pink sweater, short skirt, and matching pink ballet flats. Her pink Chanel handbag swings off her arm. We look at our own handbags, which are Coach, Nine West, and Gap. But why am I feeling inferior over a handbag? Handbags come in and out of style. Still, we dislike her for her beauty, her Chanel bag … and for her sharp tongue, which scorched me the other day.

"Hi Shakira," Maria mutters.

"Hi," Shakira says breezily. "Are you all shopping for Parent Night?"

"Yes, and for other things as well," Lisa says.

"Are you going to wear that dress for Parent Night?" Shakira asks me.

"Yes," I say.

"It doesn't suit you at all," she says.

"Why not?"

"The hem hits the top of your calves and the waistline is at your hips. It's for someone much taller."

She's right. I hate it that she's right.

"So, we'll find one in a different size," Lisa says.

"I don't think they have one for her size."

Ooh, cutting me down. She means that I'm fat, that the store doesn't have a size seven for my height. "I'm sure they have the same style in my size," I say, trying to maintain some dignity.

Maria narrows her eyes at Shakira. "Almira has a wonderful figure," she says. "So I don't know what you're talking about."

"I didn't say she doesn't," Shakira says. "She looks normal for a high school girl."

Now I'm a freak and I have to be mollified by the "normal" label. I know I'm short, therefore the slightest sign of chunkiness makes me gargantuan, but she doesn't have to rub it in. I worry that my legs are short compared to my long torso or that my head is too large for my body. I look at Shakira's long legs, perky boobs, sticklike arms, and model's face. I hate her. There, I think it. I don't even feel bad for thinking it.

Shakira shrugs her shoulders, not offended by our obvious ire, the hatred spewing from our eyes. Lisa presses one foot forward, as if she's ready to leap at her.

"Yeah, right," Maria says.

I raise my shoulders high, even though I really feel horrible by what she's implying.

"I went to the Orlando store all the time and know what this chain has and doesn't have," Shakira says. She turns around and walks out of the store.

To prove her wrong, we look through the racks. Shakira is right. All of the lavender dresses are made for Amazon women. I can't find one that hits above my knees. Lisa finds a deep-purple dress in a slightly different style, with a V-neck collar, and it's the perfect length for me.

"Don't listen to her," Lisa says.

"What a nasty twit," Maria growls.

My friends are trying to make me feel better, but they can't. First Shakira said that Peter could never be my boyfriend, and now she thinks I'm short and fat. I shouldn't care what she thinks about me, yet I do. I'm not going to let her have any power over me, I decide. She's living in her own fantasy world of snobbery and shallowness, where she thinks she reigns supreme. She isn't going to drag me into her pathetic fantasy. There are already rumblings at school, mainly from girls, that no one wants to be her friend and that she's stuck-up.

After buying our Parent Night dresses, we go to the food court and of course I can't have anything. Being in the food court is aggravating, because I normally sample everything. An ice-cream cone here, Thai food there, yellow rice, beans, a warm pretzel, lots of soda. My mouth waters, as much as it can considering that I'm dehydrated. Drool can't collect in my mouth because my body is withering up the longer I'm without food and water.

"Do you want some?" Maria asks, waving an egg roll under my nose.

"I can't," I say. Egg rolls. Oh my God. So crispy looking. I can't eat it anyway because it has pork in it and Muslims can't eat pigs, but I sure wouldn't mind a spring roll. And the fried rice looks so delectable, loose and steaming. Why do I have to starve myself like this?

"Are you sure?" Maria asks, a wicked grin on her face.

"Don't tempt her," Lisa says. "She's trying to be good."

"Sorry!"

I watch Lisa and Maria heartily eat Chinese food, which I love. Before Ramadan, Mom would order Chinese food and I would gorge myself on vegetable chow mein and beef fried rice, but now I have to wait until I break fast. Maria slurps on a smoothie and I want one so bad. I'm thirsty. My stomach growls. Going to the mall used to be pleasurable, but the reminders of food, and having my archenemy tell me that I don't look good in clothes, really sucks.

There has to be some solace for sitting here not being able to eat with my friends. I know the solution: being even more alone in my thoughts by daydreaming. Robert Pattinson swims in front of my eyes. His face looms over me. He glitters in the sun. "Almira, my love," he breathes.

"Yes, my love," I say.

"Come away with me."

"Whatever you say."

I close my eyes. The sounds of screeching children and

laughing teenagers vanish. All I see is Robert. All I know is Pattinson. He grabs my hand. We're on the beach. He's wearing these flowing, white pajama thingies that I see in newlywed photo shoots, and when I look down, I glimpse a white skirt swishing around my ankles. We're married! That has to be it. The sun is rising and he puts his arms around me as we watch the sun part the clouds. I take the opportunity to run my hands through his wild hair, something I've always wanted to do.

"Cool," I say.

I'm so caught up in my fantasy that even with my eyes open, my mind isn't in the real world. There's a bowl of complimentary noodles in front of me. They look so flaky and crispy. I see my fingers grab one. I really, truly am not thinking at all when I put it in my mouth. The same reflex that grabs candy off the desk at Dad's dental office and reaches for chips at parties compels me to put that noodle in my mouth and start chewing.

Then it dawns on me. Duh, I'm not supposed to eat. I'm ruining my fast.

Maria and Lisa are busy checking out guys. They don't notice my Ramadan faux pas until I stand up so fast that my chair falls back.

"What's wrong?" Maria yells.

I rush to the closest bathroom and spit out the noodle. I spit some more to get the taste out of my mouth. None of it has reached my throat, but I can taste the fried goodness on my taste buds. I don't even want to rinse out my mouth, lest any drop of water reach my stomach. I take a paper towel and wipe my tongue with it.

A blond toddler and her mother look at me and back away. Some girl I recognize from school stares at me and then also exits. A girl scurries behind me and shakes her head with distaste. Yeah, I'm a crazy lady all right. I grip the edges of the sink and take a good look at my reflection. My brow is sweaty and my eyes are glazed over.

I open my mouth wide to see if there are any crumbs left there. What have I done? I almost destroyed the rhythm of my fast. As much as I hate other things in my life, not keeping my word to fast for an entire month seems like the worst thing in the universe. I'd be a big, huge failure. I imagine the fat F in red ink my math teacher gave me years ago on a quiz. It was my first and last F, because I hate failing. I don't want to fail Ramadan either. That would be, like, a big event, something God is surely watching for. I won't repeat what happened during last Ramadan, when I cheated ... and Dad's mouth formed a thin line, Mom tried to console me, Grandma shook her head, and Grandpa roared about my lack of discipline. Now my whole family wants me to win at this thing. People change. I've changed.

"Almira, what's wrong?" Lisa asks. Maria and Lisa open the bathroom door so hard that it bangs into the tiled wall behind it.

Maria grabs both of my shoulders and gazes deeply

into my eyes. Neither of them knows. They didn't see me put that dreadful noodle in my mouth.

"The smell of food was making me nauseous," I say.

"We're done anyway, so let's go," Lisa says.

Both girls are frowning and fussing over me. They take turns patting my arms and smoothing down my hair. I don't like the attention, because it makes me feel guilty. But at least that noodle hadn't gone down my throat. I feel like an anvil was about to fall on me, but it missed me by a few inches. Walking away from a near tragedy, I shiver from the cool air conditioning of the vast mall.

8

It's Monday and I ponder on what to do with my pretty brown eyes. Many people compliment me on my long lashes, but I believe that glasses hide my eyes. I try to put in my contact lenses, but they feel itchy on my irises. I quickly take them out and look at my cases of glasses. I normally wear my wire-rimmed ones, since they're the thinnest, but today I settle on a pair with thick, black frames. They make me look artsy. I'm hoping to make Peter, an artist, feel like he's with a kindred spirit.

I wear black leggings and a black tunic to enhance my artist appearance. If I could carry around a palette of paint and an easel, I would. I even wear a beret, but I know I'll have to take it off once I'm inside school since we can't wear hats of any kind.

"You look like you're going to a funeral," Dad says.

"Black is very slimming," Mom says.

"You're not turning into one of those Goths, are you?"

"Dad, no, stop it," I say.

A brand-new sketchpad that I bought at the drugstore last night rests in my bookbag. Maybe I can try to become better at drawing to impress Peter. This makes me nervous, because art has been the most challenging subject in my whole school career. In elementary school the art teacher who visited the classroom once a week always gave my drawings back to me and made me redo them. "That's not a drawing. You did that too quickly. The crayon marks are all over the place." Those comments affected my artistic self-esteem. Maybe under Peter's eye I'll blossom as an artist. I've practiced doodling in my notebooks over the past few days when I was bored in class. I began with geometric shapes and flowers. Soon I'll start on the human figure.

In English class I sit down and feel something hard underneath me. I get up expecting to see a pencil, and I find a Hershey's Kiss instead. I don't know where it came from, so I throw it out. I hear some lame remark behind me by some anonymous boy: "Ooh, Almira has a secret admirer who wants to give her a kiss." I wish. I hope it's my future boyfriend sending me messages through chocolate morsels. I picture someone tall, suave, dashing. He'll leave a trail of chocolate toward my locker. I'll open my locker and there will be a dozen roses. The dozen roses will have a note saying to meet him at a French bistro. At the French bistro we'll have dinner to break my fast, and there will be roasted lamb and chocolate mousse and other stuff I like to eat. Then afterwards ...

"Almira, start your assignment!"

I jolt in my seat when I hear the teacher call my name. Ms. Odige just asked us to write in our journals, about something that's on our minds at the moment. I write the following:

> *I don't know why mean people suck so much. If I'm minding my own business and not doing something to someone, then I don't understand why anyone would say or do something to hurt me. It doesn't make sense and I don't operate that way myself. It really sucks. I don't like it when someone tries to hurt me or acts like I have no feelings. How would that person feel if I said or did the same thing to them? This person has really poor manners. This I know. She really needs to act nicer since she's new and nobody really knows her. Nobody will want to know her.*

Ms. Odige reads some poetry with us and then gives us an assignment to do while she grades our journals. At the end of class I get my pink composition book back.

You need to write more cohesively. You begin generally and then focus on the mystery person at the end. There's no middle. Work on that. FCAT writing is just around the corner. Please don't use the word "suck." It's vulgar.

These are the comments Ms. Odige has written in red pen at the bottom of my entry. What does she expect? It's just a mindless journal entry. Well, not really since I mean every word of it. I dislike Shakira. I don't care who knows it. And I hate tests and the FCAT, a statewide test, is in the spring. And there are certain things, situations, and people that really suck. I also think that I write pretty decent if I concentrate hard enough.

I wonder if my breath is okay. Fasting means that there's no food or liquid passing my lips all day, so I worry about my breath. I blow into my hand, trying to figure out if the pigeons in the courtyard will drop dead if I walk past them. That doesn't work, because all I smell is the soap on my hands. I can't even have a Tic Tac, because that would be considered cheating.

During lunch I observe—stalking is too drastic a word, even though that's what I'm doing—Peter walking outside along the main building. I quickly walk over to the gazebo, which is a large, covered, wooden circle with benches. I plant myself on a bench and take out my new sketchpad. What to draw? I see a patch of violets to the side of the gazebo and decide to draw it.

I goof up instantaneously. The violet I'm drawing has

one huge petal compared to its other much smaller petals, and the shading is messy and unrealistic. I have to learn about lighting, coordination, and everything else artistic. How am I going to impress Peter? I look up and he's watching me. I lift my knee higher, balancing my sketchpad so he can see I'm hard at work.

He climbs the short steps to the gazebo's platform. "Hey, what are you drawing?" he asks.

"Flowers," I say.

"Oh."

That *oh* says so much. He thinks I suck. I know I suck.

"I've been really interested in art lately," I say.

"Do you need any tips? I can help you if you want."

"Would you?"

He sits down next to me and grabs my sketchpad. "First off, you started drawing to the far left and off center. There's going to be a lot of white space to the right. You also have a very heavy hand shading … "

He rattles on about all of my shortcomings. He isn't mean about it, so I calmly look at his wavy hair and arched eyebrows. He's wearing a dark green shirt that's the same color as his eyes. His hands look strong, yet he holds my sketchpad with a light touch. He's amazing.

"What's that?" asks someone behind me.

I turn around and Shakira is standing next to me. Why is she ruining this moment with Peter? Does she have no heart at all? I look at her and I see no flaws, except for the sneer on her face.

"Violets," I say.

"You need to take art class with us," Shakira says.

Everything that comes out of her mouth is in a harsh tone of voice. There's nothing soft and nice about her. She's all about being rough and nasty. Yet Peter is looking up at her with admiration.

"You *should* take art," Peter says to me. "Shakira's becoming a pretty good artist, and she took art at her last school. It helped her a lot."

"Yeah, like, you have to learn to draw."

She's pointing out the obvious, with a voice dripping in sarcasm. I don't want to hear her anymore. I take my sketchpad from Peter and tell them that I have to go to the restroom. I really do need to go, but I also want to get away from Shakira's sharp tongue. I'll be mortified if she embarrasses me in front of Peter. Is she going to call me fat again? Also, the way Peter looks up at her with worshipful eyes is unbearable.

• • •

Before biology, I catch Lisa opening her new tube of *Fierce Pout* and spreading it on her lips. Within minutes I notice that her lips are considerably larger. She doesn't have Angelina Jolie pillow lips, but they are poutier.

"Wow," I say.

"Do you want to try some?" she asks.

"Maybe later," I say.

We both sit next to Peter in class. He closes his pad

when we plop our butts down on adjacent stools. I wonder who he's drawing. I only saw dark swirls of hair and the sweep of a cheekbone. It's definitely a girl he's drawing. Maybe someone is posing for him in art class.

"What are you drawing?" Lisa asks.

"Nothing," he says.

"Will you draw me someday?" I ask.

"Sure."

I smile. I want him to see my brilliant smile before I have dreadful braces placed in my mouth.

"Your glasses are cool."

He notices! Mom and Dad thought I was crazy dressing like an artist this morning, but I know what I'm doing.

"I think I saw those same glasses in *Revenge of the Nerds*," Lisa says.

I know she meant to say that in an innocuous way, but I shoot her a look of fiery anger. *DO NOT RUIN THIS FOR ME.* I'm hungry and boyfriendless. I need the simple pleasure of a boy's compliment. Lisa is pouting to make her artificially enhanced lips even fuller. She's getting trout pout and it looks ridiculous.

"There's something different about you," Peter says, shifting closer to Lisa. "I don't know. It's like you're glowing."

"I moisturize," Lisa says. She rubs her lips together and pouts some more.

"Peter," Shakira calls out. Boy, she pops up unexpectedly.

"Hi, Shakira." Peter becomes googly-eyed, getting lost in her olive skin and long lashes. She swishes her hair above one of her shoulders. She tugs at the waist of her dress and her boobs pop out an extra inch from her V-neck. Slut. Lisa must share my feelings, because her nostrils flare and the corners of her lips dip into a snarl.

"This is the picture you asked for," Shakira says. She slides a picture across the table. It's one of those studio shots where the lighting gives her a halo effect, and she's heavily made up. She's wearing an off-the-shoulder dress, giving a come-hither look to the camera. *Why is she giving this picture to him?* I want to shout out. But I can't play the jealous girlfriend when I have no boyfriend.

"Thanks," Peter says, tucking the picture into his binder.

Shakira walks away and sits next to Luis, a football player who instantly begins to hover over her like an eager dog waiting for a bone to be thrown at him. Lisa and I both expectantly look at Peter. He notices our curiosity, so he gives us an explanation.

"We're drawing portraits in art and she's my partner," he says. "She has my picture so that she can work on it at home."

"Is she any good?" I ask. I know he said she's improving, but I want to know if the slut has any *talent*. If she has beauty and talent, I just don't know what I'll do with that information. I want to hear that she's stupid and talentless, rather than smart and skillful.

"She's working on it," he says. "She's okay, but she has a lot to learn about sketching."

I feel better hearing all of this, but I still have a lot of competition: Lisa, who is pretty in her own right, and Shakira, who is drop-dead gorgeous. I take out some cherry lip-gloss and slather it on my lips. If I do have bad breath, then the heavily scented gloss will mask it. I lean over Peter throughout the lesson, but he doesn't notice my love for him. He pats my shoulder as if I'm a friend.

I don't want him to be my friend. I have plenty of friends. I want him to sketch me in his pad as if I'm his muse. I want to be his Mona Lisa or Duchess of Alba (maybe I'd be uninhibited enough to pose naked, but I'd probably chicken out). Knowing that he's sketching Shakira further infuriates me and makes me hate her all the more.

9

After school, Mom picks us up to take me to the ortho-dontist. Tina Turner's "What's Love Got to Do with It" plays on the radio and Mom sings along. The same boy who blew Mom a kiss last week does so again. His friends laugh at him, which makes me feel like he's laugh-ing at me and my mom. I see Peter walking home, and he thankfully doesn't look in our direction. Good. I don't want him to know that my mom is an exercise freak/kara-oke singer. Yeah, she sings karaoke like it's nobody's busi-ness during parties.

I'm also not in the mood to hear love songs since my heart's all torn up and gouged out. It's so hard trying to get Peter to look at me as girlfriend material. Lisa and Shakira are totally in my way. Lisa is hanging all over him shamelessly, and I'm attempting to be bolder than her without stepping on her toes as her best friend. I also want a relationship to happen naturally, yet I feel like I'm going out of my way with Peter by trying to get noticed. I don't know if I can take the chance of looking like a fool and being rejected with all the extras I'm doing (like pretending to be interested in sketching). Then there's Shakira, who is beautiful and more of an artist than I am. I did take a peek at her sketchpad today and she isn't as good an artist as Peter, but she's good enough to draw people who look like people, without outrageous features or any other oddities. Still, I feel like I'm able to compete with Lisa and Shakira. With or without braces, with or without glasses, with or without an extra ten pounds, I know that I'm girlfriend material.

Mother starts yowling like a cat in pain (or heat) when Tina Turner hits a high note.

"Mother!" I snap.

She keeps singing. The woman is tone deaf. I sigh. The sight of the road pleases me, because now we're far less likely to be spotted by my classmates as she sings off-key, dances in her seat, shakes her shoulders, and puffs out her chest. I want to walk home, but I have to go to this appointment with the orthodontist. Lisa slicks on some more *Fierce Pout*. Mom asks her what it is and they start to talk about makeup. I look out of the window, wanting to be somewhere else—in Peter's arms, in a size-four dress, on the beach. My stomach growls loud enough for me to hear it, but nobody turns my way. Tina Turner is drowning out my hunger pangs, but I want people to know about my pangs. I want everyone to know that I'm hungry and starving during Ramadan, I'm afraid of Grandpa's driving, I don't want braces, and I'm madly in love with Peter. I want to be heard.

"Do I look like Angelina with this?" Lisa asks my mom.

"More than you used to," Mom says. "But Angelina has big lips and I don't think you can buy anything from the store to get that pout."

Everything is about what Angelina would do. Since Lisa wants to be just like her, it means being slinky and seductive. She's going to take Peter from right under my nose. I'm going to be like Jennifer Aniston, spurned and lonely, and with braces. Dad always tells me that life isn't fair, and at this point I know what he means.

Dr. Abdelwahab and Dad work in the same building. The building is three stories high and is packed with doctors. There's a gastroenterologist (someone who fixes gastric stuff), urologist (a urine doctor, I guess), endocrinologist (a doctor for the endocrine), and hematologist (someone who studies hemas, whatever those are). On the top floor is Dad and Dr. Abdelwahab. Mom and Lisa stay with me for extra support, even though I don't need it. I'm not dying or anything like that, unless braces are going to look so disgusting on me that I want to die.

The doctor is tall and skinny, with a handlebar moustache. "How are you?" he says, loud and happy.

"Okay," I say.

"Fantastic!"

I frown. He reminds me of Borat, who is funny on screen but probably obnoxious to the extreme in person. There is no need for him to be so peppy when he's going to uglify me and ruin my life. I open my mouth. He pokes, he prods, and then he sticks this contraption in my mouth to take an X-ray. After a few minutes Dad comes in, taking a break from his own work to see what's going on.

"Her bottom teeth are crowded," Dr. Abdelwahab says, a large smile plastered on his face. "And they will get even more crowded because her wisdom teeth are coming in."

"What?" I say. "I'm too young for wisdom teeth."

"They usually appear after sixteen years of age, but sometimes they come in earlier," he says.

"I'll pull them," Dad says. "Then she can get braces."

Pull them. Out of my mouth? "Um, Dad, how are you going to take my wisdom teeth out?" I sputter.

"You'll need surgery."

Oh my God, I've never had surgery before.

"It's just Novocaine. You'll be awake."

I don't want to hear this! If I'm going to have surgery,

I don't want to be awake during it. I want to be knocked out cold so that I won't feel an ounce of pain.

"I can do it tomorrow—my four o'clock cancelled, so I have an opening," Dad tells Dr. Abdelwahab. He turns to me. "After you heal, you'll get braces."

"Dad!"

"Don't whine, Almira," Dad admonishes with the shake of his head. "We're the professionals."

That doesn't mean anything. Professionals can cause a lot of pain. They have the needles and knives. I shouldn't have smiled and laughed in front of Dad last week, because then he wouldn't have noticed my funky teeth and I wouldn't be going through this agony. I should learn to keep my mouth shut.

"You're going to look beautiful!" Dr. Abdelwahab brays. "Very nice!"

"It'll be okay," Mom says.

"Yeah," Lisa says. "I had my tonsils taken out when I was little. We all get surgery some time in our life."

"But I don't want to have this surgery before Parent Night." So that I can arrive there with a swollen, ugly face when I want to eat dinner with Peter afterwards? Noooooooooooo.

Whatever. There's nothing I can do. I'll be grown up and suffer through it. It's bad enough that I wear glasses, but now I'll wear braces to boot, with wisdom teeth extraction as a prerequisite. Mom stops by Starbucks to get us iced lattes, as if that can make me feel better. The sun has an hour more to go, so I put the latte, which makes me salivate, in the fridge until then. Everything seems like a test of patience: to wait for the sun to go down, to wait for my braces to come on, to wait for my braces to come off, to wait for Parent Night, to wait for my first kiss, to wait for my first boyfriend ...

10

AlmiraRules: what r u eating right now?

GorgeLisa: brownies

AlmiraRules: yum

GorgeLisa: super moist with walnuts

AlmiraRules: did your mom make them?

GorgeLisa: yes

AlmiraRules: her brownies are delicious

GorgeLisa: i know, i wish i could cook as good as she does

AlmiraRules: i can't wait until the sun goes down

GorgeLisa: for dinner we're having pizza with mushrooms

AlmiraRules: stop!

GorgeLisa: it's true, because it's pizza night and mom also stopped at the bakery and got éclairs

AlmiraRules: i'm going to faint

GorgeLisa: éclairs are delish the way the cream oozes out when you bite into them

AlmiraRules: please don't remind me

GorgeLisa: but my favorite is chocolate cake with the coconut in it

AlmiraRules: german chocolate cake?

GorgeLisa: yes

AlmiraRules: STOP

GorgeLisa: sorry for teasing you

AlmiraRules: yeah! i can picture everything in my head but none of it is in front of me or in my mouth where it belongs

GorgeLisa: ur doing a good job fasting

AlmiraRules: thanks, but i'm nervous

GorgeLisa: don't be. imagine how fantastic you're going to look without those extra wisdom teeth. you don't need them. and you're going to have perfect teeth after the braces come off

AlmiraRules: do you think Peter is falling for Shakira

GorgeLisa: she better not take my man away from me

AlmiraRules: what makes you think that he's your man?

GorgeLisa: we have a spiritual connection that can't be explained. it's like when angelina signed up to do mr. and mrs. smith. she thought she was doing a regular old action movie, but she met the love of her life on the set and it wasn't supposed to happen because he was already married, but it did. i'm angelina and shakira is jen

AlmiraRules: shakira isn't jen because peter barely knows her

GorgeLisa: if you're talking about two women vying for the attention of the same man, then she is jen.

AlmiraRules: what's so great about peter anyway?

GorgeLisa: everything. he's gorgeous, but not stuck up. quiet, but he can be funny. and he's an artist

AlmiraRules: he's great

GorgeLisa: see, i'm not wrong

AlmiraRules: he's gorgeous

GorgeLisa: he's the bestest

AlmiraRules: do u think I'll ever have a boyfriend?

GorgeLisa: men will be beating down your door someday. you've lost weight and you have curly hair to die for and big brown eyes. of course you'll have a boyfriend someday.

AlmiraRules: i really hate shakira for what she's said to me and i hate hating anybody.

GorgeLisa: you are justified

AlmiraRules: i'm going to eat soon and then go straight to bed. tomorrow i have surgery

GorgeLisa: before you go, ms. odige wants us to write about an influential book that changed our lives

AlmiraRules: i picked are you there god it's me marga-
ret by judy blume
GorgeLisa: i picked the diary of anne frank
AlmiraRules: cool
GorgeLisa: the problem is, i forgot who wrote it. can
you help me out
AlmiraRules: it's a diary
GorgeLisa: so who wrote it?
AlmiraRules: who do you think?
GorgeLisa: ???
AlmiraRules: THINK
GorgeLisa: stop playing games, i really don't know
Almira Rules: ANNE FRANK
GorgeLisa: duh, thanks. bye
AlmiraRules: bye

Mom makes a huge dinner, which I pick at. I can't stop
thinking about Peter and how Lisa is dead set on having
him. What an unfair world it is that two friends want the
same boy. Lisa and I share a life together, went through
childhood together, and then this boy came into my life
last year when I was a freshman and at the moment he
has me befuddled with love—I barely know him, but he
is causing an emotional rift between me and Lisa. It feels
strange, but maybe it's a part of growing up. I've fallen in
and out of friendships before, but I always expect Lisa to
be a constant presence. If I reveal my crush to her, could
she possibly accept it? It's too scary to think about.

I think about Peter's transformation. Last year, when he was heavier, he had love handles spilling over his jeans. Even then I wanted to squeeze the baby fat rolling off his waist. When he sat in front of me in freshman English class, I saw he had pimples on the back of his neck and I wasn't grossed out at all, when that normally would gross me out. Maybe it was a sign, fate. I'll accept everything and anything from this boy. We're meant to be together. I hope that he'll accept me the way I accepted him.

Then he lost weight, his body went from soft to hard, his face cleared up, his hair was lusher … it was like he had an overnight makeover, blossoming in front of my eyes. Smoking hot. I can't stop thinking about him, and at the same time Lisa has declared her love for him. Why can't Lisa love someone else? But I know the answer. In a school, nay a town, teeming with hot boys, Peter is a rarity. It's more than his looks, but something that is indefinable, that *je ne sais quoi*. He's more mature than the boys around us, he's an artist, he studies art books as if he wants to be swallowed by the paintings, and he's even a poet (he mentioned to me that a poem he submitted showed up in the last edition of the school newspaper). So he's not just good-looking, but he's deep. While my other male classmates are making fart noises and laughing for stupid reasons, he stands out as a profound boy/man. He's special.

"What are you thinking about?" Grandpa asks me during dinner.

"Nothing," I say.

I'm thinking about an American boy. I'm thinking about kissing an American boy. So what do you think about that, Grandpa? I feel treacherous having these thoughts in front of him. I'm stung with guilt, because how can I be musing about boys in front of Grandpa? Thank God he isn't a mind reader. Thank God daydreaming is safe, that it isn't the real thing, because I don't know if I can handle the real thing.

"How is your fasting going?" Grandpa asks me. He's always asking me that question. I try not to flare my nostrils or give other signs of anger.

"Fine," I say.

"You're not, you know—" He twitches his mouth, nibbling something imaginary. "You're not sneaking away any snacks?"

This time I do flare my nostrils. "No, Grandpa, I'm not," I manage to say. I really want to yell at him for asking me that question. Sure, I cheated last year, but it's in the past. I'm trying to redeem myself, wash away that ugly memory of eating the pack of chocolate wafers when I couldn't ignore my hunger pangs, and then hiding the evidence by stuffing the wrapper in the bottom of my trash can. But I forgot to wipe away those crumbs stuck to my lip-gloss. Grandpa noticed them first, then my parents became disappointed in me and I dropped the idea of fasting for the rest of the month. Grandpa just has to remind me of this dreadful incident. He's acting like Ms. Odige. I messed up on a paper, formatting one entire paragraph in all caps, and she never lets me forget it. "Almira, remember to watch your caps lock," she says every time she assigns a paper. Grrr. Why do some people have to be like that? I can't stand it when someone doesn't let go of the past and won't accept my new accomplishments.

My anger vanishes when we dig into a tray of cookies and cups of tea. Grandpa tells me stories about his car dealership days (he was the number-one salesperson, rich infidels were always treated nicely, and ditzy young women didn't know how to haggle). My grandparents leave and soon afterwards I help Mom clean up the kitchen.

I don't go to bed right away. I read a romance book, one with a handsome teenage boy and gorgeous teenage girl on the cover looking deeply into each other's eyes. Mom says those books are trashy, but all of my friends read them. My parents couldn't care less about what I read, because they think it's good that I'm at least reading. Some of my friends don't read at all, with the distractions of iPods, video games, the Internet, and premium cable channels. Dad even gives me gift cards for bookstores, which I use to buy more romance books. I hide these books from Grandpa. I have shoeboxes in my closet just for them, because he'd confiscate them otherwise. *You're being corrupted by this Amriki trash.* His words echo in my head. I stomp them out by reading a juicy scene of kissing and light petting.

This part is really good. That's written in the margin of one of the pages. It looks like Maria's bubbly handwriting (I lent her the book months ago). I reread the page,

picturing me and Peter as the main characters. We're stuck in an elevator during a power outage. It's hot. We're rivals, both writers for the school newspaper who never see eye-to-eye with each other. He's just written a lead story that I also happen to be working on—roaches in the cafeteria—but he finished it before I could. We had a yelling match the other day, but we stumble into the same elevator that afternoon. The power outage freezes the elevator between floors. I feel faint from the heat, so he grips my arm. I hold his shoulder to steady myself. Our bitterness turns into lust. His lips are on mine. There's nothing else to do but make out. In real life our school doesn't allow students to use elevators, and they all require a security key anyway. Only teachers can use them.

Before going to bed, I study myself in the mirror. I smooth Olay cream, which Mom has given me, over my face. I rub baby oil over my lashes since Mom says it helps make lashes grow. I have long black lashes, and I bat them. No, it looks wrong. I don't look seductive enough. All of Mom's tricks, potions, and lotions don't exactly work on me.

I take a tube of lip balm and smooth it over my lips. I make kissy faces. *Kiss me, Peter, kiss me now.* The dialogue in my head sounds like it comes from the cheap, campy romance novels I'm always reading. I wonder what the real thing is like, a real boyfriend, a real kiss, a real relationship. I open *Heavenly Kiss* again, to the page of Maria's commentary. I take a pink pen and underneath Maria's words I write, *This is the bestest part of the book.*

11

There's a surprise waiting for me in math class: a small Dove chocolate on my desk. I wonder if I should throw it out or not, since it has no perforations or rips. It's probably Maria trying to tempt me, since she's been trying to trip up my fasting since I began. Maybe it's Lisa, who sometimes joins Maria in the teasing. I hope that the two of them will have to fast someday and then I can wave food in front of their faces, see how strong they are.

I put the chocolate in my bookbag. Self-control, that's what Ramadan is about. Of course eating is far from my mind with the surgery ahead of me. Pain, not pleasure, comes to mind when I think about my mouth. I probably

won't be able to eat chocolate for days since my mouth will be sore after surgery.

In between bells, I sneak off to the bathroom to look at my teeth. I'm now obsessed. I open wide and see the opaque ovals of wisdom teeth trying to break through my gums. Gross. They're really trying to burst through and become a part of my regular teeth, like weeds sprouting out of the ground. I even feel a tinge of pain. Maybe it's real or imaginary, but those suckers are really trying to break the surface.

Everyone hears that I'm having surgery after school today and I make it out to be a big deal. "They're going to cut through my gums," I say. "I'm going to be really out of it tomorrow." The gentle touch of sympathy and kind words is nice, even though I'm not undergoing a huge procedure. It's just my mouth, not my pancreas or lungs or something like that.

My friends rally around me during this time of uncertainty. Surgery is surgery, and I can die from any misstep. Dad told me he has his patients sign a consent form before dental surgery, something saying that they're aware of the complications from anesthesia. I wonder if he'll make his own daughter sign that paper.

People ask questions and hug me all day long. I have all types of friends, because I don't discriminate. I feel that if someone has a big heart and good intentions, then that person can be my friend. Lisa is slow (ergo the Anne Frank question). My friend Raul is snide and sarcastic, but he likes to fix things and fixed my computer once. Jillian gossips a lot, and I'm sure she has gossiped about me behind my back, but she's super nice. Then there's Maria. She's a chonga, an impertinent Miami Latina. She has the fast mouth, lip liner, and stiff hair. She also has a quick temper, but she's still lovable. I once tripped her by accident because my foot was extended out and I thought she was going to beat me up, but she didn't. She can be aggressive, but never toward me.

At lunchtime, I join my friends for the company. It's not like I'm going to hide in the library during my entire fast, even though my stomach is doing backflips and cartwheels as I watch my friends eat. Maria is eating a Twinkie. She offers me one. I shake my head.

"Come on," Maria says.

"Maria, I can't," I say.

"You know you want to." Maria licks the crème filling, her red lipstick becoming fainter as she licks her lips. Twinkies ... I really don't like packaged desserts that much. They can be made out of anything: cow ears, cardboard, you just don't know what you're eating. I prefer Mom's cooking or things from an actual bakery, but Twinkies sure look good to me during my fast. I take the Twinkie from Maria and stare at it through the wrapper. It's golden yellow and so delicate looking. I'm sure it would melt in my mouth. I sniff it.

"You're weird," Maria says.

"I'm just smelling it," I say.

"You know she's fasting and that's very important to her religion," Lisa says, tapping her foot in irritation. She grabs the Twinkie from me and hands it back to Maria.

"Forget the both of you then," Maria says. She's in one of her moods. Not only did she fail to tempt me, but she's also failing shop class because she didn't finish making a lamp, so she's upset about that. "That man never wants to give me a break!" she says about her teacher. This morning she also had a freshman chip one of her toenails by accidentally dropping a heavy book on it.

"Look at this," she tells me, lifting one of her sandaled feet up in the air. The nail of her big toe is cleaved in half, with a line through the middle. "I should have busted that girl's skull for what she did. It hurts so much."

"I'm sure she didn't mean to do it," I say.

"Yeah, and you can get nail-repair gel," Lisa says.

"Okay, I'll try that."

We're hanging out in the halls after lunch, waiting for the bell to ring. Then Shakira walks by, looking at us up and down, inspecting us. The very sight of her is unnerving. She shakes her head and pushes her thick hair across her shoulders.

"I heard you broke your toenail," Shakira says.

"That's right," Maria says neutrally.

"It looks painful."

"It is."

"We're not allowed to wear open-toed shoes. It's against school policy."

If looks could kill. Maria shoots an irate look at Shakira and says, "Mind your own damn business."

Shakira raises her eyebrow. "I'm just stating a fact. If you were wearing close-toed shoes, then your toenail wouldn't be cracked."

"Look, I'm in pain and I don't need you to lecture me with your bull."

"If you're going to lose your temper about this, that's just fine," Shakira says evenly, shrugging her shoulders. "You should know better. But I guess you don't."

It all happens so fast. Maria rushes forward and pushes Shakira, who catapults a few feet backwards but doesn't fall. Shock transforms her face into someone I don't recognize. It's like when you've known someone for so long and he or she looks different when showing that rare expression of devastation. I once saw Lisa trip over a step (she turned out to be okay and in one piece at the bottom of the stairwell), and Shakira has that same expression: alarm, hurt, what's going on, what's happening to me.

Students start gathering around us. People our age are horrible. We always want to see a fight. I'm ashamed to say that I'm the same way. I enjoy seeing hair pulling and punching between classmates. "Punch her!" a girl in the crowd eggs on.

"Kick the new girl's ass!"

I start to feel the press of the mob against my back. I look behind me and elbow some guy who's breathing down my neck. There's a nucleus of Shakira and Maria, surrounded by a thickening mass as more and more people join this human circle. Maria and Shakira both have their feet apart, in a fighting stance, with eyes narrowed in pure rage. I wonder who'll make the next move. Maria could shove her again and topple her down. She's sturdy and has twenty pounds over Shakira.

Mr. Gregory just happened to be in the hallway when the push occurred and he cuts through the crowd. He saw everything. "Maria!" he barks out. "What are you doing?"

"She started it!" Maria screams.

Shakira straightens herself out and brushes her clothes with her hands. She no longer looks angry. She has a wide-eyed expression, yet she still manages to look lovely and unaffected. I wanted her to fall, but with her long legs she managed to keep her balance. I probably would have been knocked down on my clumsy butt if Maria had pushed me. Maria is strong. She sometimes punches me in the arm in play, and it really hurts.

A security guard shows up and tells Maria to come with him. Maria wears a grimace on her face, and her eyes are glassy with unfallen tears. Shakira follows behind Mr. Gregory, who is a witness. They're going to the principal's office.

Lisa grabs my hand. "Do you know what's going to happen?" she asks.

I nod, gulping nervously. "Maria's going to get suspended," I say. A part of me wants her to be suspended since she's so insistent that I eat during Ramadan, and it seems like she really wants me to fail at fasting, but another part of me feels sorry for her. I don't want to see her get hurt, not over Shakira.

The crowd dissipates. There's no longer anything to see, except the nervous breakdown washing over me. I feel horrible that Maria's going to get suspended, from defending me as well as herself. Her anger stemmed from Shakira's criticism of her shoes, but she was also angry about what Shakira said to me at the mall. Maria looks out for me and is a fierce friend. I remember how in middle school Maria had an elective class with us and this boy made fun of Lisa's boniness. He made Lisa cry. Lisa's always been skinny, but in her younger years she was all bones and knobby angles. She even had to drink weight-gain shakes. I can't believe some people purposefully try to gain weight. Anyway, Maria beat him up after school in a park and got into trouble with the boy's parents. But this time, the fight happened on school grounds. There's no way for her to get out of this.

"I hate Shakira," Lisa says.

"We all hate Shakira!" our friend Jillian bellows in the hallway.

"Let's start a petition!"

"Maria cares about us! What has the new girl done? Nothing but cause trouble!"

There are grumblings of agreement, because Maria has many friends and Shakira is the new girl who gets on everyone's nerves. I take the Dove chocolate out of my bookbag and stare at it. It's mighty tempting. I used to eat chocolate to calm down, but now I have to turn inwards to calm myself down.

Lisa watches me tear apart the foil. I tear it quickly, the same way I unwrap gifts. I look at it. Such a square piece of wonder. Such joy.

"You're not going to eat that, are you?" Lisa asks, her eyes bugging out.

I bring the chocolate to my lips.

"No, don't!"

I bring it under my nose.

"Almira, please, you've gone this far and you can do it!"

I sniff the chocolate and all the memories it contains: Whoppers when I was a kid, chocolate ice cream during summer vacation, and fun-size Snickers that Mom puts into my lunch bag occasionally. It smells like all the good things of the world. It reminds me of comfort, a toasty bed on a cold night, a bubble bath after a bad day, a good book that I can escape into ... it even reminds me of nonfood things, just because it has that power. I get a good whiff. It smells heavenly. Then I throw the chocolate in the nearest trash bin. I can't eat it, but the smell of it made me feel better.

"Someone's been leaving chocolates for me," I say.

"Who would do that?"

"Someone trying to sabotage me."

"Or someone who likes you," Lisa says.

I don't know. Is someone trying to purposefully make

me eat or trying to give me a message of love? At the moment I want the chocolate game to end ... and for Maria to have her suspension cancelled.

. . .

The whole afternoon goes downhill after the brawl. One push and all hell breaks loose, it seems. One shove, one hand moving against another person's body, and there's so much misery. Shakira comes to biology late, probably from taking her sweet time giving all the dirt about Maria to the principal. She spends the rest of the day with her head down, avoiding people, while everyone stares daggers at her. Who does she think she is? Seriously. She acts like some princess, walking around telling people exactly what she thinks of them, as if her opinion counts for something. *No it doesn't, Shakira. You're just another shallow, pretty, empty thing. So there.*

Maria leaves a voicemail message on my cell phone. Many of us leave our phones on vibrate or silent when we're in class, but Maria calls anyway, leaving tear-filled messages on our phones. "I'm sus-suspended," she sobs. "My parents are so, so angry at me. Call me when you get home."

Poor Maria. Despite her temper, she has never been suspended before. Sometimes teachers have to take her aside and give her a lecture on anger management, but never this. The bad kids get suspended, not people like Maria, who is an above-average student and genial when she wants to be. This is the first time one of my friends has gotten into trouble with authority. I finally know someone who is a badass. It's kind of cool, yet tragic.

After school Mom picks me up to take me to Dad's office. Two tanned, blonde women with massive chests and a man with sparkling highlights in his hair leave as we enter. Dad caters to the pretty people, after all. He will make me pretty, too.

None of it is pleasant. There's the needle of Novocain, first off. I wonder what will happen if I have an allergic reaction. I can die. Mom and Dad will have another child to replace me because they're in their thirties, which is old, but not too old. Maybe they'll enjoy this new child, who will be less whiny and insecure than me. She'll be slim and popular. Shakira flashes through my mind. Tears sting my eyes at the thought of my parents raising another person, someone better. I'm so used to being the only child.

"Da," I mumble, my jaw lax after he shoots me up.

"Almira, try not to talk," Dad says. "You'll drool."

"Da."

"What is it?"

"Nuh-in." Dad loves me. He gives me a lovey-dovey look, but he can't kiss my forehead or hug me since he's wearing a mask and gloves. Mom's less emotional. She sits on a swivel chair, busily reading about Jessica Alba's fashion sense in *InStyle* magazine. Jessica Alba's hair is windblown on the cover. She reminds me of Shakira. I moan.

"She's upset that one of her friends got suspended," Mom tells Dad.

"Oh? Tell me about it when I get home."

The surgery begins and the experience is horrendous. The instruments coming in and out of my mouth, the crunch of bone as Dad loosens and pulls out the teeth, the suction pipe hosing out my disgusting drool and blood. At the end, my face is puffed out. Dad says he'll give me painkillers to take at home. Mom puts down her magazine and swabs Vaseline on my dry lips, which feel like they're peeling from all the chafing of hands and instruments in my mouth.

I look in the rearview mirror of Mom's car and I'm horrified. The lower portion of my face is huge. I look like the boy in the movie *Mask*. "Ma, I look horibew for Paren Nigh."

"The swelling will go down," Mom says tersely. She looks tired, probably from exercising all day, when I did real work by going to school and having my teeth pulled out. I don't want to voice my thoughts, because then I'll be accused of whining. Maybe I do whine a lot. It's okay to have whiney thoughts, but I shouldn't reveal them all the time. Well, maybe I should, because I think it's totally unfair that I look dreadful and that Shakira has ruined my friend's life.

12

AlmiraRules: i can't call you becuz i'm in pain

MamiMaria: was there a lot of blood?

AlmiraRules: yes, but forget about me, look at all you went through today

MamiMaria: i have two days of outdoor suspension, so i can't come to parent night, cuz that would be trespassing

AlmiraRules: two days just for pushing someone. you didn't even punch her

MamiMaria: i know and i can do some serious damage if i want to and bust that pretty face of hers

AlmiraRules: her beauty means nothing. she's so rude

and cruel, so cold, that she's like a statue, only beautiful on the outside

MamiMaria: you're right, she's got nothing on us and don't let her sweat you, because you're more beautiful than her

AlmiraRules: get out of here

MamiMaria: i mean it, Almira, ur so cute in your glasses and that innocent look you always have on your face, and ur funny, and u nice and helpful, ur beautiful on the inside and outside

AlmiraRules: oh stop

MamiMaria: no! and she had no right to put you down and i put a stop to it, cuz i wasn't going to let her run over you, me, or anyone else

AlmiraRules: u should have seen how many people defended you and hate her guts

MamiMaria: i'm queen bee

AlmiraRules: bye mami

MamiMaria: see you soon and i'll bring you a twinkie

AlmiraRules: no, don't!

MamiMaria: i'm just kidding

AlmiraRules: no you weren't

MamiMaria: yes i was

AlmiraRules: why are you always trying to tempt me?

MamiMaria: i'm really not

AlmiraRules: and leaving food for me

MamiMaria: when?

AlmiraRules: all those little chocolates

MamiMaria: i don't know what u talking about, but i'll see u later

AlmiraRules: stop putting chocolates on my seat! i'm not stupid. your english class is across from mine the same period. your science class is next to my math class. i know u r the culprit

MamiMaria: ur crazy

AlmiraRules: maybe

MamiMaria: bye babe

I get off the computer after emailing and instant messaging my friends. My face feels tender and I don't break fast with my parents. I also walk wobbly because of the Vicodin prescription pills that Dad has given me. At least I know what it's like to be stoned. I feel dizzy and otherworldly, like the way ghosts must feel when they haunt the material world. I take an ice pack and hold it to my cheeks, switching sides every few minutes. It feels good to have my cheeks slowly deflate.

Mom feels bad for me and goes out driving to find me something soft to eat. She ends up getting me a peanut butter and strawberry smoothie, king-size, which is surely one thousand calories. I don't care. I slowly sip it as I do my homework. Parent Night is tomorrow and I lay out the purple dress I'm going to wear. I put on a pair of black heels and slowly walk around my room, getting used to the three inches that they add to my figure. The extra height makes me look trim. I love it. I place the dress and shoes back, wanting to smile but not being able to since my face is frozen.

I put out my contact lenses and saline solution, because I want to be free of glasses for one night. Sometimes my eyes behave for a couple of hours and they can tolerate the sensation of contacts. I have some makeup I want to wear. Grandpa hates it when I wear makeup, especially anything pink or red on my lips or cheeks. He says that I'm trying to look older than my age. He also says that women who wear too much makeup look like prostitutes. I haven't seen too many prostitutes, except those few times when Mom or Dad drove me up Biscayne Boulevard, and then I saw plenty of them. I haven't studied their makeup, though. Their clothes are what grab my attention.

The alarm clock, in blaring red digits, tells me that it's past ten o'clock. I can hear Mom and Dad messing around in the kitchen, eating a late night snack, and I join them to get a glass of water. They're eating tuna sandwiches. The bread, the flaky tuna, the chopped-up tomatoes. My stomach is saying yes, but my sore mouth is saying no. After Mom finishes eating, she gives me a mani and pedi, doing my fingers in pink and my toes in red. She does nails like a professional, cutting my cuticles, buffing my nails, and doing everything that a salon does, and it lasts for days and days. When I do my own nails I always create a mess and the polish chips the very next day, so I appreciate Mom for helping me get ready for Parent Night. It's soothing to have her hands massage mine. I feel a tickle of the nail-polish brush. Mom says some things, but I don't capture her words in my fuzzy haze. I don't even remember falling into bed.

. . .

It's strange to go to school and not have Maria there. She has a pretty clean attendance record, and I usually see her hang out with her friends by the flagpole before school starts. I see tight shorts, slicked hair, eyeliner, red lips, large earrings ... her chonga friends are there without her. At least she isn't here to tempt me with food, because that's something I'm starting to hate about her. It seems malicious to try to get me to eat when I'm being so good. I'm really on a roll with this fasting thing.

"It sucks that Maria is suspended," Lisa says.

"I know."

Shakira walks by us, her gait jaunty and unaffected by the glares she's receiving. People are staring daggers at her, because we're all on Team Maria. Team Shakira has no members.

"I'm going to get her," Lisa whispers to me.

"How?" I ask.

"I'll figure something out."

The idea of revenge sounds good to me, but revenge seems vindictive when it's actually acted out. In middle school, this boy named Daniel called me fat and pulled my hair. He ruined my day, because I was bummed out for hours. People felt sorry for me, but I felt that I had to save face by getting revenge. So I sabotaged his science project, some heap of electronics that he said took forever to build. I snuck in the science lab early in the morning when Mr. Engels went to the faculty lounge to get his mail. Daniel's robotic orange-juice maker was found that morning all broken and torn, with wires pulled out, and his face looked so crestfallen. He asked to go to the office to call his mother and she came over, embarrassing him by yelling at the science teacher. "I want to know who did this and what kind of teacher are you that this can happen in your classroom!" She went on and on and on. I jumped every time she raised her voice, and Daniel looked so ashamed. First his science project was destroyed, and then the whole class learned that his mother was loud and rude.

I didn't want vengeance at such a high magnitude. My goal had been to make him upset, not to ruin his life. So ever since then, revenge hasn't been my thing. I worry about what Lisa will do. Shakira is mean, but she's all talk, no action. Her words hurt, but it isn't like she's out to destroy us. It seems like she's crude and socially inept. Anyway, she's so beautiful that I don't think she cares too much about what other people are doing. Beautiful girls seem to live in their own bubble, unconcerned about the goings-on in other people's lives. She jabs at us, but it doesn't seem to be in a methodical, calculated manner. It's like she's one of those criminals who wakes up in the morning not planning to steal anything, but if she sees a purse lying in someone's car, she'll smash the window and take it. She sees our weaknesses and uses them against us when the opportunities are there. She saw that Maria made a mistake in wearing open-toed shoes, and she sees that I'm insecure about my looks. She also sees other things about me, things that I'm trying to hide from my classmates.

Between classes I wait for Lisa to come out of the bathroom so that we can walk together to our next class. I don't realize it, but while I wait I'm totally staring at Peter. He's at his locker and he bends down to pick up a book he dropped. He runs a hand through his thick, bouncy hair. Perfect.

"Take a picture, it'll last longer," someone says in my ear.

I think that the voice is my imagination, but then I notice Shakira standing next to me. She's so close to me that the filmy fabric of her sleeve brushes against the top of my shoulder.

"What do you mean?" I ask.

"I saw you staring," she says.

"Staring at what?"

"Don't play stupid. It's obvious you're in love with him."

"With who?"

"Peter," she says, narrowing her eyes.

Is this turning into a catfight? I've never been in a catfight before. I've seen episodes of clawing and hair pulling—which look fun as a bystander—and Shakira has been in her own tiff recently. Maybe Shakira is attracted to trouble. I wonder if I could take her on. She's taller than me, but her arms look so thin and wimpy. I squeeze my arm, wondering if I'm stronger than her and could take her down. But that would be silly, because I'm an honor-roll student and honor-roll students don't get into fights. That's like a law.

"I don't know what you're talking about," I stonily say.

"Okay, we'll see." She shrugs and walks toward Peter. She whispers something in his ear. Her proximity to him makes me angry. I should whoop her butt, but I don't have Maria's street confidence or muscle, and my parents would ground me for life.

Peter laughs and she giggles. Maybe they're talking about me. Peter thinks it's funny that I like him. Who am I, with my frizzy hair and glasses? And I'm not popular, either. Shakira isn't popular with the girls, but she is with the boys, and she's so enchanting that she'd be a better fit for Peter. Not me. Not Almira, boyfriendless girl that she is.

No, no, no—I can't think so negatively. Just because Shakira is flirtatious with him doesn't mean there's dead space between me and Peter. I don't imagine it when he squeezes my hand or arm, or sits too close to me when he has a question about a science lab … maybe he sees me as a friend, but the moments we have together are precious and electric to me. There might not be explosive fireworks between me and Peter yet, but with time they may develop. I can't give up on that idea. Maybe my desires will become a reality some day and I just have to wait. I have to step things up if I'm going to compete with Shakira and Lisa. I have to find a way ...

· · ·

"Good afternoon," Mr. Gregory says. Lisa ignores him and I give him a weak smile. He escorted Maria to the principal's office. I know why he did that—because he's an adult and an authority figure—but Lisa doesn't want to forgive him.

"Girls, can I talk with you for a minute?" he says.

Lisa groans. She hates it when adults lecture to her. She rolls her eyes and frowns, whereas I space out and don't pay attention. We all rebel in different ways.

We stand in the hallway as students walk past us to get inside the lab. "Do I detect an attitude over what happened yesterday?" he asks.

"No," I say.

"Yes," Lisa says.

It's just like Lisa to be more brutally honest than me, whereas I hate being confrontational.

"Maria's our friend, Mr. Gregory," I say. "I know you were just doing your job—"

"She didn't deserve to be suspended," Lisa interrupts.

"Actually, she did," Mr. Gregory says in an even tone. "She laid her hands on someone and that's something that should never be done, even during a volatile argument. How would you like it if someone pushed you?"

"I don't say things that make anyone want to push me," Lisa says, crossing her arms under her chest.

"Oh, really? You haven't said or done anything offensive to anyone, ever?"

Lisa silently fumes, because she can't agree to that. We all do something offensive every once in a while, whether we mean to or not. But the problem with Shakira is that she *always* acts with disregard to people's feelings.

"We'll get over it," I say.

"I hope so," Mr. Gregory says.

"I'm sure he's acted in softie Lifetime movies," Lisa whispers to me when we head toward our seats.

We giggle, thinking about Mr. Gregory's pre-teacher life as a struggling actor. Peter's sketching and, as usual, closes his sketchpad when he sees us come in. He gives us quizzical looks when he sees us laughing.

"What's so funny?" he asks.

"Nothing," I say. I look at him and wonder if Shakira has said anything to him about my feelings, which she guessed about correctly. Peter looks at me like he normally does. There's no mischievous glint in his eyes, and he doesn't act or talk like he has a hidden agenda to play games with me. He seems good-natured and even switches my dirty stool, which has a piece of dried gum on it, with a cleaner one. He's the perfect gentleman.

I touch the richly textured cardboard cover of his closed sketchpad, wondering what's inside of it, who he's drawing, and why he always closes the pad when we walk in. He takes the pad and places it in his bookbag, away from my prying eyes. He has good instincts, because I'm the type of person who goes through other people's medicine cabinets. I can't help it. I know which of my friends' parents has a bacterial infection and who's on birth control.

Our lab assignment for the day is to look at slides of various animal and plant tissues and identify their cell structures. Peter stands up to get our microscope, but Lisa says, "No, sit down, I'll get it."

She grabs her purse and goes to the back room where Mr. Gregory keeps books and lab supplies. Shakira is closer to the back room than Lisa is, but Lisa speeds ahead of her so that Shakira falls right behind Lisa in the line. One student after another goes inside to get a microscope. I watch Lisa come back to us with a microscope, one hand grasping the arm and her other hand supporting the base. She plugs it in and the light source at the bottom beams up toward the stage. I love working with microscopes and can't wait to get my hands on it. Mr. Gregory walks around the room giving each group a small box of slides to work with.

I take a slide that's labeled "fern" and adjust the focus controls until I see discernible green blobs. Peter leans toward me. "It's still blurry," I say.

"Let me see," he says.

Our heads gently collide and I look into his eyes. We smile at each other, and today I'm able to smile. The swelling in my face has gone down, so I don't look too freakish. I'm chipmunk-cheeked, but cutely so, I hope.

A burst of laughter erupts from the back of the room. All of us turn around. Shakira has a black eye.

"Who punched her?" a girl next to me asks loudly.

"Maria! Maria! Maria!"

"What! Maria's in the room?"

There's confusion. We all think Maria or one of Maria's friends gave Shakira the black eye. People are yelling, wanting to believe that there had been a brawl while we were all busy with our microscope work. Shakira touches her eye. She takes a mirror out of her purse and her eyes widen as she looks at her reflection. I want to know who punched her when none of us saw anything.

Mr. Gregory holds his hands up and we quiet down. He inspects Shakira's eye and the microscope she was using. "Her microscope is dirty," he says. After he runs a finger around the lens, it comes back with some black, charcoal-type substance on it. "It's probably dust or someone spilled soil on it. I have plants back there."

"May I go to the bathroom, Mr. Gregory?" Shakira asks in a muted voice.

He hands her a pass and she leaves. Shakira won't look at anyone and I can swear that her eyes are glassy with unshed tears.

"That was rough," Peter says. "Mr. Gregory should clean his things better."

"Absolutely," Lisa says. "I bumped into a shelf back there and my skirt got covered in dust."

"Yeah, that room's pretty grungy," I agree.

Peter goes back to looking at a slide. As I admire his good looks, Lisa grabs my arm.

"What?" I ask, turning to her.

"Didn't that feel great?" she whispers in my ear.

I stand back and look at her. Then she opens her purse and takes out an eyeliner pencil that's worn down to a nub. My jaw drops.

Peter puts his hand on my shoulder and I turn around. "You have to look at this," he says. He adjusts the microscope, so now I can see everything clearly. The cells look exactly as they do in the illustrations from the textbook, but I don't care. My mind is reeling from what Lisa did. Shakira looked so upset. We want her to feel that way, but now that she's visibly shaken, I feel bad. Lisa, on the other hand, has a smirk stuck on her face.

"So I'll see you tonight," Peter says.

"Sure," I say. The fact that he looks happy that we're all meeting up again for Parent Night doesn't appease me. Usually any morsel of his attention shoots my spirits straight to the sky, but not this time.

13

"Mom, I'm going out with some friends after Parent Night is over," I say.

"Where are you going?" Mom asks.

"A pizza place."

"That's fine."

"Who's going to be there?" Grandpa asks.

"Lisa, Jennifer, Jillian, Erica, Peter—"

"Peter!"

"Yes, he's in our classes."

Grandpa sits in our living room, frowning. Grandma sits next to him watching Dr. Phil. Dr. Phil is yelling at someone to get her life straight. I'm so glad that I don't have a Dr. Phil in my life. All day with someone telling me what to do? It's bad enough that my parents and grand-parents constrict the goings-on in my life. Dr. Phil seems much worse.

"Why is this Peter coming?" Grandpa asks.

"She already told you that he's a boy in her class," Mom says.

"Well, I don't think she should be going out with any boys," Grandpa says, the old country seeping out of his voice.

"He's Lisa's date," I say. She asked him out and she wants to claim him, even though it hurts my heart to think that he's going out with another girl.

"Oh, okay," Grandpa says, dropping the subject.

Mom has already straightened my hair with a ceramic iron. She makes it look so easy, but whenever I use the iron by myself, my hair looks crunchy and slightly wavy. I stare at my reflection, running my hands through my straight, tangle-free, shiny hair. Amazing.

I really don't want to wear my glasses. My fickle eyes reject contacts most of the time, but I want to see how they react toward Parent Night. I slip in my contact lenses, blinking at the sensation of foreign objects on my irises. They're comfortable enough. So it's a good eye day for me. I toss some eye drops in my purse just in case.

I shimmy into my purple dress and swish around the full-length mirror attached to my closet. My high heels feel tight, but I'll get used to them. I put the thinnest amount of eyeliner on my eyes, the pencil reminding me of Lisa's dastardly deed. So wrong. Next comes blush and mascara, and I'm done with applying makeup since I don't want to put on too much with Grandpa still in the house. I touch my tender cheeks. The makeup will distract people from the puffiness in my face.

I want to leave early, but Mom is taking forever to dress. Dad and I are watching the news in the living room when I remember something: I never found a knight and maiden picture for Peter. If I find one for him, then he'll know that I think about him and care for him without coming on too strong. (I don't have enough experience in the love department to know if boys like it when girls throw themselves at them.)

I tell Dad I need more hair spray, and instead of heading to the bathroom I go to my computer. I look through Google. I watch the clock nervously as I skim through pages of images. I want the best picture that exists of a knight and maiden. Then I find one. The knight is handsome. The maiden is wearing a billowing dress that flows around her like an upside-down flower. The colors are very lively, as if the painting was restored or enhanced by computer imaging. There are horses and a stream in the background. There's no time to daydream about the knight and maiden being me and Peter (I can daydream about that before I go to bed tonight or during school tomorrow). I hurriedly stick photo paper in my printer and print it out. But when will it dry? I slip the picture in a small envelope and hope it won't smear too much by the time I see Peter. I save the picture on my desktop in case I need it again.

My grandparents leave and Dad drives us to school. Mom is looking smoking hot as usual with a tight brown dress, and Dad wears a navy suit. The front of the school is packed with cars, so we have to park on the lawn. I watch people step out of cars. Parent Night is such a major affair. Everyone is dressed so nice, as if they're going to a fancy dinner rather than to a get-together with teachers. Opulent Parent Nights are the norm in my school; it's more important than freshman orientation, although far less fancy than prom. My friends at other schools say that their Parent Nights are nothing special, but Coral Gables Preparatory makes theirs seem like a big deal. It's exhilarating to see my grungy-looking classmates, who wear shorts and T-shirts during the day, come to Parent Night dressed glamorously. I don't recognize my classmates in their designer ensembles, with their hair done and faces made up. Boys who look average during the daytime are handsome in their suits and ties.

I find Lisa and we screech at each other. Lisa has bouncy curls swept into a loose ponytail, heavy makeup, and a little black dress. I give her a hug. Mom and Dad look at each other as if I'm crazy. They don't get the meaning of this night for us—we get to look like grownups and we'll eat dinner with Peter at the end of the evening.

Lisa and I share almost every class, so we're following

each other. "She needs to revise her writing before turning in assignments," Ms. Odige tells my parents. Oh, I didn't expect anything negative to be said about me, but teachers are honest on these nights, unleashing the hard truth on our parents. "I have to separate her and Lisa sometimes," my history teacher says.

Dad gives me a stern look whenever he hears these bad reviews about my school behavior, but I do have straight A's, and all of my teachers after berating me say, "She's highly intelligent." Thank you. I know that.

We're about to go into Mr. Gregory's class, the only class I share with Peter. I dash into the bathroom to make sure I look spectacular. I wince when I hear Lisa mooning over Peter.

"He's so handsome tonight—" she begins.

Don't show any emotion, I think. I'm standing in front of the mirror and I force myself to relax my face, because I'm doing too much scrunching and frowning out of jealousy and heartache.

Lisa talks a while longer, praising Peter's looks and personality as I reapply some cream blush. She rummages through her purse so that she can redo her makeup as well. She dabs *Fierce Pout* on her lips.

"Can I have some?" I ask.

"Sure," Lisa says, handing me the tube.

I slick some of the clear gel onto my lips with the wand applicator. My lips burn on contact with the gooey substance. "Is it supposed to hurt?" I ask.

"At first."

"It's, like, really painful."

"You'll get used to it."

I stare at my reflection and I can swear that my lips are inflating like balloons. "At least it's working," I say.

"It better," Lisa says. "It cost a fortune."

There's a price to pay for beauty. I see this everyday as Mom exercises and later complains about sore muscles. And now I have these stinging lips to deal with.

"You look really pretty without glasses," Lisa says. "And your hair looks great straightened."

"Thanks." I think so, too. Now to see what Peter thinks.

We strut on our high heels toward Mr. Gregory's class. I have to walk through an open hallway to get to his room. It's windy and leaves and twigs are blowing everywhere. Something flies into my eye, and I take a mirror out of my purse to see what's making me blink. I don't see anything. Sometimes my contacts bother me for a few seconds or minutes and then the pain goes away. I blink furiously and even close my right eye for a minute just to soothe it, but open it again when I see Mr. Gregory.

He's talking to a group of ten parents, giving an overview of his lessons and what students do during lab. Peter is in the front with his mom and dad. His dad is hot. He has the same light brown hair, with a wave in the front, and crinkly green eyes.

"His dad is gorgeous," Lisa whispers to me.

"Hmmm."

"Peter looks good enough to eat. Wow!"

"Yeth," I say. Whoa, I'm lisping all of a sudden. The burning sensation in my lips increases. The skin around my lips feels like it's bubbling. It's uncomfortable to talk.

"Lisa, is *Fierce Pout* FDA approved?" I ask.

"I don't know. What's FDA approved?" she says.

"Like, when the governmenth says something ith safe."

"Let me read the label."

I sigh, because now I'm sure that *Fierce Pout* was made in some loser's house and he somehow finagled his way into selling it in stores. In the news, I see many stories about people without medical degrees performing dentistry and collagen injections in their garages, horribly mutilating their patients. I'm sure *Fierce Pout* is made by one of these phony doctors. I can't believe Lisa paid fifty dollars for the stuff. The things females do for beauty, and I'm no exception. *Fierce Pout*, combined with my fresh surgery, does not do wonders for my mouth. I won't do much talking, I decide. Not only are my lips a problem, but whatever's in my eye becomes more prickly. My eye is burning.

Mr. Gregory is smiling at Dad. Dad is eyeing his teeth. Mr. Gregory is biting down and Dad is actually looking at his mouth. He's probably telling my teacher that he can get him a deal on bleaching or veneers. Dad's a smooth talker and likes to rub elbows to get new customers.

"Stop making my teachers bite down," I whisper. Dad

is always telling me to bite down and now he has to do the same with my teachers! He's embarrassing me. The evening has been pretty perfect so far.

Lisa turns to me and says, "Oh my God!"

"Wha?" Oh dear, I have no control over my lips anymore.

"Your mouth is, is, oh no, covered in bumps and your eye is really red."

No! I look like a mess. I pull my mirror out again and it's like looking at a monster. The corners of my mouth have tiny bumps, like the taste buds of a tongue. My eye is as red as a tomato. All the preening and primping I did before leaving was for naught, because I'm grotesque. I look like a gargoyle that should be hanging over a medieval castle. I can surely scare away innocent animals and children.

Lisa looks like she's going to cry for me, her best friend who now resembles a circus freak on one of the most important nights of the year. I panic and don't know what to do. I want to run out of the door and into the comforting darkness of the impending evening. The sun is starting to set and I can hide in the blackness of the night as if I'm a vampire. Will I sprout fangs next? I won't doubt it.

"Oooh, Almira, are you okay?" one of my classmates asks me.

"Almira, are you sick?" someone else says.

"Almira! Your mouth!"

I want to cry, but then that would make my eye worse

than it already is. And Peter is turning his head. No, I don't want him to see me like this. He's the reason I picked my dress and groomed myself so meticulously. My plan for how he's going to find me irresistibly attractive and whisk me off my feet isn't working. The mélange of mouth, lips, and eyes is destroying me. What next? Will all the weight I lost magically appear? I can imagine seven pounds ballooning over my figure for no reason at all, since everything else is taking a disastrous turn. Maybe my hair will fall out. Maybe the heel of my shoe will break, so that I have to walk with a limp or be forced to walk barefoot.

Peter's parents continue to talk to Mr. Gregory, but Peter sees me trying to hide in the corner, surrounded by friends. He walks over and reaches for me. "Almira, are you okay?" he asks, a frown marring his face.

"Yeth," I lisp.

"Your eyes, your lips—"

"No, I'm not okay." Why bother lying? My face is obviously falling apart.

"Come with me." Peter grabs my elbow and takes me into Mr. Gregory's back room, which is full of microscopes, books, trays, beakers, and such. There's a small sink with a greasy mirror above it. The room is dimly lit. The moment could be romantic if I wasn't transmogrified into some crazy lunatic with a bad eye, puffy lips, and ballooning cheeks.

Peter takes a paper towel, runs water over it, and wipes my lips. "What's the gunk on your lips?" he asks.

"This fancy lip-gwoss I bowwowed from Litha," I say.

"The things you girls do to be pretty."

"We can be cwazy."

Is he calling me pretty, or telling me that I'm trying to be pretty but I'm not quite there yet? My eyes are mesmerized by his beauty. His skin is slightly tanned and the planes of his face are angular and manly. I so wish for this to be a scene in one of those romance novels with a pirate and half-naked wench on the cover, but Peter's dressed like a businessman in a suit and tie and I'm horrid. If only he could be shirtless, holding me while I'm in a scanty, wind-whipped dress.

"You don't need this lip-gloss. You already have full lips."

I look into his eyes, which are darkened into a forest-green shade in the dim room. His eyes bore into mine. He wipes my lips with one hand and his other hand is gently gripping my chin. I always imagined this was the way my first kiss would begin, but who would dare to kiss my diseased lips? I have the lips of a leper.

"Your lips aren't as bumpy, but you have to do something about your eye," he says.

My lips do feel better, and the bumps are less noticeable. I open my purse, put my contacts back in their case, and pull out my glasses.

Peter smiles when I put them on. "There, you look like your old self."

My eyes feel the cool breeze of air conditioning. I believe

that Peter has made everything better again. My lips feel good. The redness of my eye is vanishing. I don't want this moment to end. Again, I wonder if Shakira has said anything to him. Shakira has no right to tell him that I like him, even if it's the truth. If that's ever revealed, then I'm the one who should be telling him to his face how much he means to me. He's the total package: polite, smart, and handsome. But I can't say anything to him. Not here and now. Not when Lisa likes him. What the hell! It isn't like he's Lisa's property.

"I have something for you," I say. I reach into my purse and take out the envelope with the knight and maiden picture. "You said you were looking for something like this."

Peter opens the envelope and his mouth slowly stretches open into a big smile when he sees what's inside. "Almira, this is beautiful," he says.

"Really?"

He flips the picture over so that I can take a good look at it. I was in such a rush to print it out for him that I didn't notice how truly beautiful it is. The maiden's dress has an elaborate curlicue pattern and she's wearing a heavy ruby necklace. The knight's armor gleams in the sunlight. His helmet is under one arm and his hair is golden, just like Peter's. The trees are so detailed that I can imagine them fluttering in the wind. And it isn't smeared at all from when I shoved it in the envelope seconds after printing it.

"Be careful," I say. "I didn't give it enough time to dry."

Peter slides it back in the envelope. "This is such a huge help, you have no idea. When you're an artist and have no clue what something is supposed to look like, you don't know when to begin. I haven't watched any knight movies or seen armor in person, so this really gives me a good idea of what I should do."

"And I'm sure Lisa's book helps, too," I say.

"She told me she never found it," he says.

The competitiveness in this unannounced competition flares inside of me. I'm ahead of Lisa, whether she knows it or not. He specifically needed something. She didn't deliver. I did. It's something small, a teensy favor, but it's a gesture of my intense like for him. I'm so proud of myself. I did something, rather than nothing. In my own way, I'm letting him know that I'm pursuing him.

"Are you okay back there?" Lisa asks, walking in, intruding.

"Yeah, Lisa," Peter says. "Almira will be okay."

"You're such a future doctor, Peter," Lisa jokes.

"Thanks. My dad would love to hear that. He's a cardiologist."

"My mom's a podiatrist," Lisa says.

"My dad's a dentist," I say.

The three of us crack a smile. There's a sense of intimacy between the three of us, but I want Lisa out of the picture and I'm sure she doesn't want me to be there either.

And what does Peter want? Who does he like? What's his type of woman? Shakira walks past the door, mini-CZJ that she is. She's wearing a knockout black dress. Peter looks, of course. Lisa and I both glare at our enemy.

Lisa pulls at Peter's arm, and his eyes disengage from Shakira's loveliness. When Lisa links her arm through Peter's, I feel a stab of jealousy. There's this whole triangle of jealousy. Lisa and Shakira. Shakira and me. Lisa and me. I don't think Lisa feels any ill will toward me, because I haven't expressed my interest in Peter. She probably doesn't expect me to be treacherous in any way. But I'm trying to betray her by liking the same guy she does. My impulses are raw and unstoppable. I want Peter just as much, if not more, than she does.

We all say goodbye to our parents and go to a pizza parlor. The sun is long gone and I slowly chew on a slice of pizza, the crust a wee bit too hard for my sore mouth. The evening was both a failure and a success. My eye and lips had been problematic for a brief moment. Peter nursed (caressed) my face, but now he's focusing on Lisa. The two of them sit close together, whispering into each other's ears. I talk with my friends, but my eyes constantly drift to them. I want that for myself, to sit with a boy and just relax and talk in a corner booth, to be a couple. I put drops in my eyes and slick soothing ChapStick over my lips. Peter doesn't notice my normalcy since he's too busy laughing at Lisa's jokes.

14

I hate depression. I know when I'm depressed because my whole body feels heavy and sleepy, as if I have to drag it around. My eyes also feel heavy with tears. And deep inside, I know that I shouldn't be depressed. I'm not ugly. In fact I'm cute, I know it. My facial features are in proportion, although I have to tweeze my eyebrows into arcs or else they'll look like caterpillars, and I think my nose is too pointy. Still, I get compliments. I'm not stupid, because my grades are excellent. And what takes most people a half an hour to figure out I can solve in minutes. When it comes to writing research papers, I do them the night they're assigned, rather than waiting until the last minute like everyone else. I have a drawer full of trophies and certificates dating back from elementary school. So I have plenty of things going for me.

I believe that there's happiness in the future—so many things to do and explore—but something is blocking me from it. One of my teachers long ago mentioned how many third world countries have slums, and not too far from the dirt and grime are beautiful beaches and sprawling hotels for tourists. She showed us a book with pictures of South American ghettoes a few blocks from luscious water views. There were photos of buildings falling apart, and on the other side of these cities were hotels bustling with room service attendants and rich people. I want to leave the slum. I want to be in the paradise that's a stone's throw from me.

Maybe I'm the problem. Maybe I need to make things happen. I feel my spirits lift up at the idea of that. I know I can get things for myself. I've done it before. A few years ago, Dad pleaded that he was too busy to go to the store to get me science supplies and that he'd have to take me another day, but I couldn't wait. Our house is deep in the suburbs away from most stores, in a driving town, but I walked in the hot sun until I found a drugstore. I used my allowance money to buy different colors of wax paper, construction paper, and paper plates (I was making large models of cells) and when I came home, I did my project. The next day I won the sixth grade science fair. I made it happen, even though Mom and Dad both told me that I wouldn't know what to buy. There was also the time that I had a paper due but my computer was infected with a virus. I spent all night deleting things from the registry and running my virus scan over and over until the computer was free of viruses and I could finish my paper. Of course I got an A. My parents both told me on that occasion to wait until they took the computer to a repairman, to tell my teacher about my problem, and to get a lesser grade. But I didn't want a lesser grade. I didn't want a lesser anything.

In the past I was able to get tickets to sold-out concerts, soothe over hurt feelings between my friends, talk other people into and out of things ... so there were countless times when I had the burst of energy to save myself from a situation and ensure that only the best happens to me. I deserve the best, just like everyone else believes they should get what's right. Why should I be unhappy and boyfriendless?

I want to know exactly what's in Peter's sketchpad. Curiosity hits me hard. I really need to see what's on those pages. Maybe I'm on them. Maybe he's secretly longing for me and deep in that sketchpad is a picture of me, his secret crush.

It's early in the morning, with ten minutes left until the first bell rings. Buses and cars are still pulling up. People are busily talking about Parent Night. Who wore what? Who pulled off their look and who didn't? Lisa simpers, as she imagines that Peter is infatuated with her.

"Could you believe how he couldn't keep his eyes off of me?" she says.

Our friend Jillian sits there, nodding. Jillian is emo and wears a lot of black—dyed hair, clothes, shoes, nail polish, bookbag. She keeps nodding as Lisa speaks. I see a white tendril of a headphone running from her left ear—the ear away from Lisa—which means she isn't paying an iota of attention to any of us. I feel like doing the same, nodding off as Lisa speaks, but she's my best friend. She's so happy about having Peter in her life, even though they're not boyfriend-girlfriend. I want to be happy, too. But I don't want to live a lie like Lisa is, imagining things between me and Peter. I want the real thing.

Peter darts into my line of vision.

"Peter is the darlingest boy I have ever known," Lisa continues.

"Yeah," Jillian says.

"Hmmm," I say.

My eyes follow Peter. Lisa hasn't spotted him yet, which means I have strong radar for him and she doesn't. I see him head toward the west wing of the school. I decide to follow. "I have to go to the bathroom," I say.

Lisa doesn't even notice that I've said anything. Her eyes are rolled to the sky as she rhapsodizes about Peter. "He's the only man for me," she says.

"Yeah," Jillian repeats, bopping her head to AFI, or maybe it's My Chemical Romance. Her heavily lined eyes are glazed over and Lisa doesn't stop talking, happy to have something of an audience listening to her ramblings. I know that Peter is a great guy, but even I think Lisa is being a bit extreme. There are other things to talk about, other things in life, other great concerns. And he isn't her boyfriend! There's nothing for her to discuss. She should keep her feelings inside, like me, but then that would be dishonest. At least she's heartfelt by being out in the open. I love him, too, but if I revealed that I would hurt Lisa tremendously.

With ninjalike moves I follow Peter to the other side of the school. My footfall is barely perceptible amid the hubbub of hundreds of high schoolers ranging from runt-like freshmen to sophisticated seniors. I see these two thousand people every day, and I don't know most of them. I half-recognize faces as I stay a few feet behind Peter.

"Hey, bro," a boy says as he approaches Peter.

"What's up?" Peter gives a high five to his shaggy-haired friend. His friend has a large, black portfolio under one arm—he has to be an art-class buddy. Peter takes his bookbag off and tosses it onto a bench.

"Finished your assignment?" the friend asks.

"Yup. I'll show it to you. An easy A."

"For you. You must be the best artist in the class."

"No, I think Eric is much better than me."

"Nah, Eric has nothing on you," the friend says.

"Well, see my sketchpad first and then you decide," Peter says.

They go on for a few minutes about who has the best

artistic skill in the class. I don't recognize the names because I'm not in that clique. They also mention techniques and artists that I have no clue about. And my eyes are glued to the bookbag, or they try to be. People walk in front of me, blocking my view, but I know where the objects of my desire are—Peter and his sketchpad. Peter and his friend walk over to a water fountain a few feet away. They leave their bookbags behind. First Peter's friend dips his head down for water, and then Peter.

I'm fast. I scamper from behind the bushes, grab Peter's bookbag, and then return to the bushes. It happens like lightening—flashes of the blue sky, the greenery of the courtyard, people's jumbled faces—and now I have one of his possessions, even though it's the owner I'm really after. I flatten my body against a building and go inside of it, to a bathroom. I have it. I have his bookbag. I actually stole someone's bookbag! I have never stolen anything in my entire life.

It isn't stealing, because I'll make sure he gets it back.

Yeah. Anything to make me feel less bad.

Inside the girl's bathroom, I hold the bookbag to my chest. It smells like him: cologne, sweat, and the graphite of pencils. It's a heady combination. I imagine this is what boyfriends smell like—a mixture of the things that they love. So if I were to date a baseball player, then he'd smell like the outdoors and the leather of his mitt. One of those hippie-wannabes who listens to Hendrix and Joplin would smell like incense and whatever it is he smokes. But it's Peter's smell that I've been after. And if any boy got to know me really well, then my perfume would become mingled with his scent so that we could become one. That's so romantic.

I look at my watch. The bell will ring soon. So much time has passed, from stalking Peter to making away with his bag.

It feels so wrong … I slowly unzip his bookbag. I never noticed before that he has several patches and pins on it. He has a Greenpeace pin, a patch with Vincent Van Gogh's face on it, and a Humane Society pin. He's so sensitive! He loves animals and art and the environment. I get even more excited as I stick my hand into his bag.

Math book, pencils, a scientific calculator. The bookbag is heavy, but I didn't realize that so much junk would be in it. Then again, my bookbag has plenty of stuff in it, too. I assumed that boys would carry fewer things, but I'm wrong.

I want the sketchpad!

There's an assortment of notebooks and folders with his slanted writing all over them, but no sketchpad. Where is it?

Well, see my sketchpad first and then you decide.

Oh no! Peter must have taken his sketchpad out during a moment when people were blocking my view. He probably had his sketchpad either in his hand when he drank water or he left it on the bench so that his friend could look at it. I've stolen his bookbag for nothing. I search through the whole thing and there are no drawings. How I wanted to see the contents of that pad! I'm dying to know what's inside of it.

The bell rings. I don't want to be late to class. But how am I going to get rid of the bookbag?

I stick my head out of the bathroom to take a peek at what's going on. People are walking to their lockers and to class. I have my own bag slung on my back, so it'll definitely look weird to come out with another bag. And I still don't know how I'm going to get it back to Peter. I leave the bathroom, thinking about how I should approach him with his bookbag. I'll tell him that I found it and knew it was his. Some pranksters must have taken it from him.

"Miss!"

The adult female voice cuts through the air.

"Miss!"

The voice is getting closer to me.

"Miss!"

A hand is on my shoulder, and I spin around to see a short, burly woman in my face. It's one of the security guards. "Come with me," she says.

"But, why?" I ask.

"Come."

"I didn't do anything wrong," I say

"I saw you take that bookbag," she says.

I gasp at the accusation. Okay, she really must have seen me steal the thing, but she doesn't know why. I'm after Peter for platonic and romantic reasons. I meant no harm by taking the bag, other than to look through someone else's possessions and rob him of his privacy. I did nothing wrong.

I gulp. I'm seeing stars. This is the first time security has ever had to talk to me about anything other than moving it along to clear the hallway before the bell rings. The chongas with a bad attitude—rolling their eyes and talking back to adults—are the ones who are always led away. Not me. Not Almira Abdul, honor-roll student with no boyfriend.

I follow her, feeling surreal, as if this isn't really happening to me. This is what it must be like to be handcuffed and booked (I hope that will never ever happen to me, but with the way things are going, maybe it will). I'm doing crazy things in the name of love. I've become a bona fide stalker. She takes me to the waiting room outside the principal's office. The principal's office! The only time I go in there is when the principal wants to talk to the high achievers about how great we're doing and to tell us in advance that we'll have luncheons and breakfasts in celebration of all our outstanding outcomes. I'm always invited to any honor roll or perfect-attendance function. Now I'm in the office for stealing.

I feel so ashamed. Shame is a big emotion with Muslims. Shame on me, shame on you, shame on everyone. How dare you shame the family name! The family name, such a precious commodity. My parents will be so embarrassed by my actions, because they think that I'm a direct reflection of them. I imagine Grandpa's face if he were to hear the news ... a dark cloud falls over me. The Abdul name will be tarnished forever unless I get out of this muck and mire.

15

"The principal is ready to see you," a secretary says.

I get up and walk inside the office. I see a lot of brown and red furniture, which almost obscures the people inside it. Behind the massive wooden desk is the principal, Mr. Lopez, and framed by a large red-leather chair is Peter with his sketchpad in his lap. He indeed had taken it out of his bag, and I wasn't able to see it at all during those few minutes in the girl's bathroom.

Mr. Lopez is in his fifties with bushy white hair and a wispy mustache. "Almira, have a seat," he says in his deep voice.

I swallow a lump in my throat and sit down.

"Peter, you approached me in the hallway before class saying that your bookbag was missing, and a security guard saw Almira in action as she took it," Mr. Lopez says.

"Almira isn't the type to steal," Peter says. He wrinkles his brow because no one associates me with thieving, even though I have sort of done that.

"Well, that appears to be what happened. Unless Almira has another explanation."

"I do," I say. I clear my throat to strengthen my voice. I have to bluff my way out of this. There's no way I'm getting suspended for this, for following my heart. I had been nosy and wrong, but love makes people do foolish things.

"Well, Almira, I'd like to hear this," Mr. Lopez says. "You're a wonderful student and I can't believe that you're sitting here for something like this. On prior occasions you've come here for your accomplishments, but now it's for this offense. I rely on you and other students like you to raise the school's name. Look at the certificate behind me; it's from when you and your classmates raised money for the community. Look at the trophy outside of my door from the math bowl that you helped us win. You've helped make the school successful, and now you want to bring it down by stealing. Trust me, I deal with issues like this all day—petty theft, fights, vandalism, things that go on in every school—but when I have someone like you doing these things, then it's a cause for great concern."

I gulp. Mr. Lopez is just as good as my parents at making me feel guilty.

"Okay, but I have a really, really good explanation," I manage to chirp out.

Mr. Lopez and Peter continue to look at me. And I still have nothing to say.

"It was really quite simple—"

Both males wait for me, and then the lies pour out of me.

"I saw Peter's bookbag by itself on a bench and I figured that his first period is right next to mine and that I'd give it to him."

"But I didn't leave my bookbag alone," Peter said. "I mean, I was at the water fountain. Maybe you didn't see me."

"Peter, I swear you weren't around. I know where you go for first period, so I thought I'd give you the bookbag."

"The security guard said that you were watching him until the coast was clear for you to take it," Mr. Lopez said.

I gulp again. All this gulping and not a drop to drink. "I don't know what she's talking about," I say. "I was going to the bathroom and saw Peter's bookbag lying there. I recognized it because of his pins and patches. Sir, I really meant no harm."

Peter has a strange look on his face, as if he might believe that I'm some crazy stalker chick.

"Almira, you have an excellent record with us," Mr. Lopez says. "I'm sure this was some harmless prank. I don't feel like doing anything except letting you go with a warning. But next time this happens, we'll have to bring your parents in and you'll get a few days of indoor suspension. We don't have time to be chasing stolen bookbags. Students need to get to work and so do we."

"Mr. Lopez, this is just a big misunderstanding," I say.

"I hope so," Mr. Lopez says.

Peter's face relaxes. Yes, I'm normal, there's nothing wrong with me, there's no reason to take a bookbag. He shifts his sketchpad in his lap. All because of that thing! And I never got a chance to see it.

Ten minutes have passed since the bell rang, so Mr. Lopez issues us hall passes. This is the first time I've ever been late to first period. And for what? But at least I can say that I tried to go after something, somebody I wanted. I'm not standing in the sidelines. I'm an active participant, even if I fail miserably.

Peter walks alongside me. I steal—there I go stealing again—glances at his gleaming hair and broad shoulders. I want him to put his arm around me absentmindedly, but we aren't there yet. We aren't anywhere yet. A big idea starts forming in my head: He will be mine.

"That was pretty stupid," Peter says. "I know you don't steal things."

"Yeah," I say.

"That security guard must be seeing things."

We walk slowly, taking our time to get to class since the principal has excused us on the hall passes he wrote. Kids skipping class for real are ducking into bathrooms and stairwells. I'd like to do that too, so I can have more time with Peter.

"I'm glad he didn't call my parents," I say. "They'd flip out."

"You were only trying to help," he says.

"I know." *I was also trying to look through your things without your permission because I want you.*

He looks so calm. I must look calm too, but there are all these turbulent emotions inside of me. He has no idea. Well, I tried. His sketchpad is under his arm. Now I don't know who he's drawing, if by chance he has a sketch of me. Maybe he stays up late at night picturing my face in his head. *Let me remember what Almira's cheekbones look like. Ah, her eyes. I need to add more definition to her chin.* Yet I doubt it, because he isn't acting any special way toward me. He's just his usual friendly self.

We stop in front of Peter's first-period history class. "Well, thanks for trying to help," he says. He puts a hand on my shoulder and gently squeezes. I want him to reach down and squeeze my hand, so that we can be seen in the hallway as a couple. A couple walks past us, hand in hand, smiles on their faces, laughing about something. A couple. Two people become one.

Peter gets closer to me. His skin has a moist sheen to it (okay, it's oily). His lashes look super long, up close. I think this is it. I hold my breath. I close my eyes.

"Almira, did you notice what we had between each other in there?" he asks.

I open my eyes. He's half-whispering into my ear, his breath strong enough to make my hair flutter. Okay, he doesn't kiss me—yet—but at least he notices the chemistry between us.

"Of course," I say. My eyes start to feel heavy as tears collect, but I blink them away. This moment is so sweet that I'll cherish it forever.

"The way we interacted was amazing."

"I agree."

"I mean, we really got together and backed you up so that you wouldn't get into trouble," he says.

"Huh?" I say.

"I didn't believe any of his accusations, and you were so cool, calm, and collected. I remember the first time Mr. Lopez spoke to me, when I was outside of science class with a water balloon when Mr. Gregory was teaching us about water pressure, and he thought I was going to throw it at someone. My legs turned to jelly and I was stammering. But you were so confident."

"I was?" I ask.

"Yes," he says.

"Oh." He isn't going to kiss me. He isn't talking about any emotional connection I have with him. He's straight up talking about Mr. Lopez and how he bore down on me and my excuses when I in fact had taken the bookbag. Not to steal it forever, but just to see that sketchpad, to see if he likes me. But it doesn't seem like he does.

Peter squeezes my arm again and his hand lingers

below my sleeve. Maybe he does like me. He's perplexing. It's like chasing the cookie chunks in a Burger King Oreo Shake with my straw. They're elusive, but I manage to get them. But I usually have to wait until they're all at the bottom to scoop them out with a straw or spoon. Peter is my cookie chunk. How I want to bite into him and have him for myself. My stomach growls. I could really use a BK shake. Images of creaminess, coldness, and cookies float in my head. *Focus!* I tell myself. Peter is still in front of me. We're alone in the hallway, not a soul in sight.

"We really have to get to class," Peter says. "The time on these hall passes is five minutes old."

That's true; our teachers will think we're skipping. But I don't care. I don't want the moment to end. I wish for the school halls to disappear and a beach to appear, and then Peter and I can run off into the sunset. Instead, it's early in the morning and we're at school. Blech.

"I'll see you later," he says, ruffling my hair casually.

"Okay," I say. I raise my hand to pat him on the shoulder, but he turns around and all I hit is air. How awkward. I don't know how to touch a boy, even in a friendly way (and I imagine that if it were in a perverted way, I'd somehow mess up).

I get to English class, hand the teacher my pass, and sit down. People stare at me. There's some whispering behind me. People know I've been in the principal's office. It's ridiculous how exciting that is to some people. They will ask me after class what happened. Nothing happened.

What I wanted to happen didn't: to see Peter's sketchpad and for him to kiss me.

Even though I feel down-and-out, I'm not going to give up. I console myself that next time, if I want something badly enough, then whatever I want to happen will happen.

16

"He's going to be my boyfriend," Lisa says.
"How can you tell?" I ask.

"Because of our chemistry. We're like oil and water."

"Oil and water don't mix," I say.

"Okay, then we're like oil and oil or water and water," she says.

I sigh. No wonder Lisa always needs help with science homework. She still doesn't know that mushrooms are fungi (she insists they're vegetables) and that brown isn't in the color spectrum. She has so much to learn, but I don't have the patience to teach her things.

"Has Peter asked you out?" I ask.

"No, but in time he will."

"He acts friendly toward the both of us."

"But he's into me. We really connected during Parent Night."

Yes, and she had a piece of basil stuck in her teeth half the night from eating pizza, but I didn't tell her. She was seated far from me. Anyway, I wanted her to fail at our group date. I ache for Peter, but I'm not sure if he likes me in any other way than as a friend. This is what unrequited love is. This is what Ms. Odige talks about when she makes us read those boring poems in Middle English, which is English, but old and incomprehensible. I want to cry every minute of every day that I can't have Peter.

We sit in front of the school before the first bell rings. It's another day. Yesterday morning started out horribly with my theft and sitting in Mr. Lopez's office, but today is a new day, hopefully a better day. Mornings are like almost-clean slates. I say almost-clean because the residue of yesterdays is sometimes stuck on them. Like if I had an argument with a friend or my parents, I'd wake up the next day feeling crummy. Today I still feel weird about stealing Peter's bookbag. With time, I hope all that entirely washes over. Maybe by this afternoon Peter will think absolutely nothing of it, even though he assured me yesterday that he didn't think I was capable of stealing. I watch Lisa make another Bic tattoo on her wrist: *L and P.* Lisa and Peter.

"Your P looks like an upside down 6," I tell her truth-fully.

Lisa adds more ink to the artwork, but botches the job even more. She then puts some *Fierce Pout* on her lips, even though I told her the stuff is poison. She's now Jolie-like enough to enter school, with her fake tattoo and temporarily full lips. The morning is uneventful, unlike yesterday's debacle with Peter's bookbag. Mornings are like that: you can start the day off all wrong or all right. The meeting with Mr. Lopez is starting to fade away. He walks by me and doesn't even look at me because he's eyeing one of the football players who threw a milk carton at a bench, missing his goal of the garbage can.

In English class, Ms. Odige tells us to write in our journals about our thoughts on Parent Night since all of us were there. Ms. Odige tolerates all ink colors in journals, so I take out my pink pen and write my entry.

> *Parent Night was cool. My parents heard teachers say good and bad things about me, but mostly good. Anyway, I had a mishap with my contact lenses and this lame lip-gloss that I borrowed from a friend, but I quickly bounced back. That experience taught me that I have a very resilient spirit. I think Parent Night went well, considering that I was bothered by my eyes, my lips, and the empty sockets in my mouth from all the teeth Dad pulled out of me ... four wisdom teeth. I can put my tongue in these sockets. It's so*

weird walking around with my tongue finding these holes in my mouth. And I think I'm in love, but I'm not sure the boy is into me as much as I'm into him, which sucks.

Ms. Odige's comments are typical, written in red ink at the bottom of the page when she hands our journals back to us at the end of class. *You stray from the topic. Be careful about starting sentences with "and."*

Blah, blah, blah. I put my journal in my bookbag and head out to my next class. Maria is back in school and she eyeballs Shakira. Shakira looks unfazed, giving Maria a cool glance before walking away.

"Shakira," people mumble. "Go back to Orlando."

"She got Maria suspended."

Shakira holds her head high as these comments are hurled at her. I almost feel sorry for her. To have people say such bold things to her in an attempt to drive her out and make her uncomfortable must hurt, but then again, she has hurt others. It's tit for tat. It's karma returning to her with a slap on the cheek. Karma can be good that way.

"So how are your driving lessons going?" Maria asks.

"You're so lucky!" Lisa brays. "My mom just started teaching me."

"My lessons are going okay," I say. "I'm getting the hang of it. Maybe I'll pass my test right after my sixteenth birthday."

"Which is in two weeks!"

I'm going to turn sixteen soon. Many of my Latin

friends had quinceañera parties to celebrate their fifteenth birthday, dressing in beautiful gowns and having lavish parties in rented ballrooms. The American version, sweet sixteen, is something I can't wait for. I'm about to become a real adult on that landmark birthday, but I'll still be boy-friendless.

Peter is behind us, getting things in and out of his locker. He opens his sketchpad, the one that he takes so much effort to hide from me when I sit down next to him in science class. He flips it open and there is Shakira's gorgeous face. I lose my breath. Even Lisa gasps. Maria narrows her eyes at the image of enemy number one.

It was her that he was sketching so painstakingly, so lovingly. Tears prick the corners of my eyes. Lisa grimly turns to us and says, "I'm going to make Peter forget about her, and he'll sketch me next."

"Fat chance," Maria says.

"What's that supposed to mean?" Lisa asks.

"She's bewitched him. She's the person all the girls are going to hate and all the boys are going to love, just like in the movies."

"We're not living in a movie," Lisa says.

Seeing those pencil marks, so congruously put together to create Shakira's face, feels like a stab in the heart. It does something to me. I can't even explain it, but I want to be sketched and fussed over. I want Peter to love me. "I'll be right back," I mutter. I run to the bathroom and lock myself in a stall. He isn't drawing me ... but her.

I took his bookbag for nothing. I was escorted by a security guard to the principal's office for nothing. I had to listen to Mr. Lopez's guilt-inducing words for nothing. A few tears slide down my cheeks, but I wipe them off as soon as they fall. My breathing is out of control, but then it steadies. I shove my hair across my face to distract people from the redness of my eyes. I come into computer class a few seconds before the bell rings, sit down, and avert my gaze from everyone. I sluggishly start the daily assignment, typing slower than I normally do since I'm so sad. Peter can never be my boyfriend when he's smitten with Shakira.

He even has the nerve to bring her up during lunch—he leaves the cafeteria early and he finds me sitting alone in the library. I'm at a round table behind the biography section and he sits down next to me. On the back of my notebook, on one of the end pages, I've been drawing graffiti pronouncing my love for Peter. *Almira and Peter 4ever.* *ALMIRA LOVES PETER.* I close my notebook and look at him as if he's an alien from another planet. We've never sat with each other during lunch. It would be a treat, if Shakira didn't have his heart.

"Have you seen Shakira?" he asks. "I didn't finish sketching her for my art project."

"No," I say.

"You look upset," he says.

"I'm just studying," I lie.

"It's Maria, isn't it? Are you still upset about what happened?"

"Yeah," I say, even though I've gotten over it.

"Shakira—how should I put this—isn't the warmest person," Peter says. "But she's nice when you get to know her. She does have a sharp tongue, and she's opinionated."

"No kidding?"

"But she's very patient. She can sit for an hour while I sketch her, and she doesn't move like other people do."

Great, she's patient and a true model. I don't want to hear anything good about her. "Are you here to study?" I ask.

"I'm going to check out a book to read over the weekend," he says. "I love mysteries, especially the old ones."

"Me, too. I have all the old Agatha Christie paperbacks. Every book she's ever written is at my house. They're really my dad's, but I'm hooked on them."

"No!"

"Yes. I even watch the Agatha Christie movies on public television, even though that sounds dorky and I'm probably the only one who watches them."

"I sometimes watch them." He looks at me, mesmerizing me with his green eyes. My heart skips a beat, but I have to extinguish my love for him. He belongs to another.

"You've lost a lot of weight," he says. "You're not sick or anything?"

"No," I say. "You know I'm fasting."

"You look good, but be careful."

"Why?"

"You won't know who's real or not if you look too good. I remember a year ago, how I was chunky and had a lot of zits, and now people treat me differently, better. I don't like that."

"You mean, why didn't they appreciate you when you looked less glamorous?" I ask.

"Yes."

I nod at this deep thought he's having (it's so hot that he's capable of deep thoughts when so many good-looking guys are really dumb). "You didn't look that bad, so don't be so hard on yourself," I say. "You were still cute then. And I always thought you were smart, and a good artist."

"I know," he says. "You always talked to me, but other girls are, like, hanging all over me now, as if they didn't notice me before. I really hate that."

"I can imagine." Setting aside my jealousy toward the beautiful people, I think that perhaps it isn't always so wonderful to be beautiful—that beauty has setbacks and people have unrealistic expectations of those who have it.

"Even with you, I see guys looking at you as if you're someone else now," Peter says.

Boys are definitely giving me more attention. For every three pounds I lose, there are three new boys who say "hi" to me and stop me to strike up small talk. What a shallow world we live in. Maybe everyone's a little shallow, since I fell for Peter after his transformation and he's all gaga over modelesque Shakira. We don't notice someone's brains across a room. We don't place someone's eloquent words into a picture frame.

"Be careful and you won't get your heart broken," he says.

It's too late for his cautious words. My heart is broken into irreparable pieces now that I know he's been drawing Shakira. But as always, when despair hits me, hope shines through.

"Hey, some of my friends are going to an art gallery in a couple of days," he says. "Our art teacher told us to pick a gallery and go, as an assignment. We're supposed to take some pictures and write down our impressions in a report. We don't know exactly what night we're going, but you want to come?"

"Sure," I say. He's asking me to go somewhere with him? OMG.

"You already know Raul and Jillian," he says. "You can bring some of your friends, too. It's abstract art. I don't know if you'll like it."

"I love abstract art," I lie. It's just a bunch of squiggly gunk on canvas, but I want to spend some time with him.

"I think I have your number, but give it to me again so I can text or call you when we're ready to go."

I give him my number. *Call me all you want,* I think.

"It's in Coral Gables, so it's not far," he says. "So, if it happens, I'll see you there."

"Sure," I say.

Peter stands up, collects his things, and walks to the mystery section to get a book for his weekend reading. His jeans hug his slender legs and his plaid shirt is tight across his muscular shoulders. I sigh. His brains and beauty are for Shakira to enjoy. I'll have to wow him at this art gallery thing to get his mind off of her. In my head I make a list of things to do: get highlights in my hair, straighten it, do my nails, buy an outfit that's tight but not ho-ish, get some false eyelashes, clean my contact lenses so that they don't scrape off my corneas like last time …

17

"You're getting braces next week," Dad tells me.

"Fine," I say.

"You seem resigned to it."

"You already made the decision, didn't you?"

"Why the long face?" he asks.

"I'm just tired."

It's Saturday, and we woke up before dawn to eat our early breakfast. I'm still upset at the thought that whatever chances I have at winning Peter's affections are diminished by the competition Shakira poses. At least he's noticing that other guys are paying attention to me. David in first period is starting to hang all over me, smiling at me and winking at me. He isn't bad-looking either, so maybe I'll have a boyfriend soon enough. I've known him since sixth grade, but I've never been close to him. He hangs out almost exclusively with skaters, while I have a more varied group of friends. The chemistry isn't there. I don't want *any* boyfriend. Just because David is giving me attention doesn't mean he's the one for me. I want magic. I want sparks to fly. I want my first handholding moment and first kiss to be just as sweet as it appears in the movies. I want my boyfriend to be hanging upside down as I kiss him, Kirsten-Dunst-style in *Spiderman*. Okay, that's far-fetched, but it could happen.

Mom is in the living room doing aerobics from a DVD. She's wearing a midriff-baring shirt and spandex shorts. She dances, swings her arms in the air, and jumps up and down. I make sure the curtains are closed because we've had quite a few peeping Toms, since Mom has a fan base and all. I wish I had an audience (Peter can be the only one in it and that will be fine by me). I pat my stomach. It's nearly flat like Mom's. Between Ramadan, the dental surgery, and my broken heart, I'm really not eating much at all.

I get ready to go to my next driving lesson. I wear a long skirt so that Grandpa can't say I look like a prostitute in any way. I put on a nude shade of MAC lipstick, an undetectable color I really like and that Grandpa probably won't notice. He comes an hour later to take me out driving. He crashes into our garbage can again and I yank it upright. Mom is still wearing her exercise gear, and he grimaces at her. She ignores him. I'm sure he thinks she looks like a prostitute showing so much skin, but she's at home. She limberly places a foot on top of the sofa to stretch.

"You let her dress like that?" Grandpa whispers to Dad in the kitchen.

"Let her?" Dad whispers back. "She's a grown woman and she doesn't need my permission to dress that way when she's exercising."

"It's not good for Almira's eyes to see her mother dressed like that."

It's fine for my eyes, but not good for my self-esteem since I feel that I have to match Mom's hot body. My morals aren't affected at all by what she wears; it's her slender legs and tiny waist that disturb me. Oh, and the entire football team at school eagerly awaiting her on days when she picks me up, so that they can ogle her. One of them even left his phone number under our windshield wiper the other day: *If this is Almara's mom's car you don't know me, but my name is Joshua and here's my phone number so you can holla at me …*

I go back to my room because I forgot my purse. My computer beeps because I have new mail. Sitting down to read it, minutes fly by and I don't realize that I'm keeping Grandpa waiting. He walks in and I turn around quickly. Knowing my computer like the back of my hand, I close the Internet browser without looking at the screen. Maria had written me a juicy email that included vivid details of a date she went on last night. It isn't something I want Grandpa to read, what with him thinking I should only have pure, virginal thoughts. I had read the email to the point where Maria's date's hand was massaging her thigh, and then Grandpa intruded. Maria's emails always read like a soap opera or romance novel (with really poor grammar and spelling) and being interrupted, all I can think about is finishing the email.

"I'm ready, Grandpa," I say.

"Who is that?" Grandpa roars.

"What?"

"That," he says, pointing at my computer screen.

Uh-oh. I usually have my computer locked when I'm away for this very reason: my Robert Pattinson desktop is in full view. He has his shirt open and is giving a come-hither look to the camera. I've never allowed any of my relatives to see the contents of my computer before. Dad would get the wrong impression—okay, it's the right impression since I have indecent thoughts about Robert Pattinson all the time. Mom might understand, but I don't let her see my file of hot hunks either.

"Who is that?" Grandpa asks again. His hands are on his hips and he wears a monstrous scowl on his face. I have to think of something quick.

"He's an in … inventor," I stammer.

"He's no inventor! He looks familiar. Was he in a movie I saw?"

"No, um, he probably looks familiar because he's on all the talk shows talking about his, um, inventions."

"And what does he invent?"

"His name is Michael Hufnagel and he invented, um, he invented these funny computer keys on my keyboard."

"What!"

"Like, you know, the key that has the moon on it to put the computer in sleep mode, and the key with the email icon to get my email running … "

I'm sounding super stupid, but the lies are coming easier to me the longer I speak. *Yeah, he invented stuff, lots of stuff, major stuff. Now leave me alone.*

"See," I say, pointing to the keys I'm talking about on the keyboard. "He invented all of them. His picture is the default for the screen. It came with the computer."

"What does this key do?" Grandpa asks, pressing a key that makes a help menu pop up.

"It has a question mark on it, so you push it when you have a question."

"You can ask the computer questions?"

"Yes." Duh! He knows nothing about computers. This is a good thing, since he can't Google Michael Hufnagel and catch me in my lie. Grandpa doesn't have the faintest idea of what a search engine is.

"Okay, this guy invented something good," he says.

"Yeah, this stuff is really, really good."

"He looks too young to be an inventor." Grandpa's voice is more sedate than before.

"He's in all the magazines as one of the richest millionaires under forty years old."

"Can't you change the picture?" Grandpa asks. "He doesn't even know how to button his shirt. Is that grease on his chest? Why is his skin shiny? I knew someone like that who had to go to the dermatologist."

"He was probably sweating," I say. "He lives in Texas where his company is, and you know how hot it is there. I'll change the picture right away." Grandpa hovers over me and I have to be careful that he doesn't see all my files, pictures, journals, saved emails ... my mind reels thinking about all the things he doesn't know about me. My fantasies and desires are something I can never divulge to him. I have this secret self, Almira II, who I can't let my family get acquainted with.

I go into the harmless *My Pictures* file and set the screen to Hello Kitty, who I outgrew years ago but still have a fondness for. Hello Kitty's big white head dominates the computer screen. Hearts and butterflies surround her stocky body. You can't go wrong with Hello Kitty. Whenever I fear that Mom or Dad may walk into my room without any notice, I turn my desktop over to Hello Kitty or Chococat.

"I hate cats," Grandpa says.

"They're so sloppy," I say to humor him. I actually like cats, but at this moment, when my cover has been almost broken, I'm willing to agree with everything he says. Yes,

Americans are infidels. MTV is full of gyrating prostitutes. VH1 is the devil's channel. *Whatever you say, Grandpa.*

Grandpa tells me he's ready to leave. He has to get away from our house of hellfire and brimstone. He averts his eyes from Mom's nakedness as we walk past her to get to the driveway. The visit has been a double dose of decadence for him: Mom's scanty clothes and a granddaughter lusting over a famous movie star/inventor.

18

This time I'll drive to the shopping plaza. It's a three-minute drive and roads are deserted this morning. My feet know what has to be done at red lights and stop signs. I still feel a tremble run through my body like a tuning fork when I drive, but for the most part I know what I'm doing. Grandpa is unpleasant on our way to the plaza, so I'm filled with a sense of foreboding. He makes a demeaning comment about female drivers when a woman makes an illegal U-turn in front of us. Our windows happen to be open when he yells at her—*PROSTITUTE*—as she drives away. I would've felt better if he said "F you" instead. The F bomb sounds less personal and judgmental than "prostitute."

"Are you fasting properly?" he asks me sharply.

"Yes," I say.

"You're not eating cookies or candy during the day?"

My entire body hardens at his assumption that I might be cheating. "No, Grandpa, I don't eat anything during the day."

"That's good."

"So what's my lesson for today?" I say, to change the subject.

"You're going to learn how to drive in reverse."

My mouth hangs open in shock. I don't know why I have to drive in reverse since people are supposed to drive forward. This lesson has to have a point to it. Grandpa tells me to park in reverse and I have to do it five times until I neatly encase the car in between the yellow lines of the parking space. Now I know why people don't drive in reverse more often. It's really hard.

"Now drive and make a turn in reverse," Grandpa orders.

I go backwards, to where the L is in the parking lot, and successfully make the turn. "I did it," I gleefully say.

"Good. Now I'm going to get out of the car so that I can see how you're doing."

Grandpa leaves the car so that he can have a visual on how I drive. Do I park properly or at an angle? Do I drive zigzagged or straight? So he watches me drive in reverse at the next L.

My throat tightens as I hold my breath. There's no one else in the parking lot, so I don't know why I feel so fearful. The strip mall, with its boring businesses, is empty this early in the morning. So I make the turn, while Grandpa watches in the distance. His form, in high-waisted pants and a lime-green shirt, becomes smaller and smaller.

What happens next is my fault, but I don't exactly know how I commit such a goof. It's probably part being a newbie driver and part feeling nervous. I keep driving until I make a reverse turn out of the parking lot and onto a small road. "Uh oh," I say. Instead of seeing store fronts, I see manicured lawns and Spanish-style stucco houses. Grandpa is nowhere in sight. I have to find him.

Another car is right in front of me, coming head-on, since I've driven into the wrong lane. The woman honks at me, which rattles me since I've never been honked at before. There's no leeway for me to get back into the entrance I just drove out of, so I go around her and keep driving. I'm looking for another entrance, but there's no other way into the strip mall on that side of the street.

Don't panic, I think. I'm sure that if I make one or more left turns, I'll be back to where I started. I make a left turn and see more houses, but at the end of that road I can only make a right turn. I want to scream. I don't even recognize the streets or houses. The biggest problem of living in Coral Gables is that all the street signs are on the ground and I have to strain my eyes to find them. On every corner I see stone slabs saying *Malaga Avenue* or *Anastasia Avenue*. Also, it isn't like the rest of Miami where you have a grid line of streets and avenues. In Miami, I know that SW 8th street is below SW 7th street and that NW 10th avenue is to the west of NW 9th avenue, but in Coral Gables you have to know exactly where all the roads are. I'm on *Palermo Avenue* and want to get off of it.

My cell phone starts ringing, but I don't want to lose my train of thought by reaching into my purse for it. I glance at the passenger seat and see my MAC lipstick roll out of my purse. My first impulse is to reach down to the floor to find it, but I have to abandon it. This requires all of my concentration.

I drive onto a main road with three lanes and I feel a little less lost. We drove on this road to get to the strip mall, and now I know where I am. The openness of all these lanes scares me. And I'm driving all alone. I want to cry, but no, no, I won't. The world is unfair, being that I'm big-boned, have a mom better-looking than me, and can't have Peter when Shakira is in the way. I have to at least conquer the roads and have something for myself. If I can't have Peter, then I can at least have my driver's license. If Shakira is going to do her best to hurt me, then I should have mastery over the county roads. I have to have this, I tell myself. I don't have much, but I will be an excellent driver.

I'm not excellent yet. A tire hits the curb when I pull

into the strip mall. Grandpa is waving at me and I stop right in front of him.

"Where were you?" he yells at me. He gets into the car and slams the door. "I was calling you!"

"Grandpa, please, I was fine. I just made a wrong turn somewhere. I'm back, aren't I?"

"You were gone for ten minutes. I'm going to tell your father. And the rim is caved in. Did you hit something?"

"I hit the curb." I don't care about that. Grandpa is always hitting something. Maybe the damage to the rim was his fault from hitting our mailbox so many times, and now he's blaming me for it. But I definitely did hear a pop of metal on concrete when I hit the curb.

"Go home now," he says, rubbing his forehead.

"Okay."

Grandpa leans forward. "What's this?" he asks. He's holding my MAC lipstick.

"That's mine," I croak.

"You're too young for this." He throws the lipstick out the car window. What! Hell no!

"Grandpa, that's a MAC lipstick!" I say.

"So what!" he roars.

So, it's only a top-of-the-line lipstick that I bought at a MAC store with my own money. That's all. And who is he to callously throw out my favorite lipstick? It was only halfway done. And he littered! That's so gross, and wrong for the environment.

I'm silent and try not to cry on the way home. I sit

with a stiff posture, pretending to be unaffected by his anger. Does Grandpa have to upset me during every Ramadan? A year ago I burned with the same intense ire toward him. When I emerged from my room with the chocolate crumbs embedded in my lip-gloss, Grandpa walked toward me while I backed away from him.

"You were eating!" he roared.

"What are you talking about?" I squeaked.

"Do not deny anything! We can all see that you've eaten something. This is the holiest of months. The Koran was revealed to us at this time. So many people are following this holy month, and you turn around and cheat! I knew you couldn't do it!"

I felt horrible after Grandpa's outburst, as if I had no will power or self-control. I knew of other family members who didn't participate in Ramadan, and even though some people looked down on them, they still led normal lives. But I really wanted to do it last year.

His words had shaken me, and I cried plenty that day. *I knew you couldn't do it!* He never believed in me in the first place when it came to fasting, and now I see that he doesn't believe in me when it comes to driving.

When I pull into our driveway, I jump out of the car and go inside without a word. It's Saturday—it should be a day of relaxation, of getting away from school and doing fun things, and this morning has started off on such a bad note. Big deal that I ruined the rim of the car! Grandpa's car is covered in dents and scratches. I guess it's fine if he messes up, but not me. I have to be perfect!

I go into my room and hear an argument ensue. It's an ugly one. It happens yards away from my room, but it sounds like it's right outside my door. I sit up in bed, blinking in disbelief at what I'm hearing.

"She is disobedient!" Grandpa yells. "She doesn't follow directions and she ruined my wheel!"

"We'll pay for the repair," Dad says. "Didn't I ruin the bumper of your car when I was learning how to drive at that age?"

"Yes, that was a stupid mistake, but at least you owned up to it. Almira is acting like a spoiled brat!"

"Hold on. You insisted on teaching her how to drive," Mom says. "That means you have to accept all her faults and give her your time and patience."

"And I'm going to listen to you? Look at you. You're dressed like an infidel."

"What does my way of dressing have to do with this? I was exercising when you came in. Do you expect me to wear a veil when I do yoga? How ludicrous."

"I once saw a woman jog in *hijab*."

"Well, this is my home and I'll wear whatever I want when I'm working out—"

"No wonder Almira acts with such arrogance and disrespect," Grandpa says.

I'm arrogant and disrespectful? Am I really those things? I wasn't aware. My heart feels like it will shatter into pieces hearing such horrible things about myself. I once heard a teacher talking about me to another teacher before school started. I was behind a door when my computer teacher told my science teacher how stupid I was and that I must be missing some chromosomes because I didn't know how to create html codes. I rushed to the bathroom hyperventilating, but that was three years ago, when I was younger and more sensitive. (Also, Raul tutored me until I conquered html, so that showed my teacher what he knew about me.) I'm older and stronger, yet I'm depressed hearing Grandpa's belittling tirade about me. I know Grandpa is old-fashioned, cantankerous, and melodramatic, but his words hurt me. I feel so small.

I put a pillow over my head, even though it doesn't do any good. Their voices are so loud that they penetrate a layer of down feathers. I realize that this argument was bound to happen, that Mom and Grandpa never seem to agree on anything, but to actually have this fight unfold within my earshot pains me.

Because cell phones become smaller with each passing year, I'm having trouble finding mine. Years ago, Dad lent me one of his cell phones and the palm-sized bulk was easy to find. Now cell phones are so lightweight and small that I can't locate my BlackBerry Pearl in my purse. I throw my purse against the wall to join in the rage of the household.

"You cannot dress like that in front of Almira, and you allow her to do whatever she wants!" Grandpa rants.

"You let her go out at night. She's probably seeing boys for all you know! And do you know how much makeup she wears? A lot! I just had to throw her lipstick out and she was defiant about it!"

My cell phone tumbles out of my purse when it collides with the wall. I pick it up and call Lisa. The line is busy. I sit down at my computer.

"And she had a picture on her computer of a man! You need to throw out her computer! It's probably giving her all sorts of ideas! I watch the news, and men kidnap girls over the computer! I see what infidels do on the news shows! Ibrahim, you must stop this nonsense with your daughter immediately and take that computer away from her!"

"Almira is intelligent and knows what she should and shouldn't do with a computer," Dad says.

I quickly unlock my computer with my password and I'm relieved to see the Hello Kitty desktop still there. I forgot about my Jake Gyllenhaal screensaver, so I quickly change it to one with a bouncing star just in case Dad comes over to see if Grandpa's accusations are true. I want Grandpa to leave. He's getting nastier and louder the longer he stays.

"You're the one who's rude and arrogant!" Mom huffs. "Don't you dare tell me how to raise my daughter!"

AlmiraRules: are you there?

"Father, please!" Dad yells.

AlmiraRules: is anyone there?

I'm typing into an empty void because I'm not getting a response. Lisa, Maria, and my other friends are not online as I expected them to be. I type in their screen names and the only message I see is *OFFLINE OFFLINE OFFLINE.* I'm sending out a mayday signal and nobody's responding.

My bedroom has a wide glass door that opens to the pool and backyard. I slide the door open, walk through the yard, and pry open the fence. I'm on the sidewalk, away from adults. I feel that I can breathe, even though I'll eventually have to return to my tense, angry family.

Without me even paying attention, my feet lead me to Lisa's house. She's out front with a cousin, the both of them washing her mom's car. Lisa tells me that she's almost done. I watch the suds roll off her mom's BMW. Lisa and her cousin giggle at the normalcy of washing a car and getting wet in the process. I stay at her house for an hour, until my cell phone rings and Dad asks me in a mollifying tone to come back home. I don't want to leave Lisa's home because she's so understanding. She's as shocked as I am that Grandpa discarded my MAC lipstick through the window. "MAC's, like, the best lipstick ever," she says.

"I know!" I say. "It's the bestest!"

Lisa hugs me and I melt into her. What a terrible day. Pattinson was discovered on my computer, the driving lesson was disastrous, and Grandpa was monstrous toward Mom and me.

"I'll get you another lipstick," Lisa says.

Her generous offer makes me burst into tears.

19

The only thing Mom says about Grandpa after the fight is, "He's not allowed in this house again."

"We'll work things out with him," Dad says.

I know Grandpa's thinking is from the past and all, but he seemed to come down really hard on me and Mom, judging us based on the clothes we wear and our American values. Mom was born in Miami and Dad came to America when he was a little kid, whereas Grandpa was already a grown man coming from another country when he moved to Florida. They don't understand each other. I used to think Grandpa's way of thinking was funny, the way he calls harmless-looking women on the street "prostitutes," how he thinks my teachers are infidels by teaching me that we come from monkeys, and how he insists that *Allah* (not sonic waves) makes thunder. It used to be ha, ha, ha, Grandpa is so loony. Dad would shake his head and chuckle, and even Mom would smirk at the things he said. But Grandpa has taken it too far. He acts like the morality police, ready to stone Mom for the way she dresses and raises me. I like Mom's clothes (as long as she doesn't wear the exercise gear outside), and I think she did okay raising me. I get good grades, never cheat on tests, and clean my room without being asked. And it isn't a crime that I want a boyfriend. Grandpa mentioned the man on my computer, the wonderfully talented Mr. Pattinson, and I'm glad my parents haven't followed up on that. My computer is guarded by my password, at least. But Grandpa is unlikely to sneak up behind me again, so I remove Hello Kitty so I can gaze at Robert once more.

I go to school Monday feeling burdened by the argument. There's a Hershey's Kiss on my seat in first period, but that doesn't cheer me up. The prospect of a secret admirer or vindictive saboteur doesn't fill me with curiosity or wonder. I feel so low. Weekends are a time to refresh the senses, but I look like a zombie. People keep asking me if I'm all right. I don't want to reveal my family problems to everyone, so I don't say anything. I'm most honest in my English journal:

> *So, old people can be really old-fashioned and*
> *they look at younger people and judge them. My*

grandfather said some really horrible things to Mom this weekend. He really crossed the line. It seemed like he was grasping at straws, trying to beat her down on these non-issues. He took these small things about her and turned them against her. My mom likes to dress in exercise clothes most of the day since she works out constantly (it's like an addiction) and he talked about that as if she wears a bikini or nothing at all. Nobody can see her stuff with what she wears. Some women wear things that become sheer with sweat and my mom wears layers, with a tank top over another tank top. She dresses G-rated. Maybe my grandfather never liked her and wanted to use something against her.

I think he hates the way I turned out, because he said that I wasn't raised right. I may not go to the mosque like he does and I don't pray five times a day, but I'm still a good person. I'm fasting for the first time ever. It's hard, but I don't cheat. I don't sip any water or have any snacks during the day. This is the ultimate sacrifice. I know other people my age who don't fast, but I want to prove to myself and God that I have this willpower and control. This is a month to become cleaner and purer, and I'm feeling lighter (even lightheaded) from fasting. This is a month of discovery, and I discovered that my grandfather can be really mean

and ugly. He refuses to understand people my par-
ents' age and my age.
    Forgive me for rambling.

At the end of class, Ms. Odige gives our journals back to us. Scrawled in red ink are her comments. *What a thoughtful entry. Yes, you ramble, but I'm sure that if you had more time to write this it would be a fantastic essay. Hang in there and things will work out.*

What a trite saying. Hang in there. I'm reminded of the poster Ms. Odige keeps above her desk, the one with a kitten hanging on a clothesline by both paws. I'm hanging on, but for how long? When can I let go, and is there a cushion under me to catch my fall?

In between classes, Maria tries to trip Shakira in the hallway. She does it in a subtle way, casually jutting her feet out, pretending that she's stretching, but I see it. Shakira stops in her tracks immediately so that a girl behind her crashes into her. "Watch where you're going, new girl!"

Shakira shakes her head and people laugh at her. Wow, that's pretty mean of Maria. Her suspension ended last week and she needs to get over it already. I'm softening toward Shakira, and I think it's best if she leaves people alone and people leave her alone. Hands off. Truce. But ill feelings linger. My classmates will always see Shakira as the person who got Maria suspended, and Mom will always see Grandpa as the rude old man who spat out harsh words about her clothes and her only child.

At lunch I sit by myself in the gazebo. About a dozen other kids are also seated here, eating bag lunches or food from the vending machines, but the gazebo is large enough that we're all spread apart from each other. I'm still in a funk about what happened with Grandpa and want to be alone.

I take out my sketchpad, which is absolutely useless since I suck at drawing. I only bought it to imitate Peter, to be closer to understanding who he is, to become an artist like he is. I think about artists and what they're like. Maybe they have dark thoughts, or ideas that are so abstract that they can only be pictured, not put into words. The other day, Peter told me that the cells he saw under the microscope reminded him of a field of poppies in an impressionist painting. Another time he told me that he drew things from his dreams (I don't even remember most of my dreams). I have no idea what he means most of the time when he talks about anything related to art, but obviously he sees things differently than I do. I see things for what they are. A microscope slide is a microscope slide. A dog is a dog. The sky is the sky. Peter probably looks at the sky and searches for the meaning of life in it.

My pencil glides over the paper. I draw eyes that are different sizes. I draw a nose that looks like an eggplant. The smiling lips are banana shaped. The ears are round like the knobs of a radio. Trying to draw Peter, I draw a fugly man from an alien planet. The picture doesn't do him any justice. In fact, it insults him. He looks like a Greek god, and I'm turning him into some untouchable nerd. In fact, this looks like a sub-nerd, someone who is off the charts as far as high school social castes go. I erase the features and redraw them, but I only make everything worse.

At least I can write, though. Underneath the drawing I write *Peter* in big, bubbly letters. I draw hearts around his name. What a beautiful, simple name. Peter. It's pronounceable, two syllables rolling off the tongue. Peter and Almira. Five syllables in total, which is still simple. *Peter and Almira are going out. Did you hear about Peter and Almira? You know that they're an item, don't you?* I imagine what people say about us if we're a couple. There will be admiration mostly, maybe jealousy. But then I think about how Lisa would react and my heart sinks. I can't hurt her. She would be mad at me forever. A lump forms in my throat as I picture losing Lisa, but then my eyes water with joy when I imagine hooking up with Peter.

"What's that?" someone says behind me.

I snap my head around and hold the sketchpad to my chest. It's Shakira. She has a smirk on her face, which makes her pouty, pink-glossed lips look unattractive—okay, not really. It's my imagination trying to induce me into thinking she's ugly, because nothing about her is grotesque. Her farts probably smell like roses.

"It's nothing," I sharply say.

She tilts her head back and laughs. "You were drawing Peter," she says.

"I was not!"

"Then why did you write his name at the bottom of the paper?"

She has me there. She's my rival, always hanging all over Peter, and now she sees me drawing him. I wonder what she'll do with this information.

As if she's reading my mind, she says, "Your secret is safe with me."

"What secret?"

"That you like him."

"I don't like him!" I say.

"Then why are you drawing him?" she asks.

"Um, because, um, I'm bored."

"I also draw boys I like when I'm bored."

"Well, I don't. I draw anyone when I'm bored."

"Didn't know you were an artist," Shakira teases.

"There are many things you don't know about me," I say.

"But I learned something today."

Lunch is coming to a close and I gather my things to leave. Shakira is watching me as I get up, and I feel clumsy and awkward. I even trip when I walk down the steps of the gazebo, but I right myself before I can fall. Not turning around to look at her, I walk evenly and steadily toward an entrance. *Don't look at her. Don't look at her. Don't look.* On my way to the bathroom, I tear out the crummy portrait I made of Peter and crumple it into a ball. I throw it toward a garbage can and miss. A group of popular girls walks by, talking loudly and giggling, and they block my way. I don't bother to pick up the paper and throw it out properly. Dealing with Shakira, I've had my fill of snotty, pretty girls for the day.

20

Lisa grabs my arm on the way to biology. "Like my new tattoo?" she asks. She sticks out her arm and I see *PH* in neat cursive on the inside of her wrist. Peter Hurley.

"Peter Hurley. Lisa Gomez Hurley. Mrs. Lisa Hurley ... "

I roll my eyes as she fantasizes about her future name with the man of her dreams, who also happens to be the man of my dreams. "Okay, Lisa, I get it," I say.

"Do you think it's meant to be?" she asks, hysteria in her voice. Her grip on my arm tightens and her fingernails are digging into me.

"Don't get psychotic on me, Lisa," I say, pulling my arm away from her.

"Almira, tell me what you really think." She's now pleading, deranged with love.

"Fine! I see you two together, for life."

She lets go of my arm, satisfied with my response. She wants her best friend to mirror her feelings, and I do. Superficially, that is. My hidden thoughts are all about securing Peter for myself.

Lisa and I come to class early. We sit on our stools and watch everyone else pour in. Shakira and Peter stand a few inches from the door, their heads together, in their private world with their secret jokes. Peter laughs and Shakira smiles. She swings her hair toward her shoulder and looks up at him with adoration. They're a good-looking couple, but I should be the one standing by his side.

"What is that heifer doing with my man?" Lisa says between gritted teeth.

Shakira twists her body around, shrugging her bookbag off her shoulder. She unzips it and brings out a crumpled ball of paper.

"Oh my God," I say.

"I know!" Lisa brays. "She's, like, flirting with him."

Shakira unfolds the piece of paper and hands it to Peter. His eyes widen and then slowly find mine. Our eyes lock. Shakira talks into his ear, her hair covering Peter's face. I want to see more of his surprised expression.

He's seen the fugly face with his name right under it.

I can't breathe. I want to escape. I feel so embarrassed. More students walk in and block my view of Peter.

"If I could just get a few minutes alone with her in a cage and wrestle her down," Lisa says. "No rules. Just fists."

Lisa is babbling stupid stuff, proclaiming her love for Peter, and I'm not paying any attention to her. All I care about are Peter's thoughts on my drawing. I hope he isn't taking my portrait of him seriously. I immediately think about what lies I should say if he asks me about it. Shakira doesn't know what she's talking about. That paper isn't mine. I drew it as a joke. No, I'm not in love with him, but doodling out of boredom. I'm making a portrait montage of all my classmates.

I remember how long ago, in first grade, I had a stomachache in the morning. I begged and pleaded with Mom to stay home, but she didn't believe I was sick. I went to school and vomited in the cafeteria. There was a pool of orange vomit (from Mom's squash soup the night before) on the cafeteria table, so I was trying to put my arms on either side of it to shield it from my classmates. I was embarrassed and had every right to be. We were in the middle of lunch and my classmates were staring right at me. A pretty blond girl named Deb, who sat in the farthest corner away from me, exclaimed, "Almira is gross." A little brown-haired boy who sat a few seats away from me vomited from seeing my vomit. The principal pulled me out, patted me on the back, and called my house to have

Mom pick me up. Those feelings come back to me now: being looked at, being judged as gross, and having people sympathize over me (poor girl will never have a boyfriend, and Peter doesn't want her).

Why does Shakira have to stoop so low? She picks up my garbage and uses it to humiliate me. Does she hate me that much? And what is the hatred all about?

The bell rings and Mr. Gregory positions himself in front of the class. Peter normally sits next to me, but Shakira holds his hand and leads him to a stool next to hers. I steal some glances back to where they are. It's a lecture day, not a lab day, and Peter studiously takes down notes with an emotionless face while Shakira smirks at me. The notes I take look like a jumbled mess. I'll borrow Lisa's notes later, because my mind isn't on biology at all. I'm so fixated on the drawing that when my mind finally strays from worries over that, I start to think about Grandpa and his nasty words. There are so many mean people in this world: Shakira, Grandpa, and Kristen Stewart, because Robert Pattinson seems infatuated with her, thus ruining my chance with him.

• • •

I do my homework, and after that I spend a good hour on the computer. I hear sizzling from the kitchen as Mom fries something up for dinner. I smell chicken, peppers, and garlic. My stomach pulsates in and out, in and out, feed me, feed me.

At least I know Grandpa isn't going to come for dinner. I think about the many times he came, invited and uninvited. My memories are bittersweet. Usually I didn't mind his presence and thought he was funny and educational. And then there were those other times when he was cruel and narrow-minded. On the news months ago there was a clip of a gay pride parade and he turned toward me and said, "Only in this country." Then I told him about how Lisa was dating a boy named Mannie, and Grandpa said he couldn't believe I was friends with someone whose parents allowed for that to happen. Sure, teenagers should never be interested in the opposite sex. I wonder how Dad survived his own teenage years under that man.

The front door slams shut due to a heavy breeze. I hear Dad's voice as he says something to Mom in the kitchen. Then his footsteps get louder, which is odd. The master bedroom, which is in a separate hallway from mine, has its own bathroom and Dad always goes there first to wash his hands. But he's headed toward me. He knocks on my door and I tell him to come in.

"Almira," he says, a frown on his face.

I wonder what trouble I've caused, and I'm pretty sure I didn't do anything wrong recently. "Yes?" I say.

"I was thinking about something that my dad said," he mutters under his breath.

He walks over to my computer and moves the mouse. *This computer is locked by AlmiraRules,* the gray message box in the center announces. *Press CTRL + ALT + DELETE.*

"Almira, unlock your computer," he says.

"Why?" I ask.

"Just do it."

"But there's nothing but homework stuff on it."

"Almira, unlock your computer!"

He rarely yells at me, so I jump up. I go over to my computer, sit down, and type in my password. My body trembles and the moment feels drawn out, as if I'm walking through a time warp. I dread the outcome, but I press *return* after typing in my password.

I hear the squeak of my door hinges as Mom peeks inside my room. She gasps when she sees my Robert Pattinson desktop.

"What is this garbage doing in your computer?" Dad asks. He shakes his head in disappointment, as if I'm an utter, unabashed failure at life. Dad is computer literate and he quickly goes into my files and deletes all my hotties. He's even faster than me, because it takes me a while to find things on my computer. Standing hunched over my computer, his fingers are fast as they click, click, click. Pattinson, Bale, Bana, Gyllenhaal, Welling, Pitt, Dempsey, Phillipe, Lautner, all three Jonases, and other guys I've fallen in love with on the small and big screen disappear.

I feel distraught and empty. They're gone. They digitally die, floating in some vast graveyard in my computer's hard drive. Dad even goes into the recycle bin and empties it so that I can't restore these men to life. It's too cruel. Tears well up and I sniffle. It's just as bad as reading about their physical deaths in the news. *Actor dies in hotel fire. Movie star accidentally drowns in stunt scene. Leading men pass away inside of Almira Abdul's Dell computer.*

Dad seems to soften up when he sees how upset I am. "Asma, will you talk to her?" he says to Mom.

"Yes," she says.

I can feel my eyes begin to roll, but I stop myself. My parents hate it when I roll my eyes. To them it's just as bad as a verbal insult. I don't know if girls in the Middle East roll their eyes, but American girls do it plenty and my parents don't like it one bit.

I brace myself for one of her lectures. I sit up in bed and fold myself into a ball, my knees to my chin and my arms wrapped around my legs. *Give it to me*, I think.

• • •

Mom sits on the swivel chair next to my Robert Pattinson-less computer. Her hands are perched on both knees. I get déjà vu, because this is the same pose she had a year ago, when I failed during last Ramadan. She sat in my room and told me that even though I'd cheated the first day by eating behind their backs, I should try again, that I could perhaps fast an extra day. But then Grandpa stormed into my room to tell her it wasn't allowed—I would need to fast a whole extra month. I'd had no reason to cheat, since I wasn't ill or pregnant. Grandpa makes everything worse, while Mom tries to add reason and comfort to the household.

"Almira, you know that you shouldn't have those pictures on your computer, the computer your dad bought for your last birthday," she says.

"But it's my computer," I say, a tear sliding down my cheek. "Isn't it mine to do what I want with?"

"Yes and no. Sometimes someone gives you something and the person doesn't wish for you to abuse it."

"But they're not porno pictures."

"I know," Mom says.

"Did you collect pictures of boys when you were my age?" I ask.

"I would hide them, throw them out, stare at them, and give them away. It's not something I wanted my parents to know about."

So Mom had a similar experience to mine, which explains why she's being so nice to me, much nicer than Dad was.

"Mom, I like it that you're not strict like your parents are or the way Grandpa is," I say.

"I know what it's like to grow up here with foreign parents," she says. "You want to dress and act like those around you, but you don't want to forget your religion. Almira, I know it's odd that you can't do every single thing that your friends do, but we're Muslim. Your skirts are shorter than mine were when I was your age, but you're still modest. We let you have the friends you want, but that's because you have decent ones anyway and we trust you. When I was your age I snuck around in miniskirts and makeup, which my parents really hated. They wouldn't let me go on field trips because they didn't trust strangers, especially American ones. I couldn't be outside after dark. School was a huge struggle for me because of my parents, but I still grew up well-adjusted and normal. Since my parents weren't born here like I was, you can imagine what it was like. They weren't as strict as your grandfather, but they were up there with their many rules. I felt frustrated most of the time, but I knew their boundaries and never hung out with the wrong people. Compared to my parents, your dad and I are very cool with the things you want, even though we don't permit everything."

"And you're totally not like Grandpa," I say.

"Of course, every generation is going to be more lenient than the previous. Your grandfather is extreme, but he isn't as bad as some other older men I've met."

"You mean he could be worse?"

"Yes."

I picture men who don't allow their girls to see the light of day, who force burqas and arranged marriages on them. How things change over time! Maybe when I have children, a decade or so from now, they'll be totally and completely American, having more freedoms than I had. And then my grandchildren will be no different than the Billys and Michelles that they'll go to school with. But in the present I live in this in-between world of being foreign and American, and wanting to do some things that my parents won't allow. Mom and Dad still have too many restrictions on me, like I can't have a boyfriend or a Mohawk (I asked for that haircut years ago when I was in my rocker phase). But I have to admit that my parents are okay. Dad's a yuppie dentist who likes fast cars and European getaways. And the kids at school are always telling me how cool Mom is (because she's hot). I look at her, sitting in my chair. She has on her tank top and shorts, light makeup, and small feet that have a fresh pedicure of burgundy nail polish. She's awesome in her own way, even though she doesn't let me do whatever I want.

"Mom, I'm glad you and Dad don't badger me about every single thing I do," I say, meaning it. "My curfew is really fair. But you still don't let me do some things I want, like having pictures of Robert Pattinson."

"Just don't do it again," she says.

"All right," I say. "I'm not going to spend a hundred hours of my time collecting pictures again when I know Dad is going to delete them."

"That's a good point. Don't save them."

I can look, but not save. Okay, I get it.

Actually, I don't absorb anything my parents have said to me. Mom leaves and I make sure the door is closed. I have a metal lockbox that's supposed to guard precious items from fires. The small box holds my childhood journal, four hundred dollars in emergency cash, and my flash drives. I find a pink flash drive and rub my thumb along-side it. It's so small, yet what it contains is more precious than gold. I plug it into my computer and wait for it to load.

What Mom and Dad don't know is that I back up my files at least once a week. My old computer crashed years ago, causing me to lose all of my homework and other personal documents, so I learned to save everything on a flash drive. The contents of the flash drive open and I hit copy and paste. My hotties are copied into my computer, so that I can make new desktops and screensavers of my favorite men. I change my password. That was a nasty run-in with my dad—thanks to Grandpa's big mouth—but Mom's conversation was a nice cushion to fall back on.

Pattinson is back, and I blow a kiss at him. Because my eyes are still blurry with unshed tears, I can swear that he winks at me. I touch the screen and smile.

21

I get a text message from a number I don't recognize. When I open it, my heart starts to flutter. It's a wonderful surprise after that run-in with my parents.

art gallery 2nite @ 7. can u come?

It's Peter. I remember that he invited me to an art gallery, but I didn't know it would be so soon, on such short notice. But he did say he would text me when his friends were all available to tag along for the assignment. This allays my fears—he doesn't think I'm silly or stalking him. When Shakira showed him my sketch, it was a nothing incident for him, although it's everything to me. My feelings were revealed in that drawing, but maybe he thinks it's funny or flattering. Anyways, I can't say no to this gallery thing.

I pop my head out of my room and yell at Mom. "Can I go to an art gallery tonight with some friends?" I ask.

"Who are you going with?" she yells back.

"Friends!"

"Like who?"

"Lisa, Maria, the usual!" I blurt out their names because I don't want Mom knowing I'm going there for Peter's sake. Actually, Lisa and Maria have no clue about this, but now I have to tell them since I need to use them as my cover for the night—my parents trust Lisa and Maria while they're wary about some of my other friends. So they're definitely coming, even though I don't want Lisa to attend this rendezvous.

First I text Peter, telling him I can come, and he texts me back that Raul is borrowing his parents' SUV and we can all fit in there. So I give him my address and write to him that Lisa and Maria are coming too. I call Lisa and Maria, and of course they want to come: Lisa is eager to see Peter and Maria has no plans for the night.

Once Raul picks me up, I'll direct him to their houses. Lisa will throw herself at Peter. And Maria might make a scene at the gallery with her big mouth. We once went to a bank together and it was pin-drop quiet, but then

Maria started raving about how cute the shoes were on the woman in front of us, and then she went on an insane tirade about how a heel broke on a new pair of pumps she just bought. Everyone looked at her, which made me feel self-conscious since I was standing next to her. Which is worse? A best friend who's thin and pretty and has eyes on Peter? Or a girl with a motor mouth and a booming voice? Definitely the best friend, since things are more at stake when she's around.

Great, my plans to look like a knockout fizzle out since this is short notice. It's six o'clock and he's coming in an hour. I don't have time to iron my hair or buy a new outfit. I look in the mirror at my puffy hair. I rub some anti-frizz serum into it and then put it in a bun. That's better. I look through my closet and find a dress that I haven't worn in a while that Peter probably never saw me in before. I put on makeup. Pink blush brightens my face and mascara makes my eyes pop out behind my glasses. I decide to forget about the contact lenses since I don't want to spend another night blinking like crazy. My efforts are good enough.

Peter comes early, fifteen minutes before seven. There's a honk outside and I walk out. Jillian is in the front seat of the SUV, with Raul behind the wheel, but when Mom looks out of the window she doesn't say anything, since she's met the two of them before. It's the person in the back seat that will confuse her—Peter, whom she briefly met at Parent Night and whom I aspire to have a relationship with.

But she doesn't see him, or she doesn't ask about him. She lets me go without saying anything more than, "Be home by ten."

I sit next to Peter in the back and smile. Then I stop smiling because it might weird him out if I'm always grinning.

"You look nice tonight," Peter says.

"Thanks." I can feel the blood rush to my face. I hope that my fake blush is hiding the real one. He's looking mighty tasty himself. He has on a tight shirt and I see muscles that I haven't noticed before (he always wears a plaid shirt at school; it helps with the frigid air conditioning in most of the wings). I think of the ugly drawing I made of him, that Shakira picked up. He doesn't mention it. He must think it was just a harmless doodle. I'm still embarrassed about it, but hopefully he forgot about it completely, and I hope he's forgetting about the time I stole his bookbag, too. I didn't realize that chasing after a boy requires so much drama and action. This whole experience of pursuing Peter is filled with firsts for me.

Lisa lives close to me, so her house is next. I can feel my lips turning down in a sneer. What's happening to me? Since when do I dislike my best friend? Can a boy really make me not want her around? I've always wanted her around. As soon as I come home from school, I text her, IM her, and if I can't do those things, then I think about her. When I'm out shopping without her, I ask myself if she'd approve of the outfit I'm about to purchase. When

I watch TV late at night, I laugh at the comedies wishing that she was there to laugh with me. Now I actually sneer thinking about her! I'm a monster. I make my lips slacken into a straight line. I feel so guilty.

She comes out and Peter's eyes practically pop out like some cartoon character's. I can't see the actual roundness of his eyes coming out of his orbitals, but he is sure looking, looking hard. Lisa's gorgeous. Her hair, which is similar to mine, looks shiny and springy. How does she get her curls like that? Why is it that every other curly haired girl has better hair than mine, and what is their secret? Lisa is bony but doesn't look it. She's wearing a dress that's baggy on the top and bottom, but cinched tightly at the waist. Her dress is black and her high heels are pastel pink, which is a combination I never thought of before. She wears large, circular silver earrings that frame her face. She looks like a runway model.

Peter complimented me minutes ago, but when Lisa joins us in the back, he whistles. "Lisa, wow, who knew," he says.

Lisa giggles and coyly shrugs her shoulders. I feel the sneer trying to penetrate my facial muscles and skin, and I have to yank my lips up with a fake smile. "Lisa, you look great," I say.

"Thanks," she says. "I just threw this on."

Yeah, right. She just put a lot more effort into getting ready than I did. But who am I to judge? If I had more time to prepare, I'd look like a million bucks, too.

Raul and Jillian sit in the front having their own conversation. Sometimes they turn around to talk to us. Jillian's flat, black, ironed emo hair is mostly what I see of her. I see part of Raul's sharp profile. He has a pointy nose and angular jaw. He laughs a lot, so that interrupts Peter and Lisa's conversation every minute. Raul nods at something Jillian says. Peter and Lisa talk about school. I feel like the fifth wheel. Maybe I am the fifth wheel. There are five of us and I'm not talking to anyone. We stop in front of Maria's house. I feel better when she gets in, because she's a hub of excitement who talks to everyone. She distracts me from Peter's obvious attraction to Lisa. We all start talking about Lil Wayne's music because she's going on excitedly about his songs, which she downloaded recently.

"Girl, let me tell you, that Lil Wayne is fine as hell," Maria says. Her large hoop earrings swing against her shoulders. She's right next to me and I have a good look at her drawn-in eyebrows and bright red lipstick. Chonga. But at least she's a chonga with a good heart. She squeezes my hand, which comforts me during this stressful time when my best friend is stealing my spotlight. Peter's eyes were on me before Lisa came into the picture.

We drive past chic restaurants that have outdoor seating, and then we're in front of the art gallery. Raul parks at a meter and we all chip in with quarters so that we have two hours of parking time. We go inside.

There are a bunch of paintings on the wall and an

equal number of rich-looking people milling around looking at them. Even though Dad's a dentist and I live in a ritzy neighborhood, I don't consider myself a fancy person, so I feel out of place. Maria loudly snaps her gum, causing a middle-aged woman to turn toward her with blazing eyes. Maria doesn't notice the stares, so she continues to chew and pop.

Peter acts as the group leader. Wherever he goes, we follow. He leads us through archways and different rooms. The paintings are all abstract. I don't see people or trees. There are lines, ropes, and ribbons of paint. Some of it looks like something a child can do, but others look really neat. One of them reminds me of a bowl of spaghetti, if each noodle were rainbow colored. Another one looks like the ocean exploded and merged with the sky. Raul is taking pictures that he can share with Jillian and Peter.

"Peter, this is wonderful," Lisa says. I can tell she doesn't mean it. She barely glances at the paintings because her eyes are always on Peter. Raul and Jillian are both kind of strange—Raul is a math and computer genius and Jillian is emo and depressed—and they study each painting as if they could fall into them. Maria couldn't care less about anything except her gum. Then there's me. I'm only halfway interested in the gallery, some paintings charming me and others boring me. I'm waiting to be wowed.

"I need to go to the bathroom," Jillian says.

Peter points to where the bathrooms are. Girls have this habit of going to the bathroom together, even if they all don't need to go. Maria and Lisa both follow her. I decide to stay behind, because I want to be with Peter. Raul drifts off to another room to take more pictures, and that leaves the two of us alone together.

"So how do you like these paintings?" Peter asks. "They're all by local artists."

"They're really interesting," I say. "Especially the two of them in there … " I describe the ones that I really liked from the other room.

"Not a lot of people get abstract art," he says. "I'm glad you do."

"Yeah, I know." Actually, I don't get it at all.

"Abstract art is about the way you feel. It's not about seeing something recognizable, like a tree or bird. These paintings give me all sorts of emotions. Come here."

Peter backtracks through an archway we already went through, to a room we visited earlier this evening. The gallery isn't that big, but since we stand in front of each painting for a few minutes, it feels like we've been there forever. Now Peter wants me to look at some paintings *again*.

We face black and red cubes that overlap each other with imperfect edges. I look at it and think about toy blocks, sugar, and other things that are shaped the same way. It isn't an ugly painting, but I'm not sure if I would want it hanging in my house.

"What does this make you feel?" he asks.

"Um, I guess it makes me feel, I'm not sure … " What to say?

"It makes me feel lonely."

"It does?"

"Yes."

That silences me. How does a painting make one feel lonely? I look at it harder, trying to see why it would make Peter think of loneliness. The colors are dark. Cubes are a solid shape, something you can depend on, but the edges of the cubes are smeared. Surrounding the cubes are swirls of blue. The painting reminds me of the solar system, how you see the planets together in a picture or three dimensional model, while in fact they're very far apart.

"Maybe the cubes are keeping each other company," I say. "Or maybe they're together, but they're not related to each other, like when you're in a room full of people and you're not talking to anyone."

"That could be it," Peter says. "But we all feel different things when we look at these pieces. Let's go to another one."

The next painting is another one we've seen. It's a sunburst of yellow and orange, with a red outline outside the dabs of color. It makes me think of sunshine and happiness. "This is more cheerful," I say.

"I feel like my heart opens up when I see this," he says.

"I know. It's so airy and bright. It's like spring and flowers and light, even though the artist didn't really paint those things." Wait a minute, am I actually feeling something toward a painting? Yes, I am. I almost gasp out loud, but the gallery is relatively quiet and I don't want to break the silence with teenage gushing.

We continue to admire the painting. I want to hug Peter. Because of him, I now have all these thoughts and feelings toward this blob on the wall. I didn't think it was possible. I actually like abstract art now that I see beyond the streaks and smears. Peter's so deep. When he takes me to the next painting, which has sharp lines of blue and purple, the anger of the artist is obvious, as if the slashes of paint are slashes against someone or something. He must have really been upset about something when he painted it. I can tell.

The evening has been so unexpected. I came here to dazzle Peter, but instead he's dazzling me. I'm thinking more about how the paintings are filling up my mind with ideas, and less about my goal of a romantic relationship with Peter. I can still feel him at my side, his presence, his body heat. But instead of thinking *Peter, Peter, Peter*, there are other things to look at and ponder about. For the first time in weeks, I don't have tunnel vision when I'm around him. I can focus on other things. It isn't all about Peter.

"We're baaaaaaack," Maria says, sashaying toward us. My friends have reapplied their makeup and perfume, so I see glossy lips and smell floral body spray. But they missed out on a lot while they were away.

My friends are loud, compared to the silence that surrounded me and Peter when we were alone together. I want to rewind time so that we're alone again, just the paintings and us, but Maria is there smacking her gum and Lisa grabs Peter's arm to lead him to a painting she likes (something pink, her favorite color). "I love pink," she says. Lisa's still looking at the surface of the paintings, rather than at what they mean. At least I see past that, and I had that sweet time with Peter when he showed me something new and different. Lisa continues to dominate his attention, but he still turns to me when we come to the last painting, which is near the exit of the gallery.

"What do you think?" he asks me.

I look at the lively colors of red, orange, and purple. The colors are in swirls and circles.

"I think it's romantic," I say.

"I do, too," he agrees.

Lisa twitches her nose and Maria frowns. They don't get it.

"This is very psychedelic," Jillian says. "It's like, wow, really touches the heart."

"I don't get it," Maria says.

Peter squints at the nameplate on the bottom. "The title is *Love and Sunset*," he informs me. He winks at me. We were both thinking the same thing. And he's super sexy when he winks. He should do it more often.

I think of the horizon in the morning time and a

couple sharing the same vision of it, just as Peter and I share this thing we have. It's an indescribable thing, the same way some of the paintings are beyond description. Even Lisa, with her hands and eyes all over Peter, can't take that away from us. I smile as we all get back into the SUV to go to a restaurant. It will be the second time this Ramadan that I'll be breaking fast with friends rather than family.

At the restaurant we pile into a booth, and it just happens that I sit next to Peter. We jostle each other constantly when we reach to get a glass of water or a fork. We all laugh and crack jokes. Raul impersonates our teachers, Lisa tears up with laughter, Maria cackles hysterically, Jillian shakes so hard that our glasses of soda tremble, and Peter touches my knee or squeezes my arm anytime he finds something funny. He's giving me mixed messages—am I a friend or something more? I silently hope that I'm something more. When we get to dessert, we all order something different. I order a sundae and he orders a Frisbee-sized cookie. He insists that I have a bite of his cookie. I'm about to reach for it, but he's faster than me. He breaks off a piece and pops it inside my mouth. I see the flash of distaste in Lisa's eyes. Even though it's probably a friendly gesture, it does seem like something more. His fingertip did graze my lips. If only we could be alone together, minus our friends and the restaurant crowd. We could feed each other all we want, and even kiss each other.

It feels like the best night of my life. Parent Night might have been a disaster, but this is the exact opposite. The night is luminous, just like the paintings we saw, just like the green sheen of Peter's eyes, just like the tinkling laughter of my friends.

22

The braces are on my teeth, and my mouth is immobile with metal and ceramics.

Dr. Abdelwahab put them on me—*very nice,* he proclaimed—grafting each bracket on my teeth with some superhuman glue that keeps them in place. Then he slid a wire between these brackets. My teeth feel tight afterwards, with some unseen forces working against them. Only my lower teeth have the clear braces on them. My smile stays the same since only my top teeth, which are braces-free, can be seen. I'll make sure my lower lip doesn't retract too much when I talk, so that people can't see them at all.

They're not a treat, even though Dr. Abdelwahab acts like braces are sparkly treats for kids. They're painful and ugly. Food gets stuck in them. The brackets rub against the inside of my cheeks. I didn't expect them to be so uncomfortable, but Dad says that I'll get used to them. I don't believe him. How am I ever going to get a boyfriend with a sci-fi mouth? I feel like I'm in a *Star Trek* episode as a specimen from the planet Ceramico. This is a disaster.

I go to school and nobody seems to notice for the first few hours. But then Lisa says something stupid—she thinks that the position of *secretary* in our government is an actual secretarial job, which means typing and filing for the president—and I laugh so hard that people see them. "Almira, you're wearing braces!"

"They don't look so bad," someone behind me says.

"They look all right," Lisa says.

"Thanks," I tell people, trying to keep my mouth as closed as possible

"You look really cute with them on," Peter says, smiling at me.

Huh? I look cute? And from Peter. I glow inside, but I try not to smile. Anyway, I'm trying to avoid Peter. After he says that compliment, I scurry away from him in the hallway. I chide myself for that: I want to get closer to him, not further away from him. But I don't want to be anywhere near him since I feel shy with these new braces in my mouth. We had such a good time at the gallery, I felt so pretty and sexy, we had chemistry—and now these uglifying braces are in the way. I'm no longer ashamed of that stupid drawing I made of him that Shakira showed him, because now these braces are the bane of my existence. Something always has to go wrong, whether it's to mess with my head or my looks. On top of my braces, Lisa is more rabid than normal about Peter today. She's coming on stronger than usual, putting her arms around him, patting him on the back, and using any excuse to touch him in the hallways.

Since Peter's locker is next to mine, I walk away when I see him at his locker. I go to class without my American History book. My teacher is surprised that I don't have it and tells me to share a book with someone. "Really, Almira, this isn't like you," she says. I know I'm not acting like myself.

Not only am I frantic about Peter's image of me, but the back of my mouth feels raw. The doctor gave me a small case of wax that I'm supposed to rub into balls and place on brackets that hurt me. I have several pieces of wax stuck to the brackets in the back, because my mouth is being ripped apart from the friction between braces and flesh. A nice, cold glass of water would feel fantastic, but I'm still fasting.

"Hi, Almira," a boy I don't recognize says.

"Hey, girl," another boy says.

I'm definitely becoming skinny and I pat my stomach, which is flat now. It's also growling like a beast. It's lunch time and I go to the library, away from the temptations of food. I sit behind the biography section. I'm trying to do all of my homework, getting so lost in my textbooks and binders that I block out the noises around me. It usually annoys me when I hear talking of any kind, and there are always study groups or students whispering into their cell phones.

What catches my attention is sniffling, coming from right next to me. It keeps getting louder and louder. I get up, look in between the shelved books, and see a head of black hair bent over a tabletop. I usually mind my own business, but I really want to see who's crying and why.

Walking around the shelf, I see that it's Shakira. Her eyes are red and puffy and she's holding a tissue to her nose. She still looks outrageously pretty with red eyes, a pink nose, and tear streaks down her face (darn it, I look like a hot mess when I cry). She looks up at me and I feel *empathic*—it's Ms. Odige's word of the day—with sorrow stirring for this enemy of mine. Shakira, of the quick mouth and hurtful words. Why am I feeling sorry for her?

"Leave me alone," Shakira whispers.

"What's wrong?" I whisper back. "Did something happen?"

"Everything happened. Nobody likes me."

She sniffles some more and I don't know what to do. Whenever Lisa cries, I hug her. When someone isn't a friend, I usually just bring over tissue, but she already has one. At this point it makes the most sense to be truthful with her. "Well, you make it very hard for people to like you," I say.

Her eyes widen when I say that.

"You haven't exactly been nice," I add.

"What do you mean?"

"Come on. You make snide remarks about how Peter wouldn't be interested in me, or that clothes don't fit me right. And you were rude to Maria."

"But I meant nothing by saying that stuff."

"It doesn't seem like it. You're vicious."

"I know I say what's on my mind, but people take it the wrong way," Shakira says. "I never called you fat, but I knew that dress in the store was wrong for you. I didn't imply that Maria was stupid for wearing those shoes the day her nail broke, but that she wasn't following school rules. I was also teasing you about Peter. I really thought you should be honest and say what you want to him, to see if he likes you back."

"It's the way you say things. It comes out wrong and arrogant."

Shakira shakes her head. "I never meant to hurt anyone. At my last school, my friends warned me that I shouldn't come to a new school the way I am, that I'd make enemies, and they were right. They knew me for a long time, since elementary school, and they were used to my bluntness. Here I am, the new girl, acting that way with strangers. I should have softened up before starting here."

I'm turning sympathetic toward her now that she's being candid and sorrowful. She finally admitted that she can be extremely blunt, to the point that everyone, except for boys, shuns her. I sort of see things her way. There are people who blurt things out because that's a personality trait of theirs, and they accidentally upset people. It looks like Shakira is one of those people. But as the new girl who is so drop-dead gorgeous that most girls are jealous of her, she has treaded on too many toes.

"I'm sorry if I ever offended you," Shakira says.

"I accept your apology," I say. "Let's get to class. The bell will ring soon."

"You must think I'm a creep for showing your doodle to Peter."

"Why did you do it?"

"I thought it was a funny picture. He thought it was funny, too."

"What else did he say?"

"That he felt flattered that you drew him."

"What else?" I ask.

"That's about it," Shakira says.

That's a relief. I want Peter to think that the portrait is an innocent, nothing gesture (when it really reflects the inner turmoil of lust and love I have for him). Shakira's sniffling stops and she packs her things, since lunch is almost over. I carry her heavy science book since her arms are already full. "Thank you," she murmurs.

"Come on," I say with the wave of my hand. "I have something to ask you."

"What?" We stop walking and stand by a trophy case to talk.

"You know I love chocolate?"

"Yeah, I heard you telling Lisa that it's your most-missed food during Ramadan."

"Have you been leaving chocolates for me?"

"What?"

"Chocolates," I repeat. "Have you been leaving them on my seats and desks in our classes?"

"No," Shakira says. "Why would I do that? It would be mean, since you're fasting. I wouldn't want anyone to leave pretzels around for me to eat."

Pretzels are her downfall! Of course they are. They're low in calories and she has the perfect figure. Meanwhile, I can't resist anything that has globs of fat in it.

"Okay," I say.

"Chocolate is really fattening," she says.

"Duh, I know that."

"I'm sorry. I guess I had a moment there. I hope I wasn't rude."

"No, you weren't."

"Are you sure?" she whines.

"Yes, that was okay," I say.

"I'm sure you think that I'm saying you eat a lot of heavy foods—"

"Shakira, I accepted your apology already. Let's get to class."

23

"She apologized," I tell Lisa and Maria.

"Wow," Lisa says.

"Hmmm," Maria hums skeptically.

"She's really sorry that she says things in the wrong tone of voice," I say.

"I hope she means that," Maria says. She's eating a Little Debbie cake. Another crème cake, this one chocolate covered. It probably tastes part chocolate, part chemical plant, but it looks mighty tasty.

"I haven't had Little Debbie in ages," I say.

"Then have one," Maria says, offering me a cake.

"No," I say, backing away as if she's offering me an apple in the Garden of Eden.

"You can take one bite," Maria says.

What if I take a bite just to taste it and then spit it out? But then the residue will somehow run down my throat and into my stomach. It's cheating.

"Maria, why do you always do this to her?" Lisa says.

"I'm testing her."

"Do I pass?" I ask.

"With flying colors."

I smile at that. I'm acing Ramadan. Food will not beat me down with its many temptations: iced cakes, marinara sauce, seasoned hamburgers. I'm winning. Just a little bit longer to go. Someone, Maria I'm sure, left another Hershey's Kiss on my science seat today. Maria isn't even in my science class, but she's next door in another class. She's really going out of her way to try to get me to cheat.

"Oh no!" Lisa says.

"What?" I ask.

The final bell rang moments ago and we're all about to walk home when Lisa turns around to see that Peter and Shakira are huddled together next to his locker.

"Get away from my man," Lisa says between gritted teeth.

They're several yards away from us and can't hear us, but I'm positive that Lisa is going to barge over to where they are and separate them.

"You can't claim him," Maria says.

"Yes I can, because he likes me and we have chemistry."

Like oil and oil or water and water. "Peter's nice to everyone," I say. "Just because he's nice to you doesn't mean that he likes you."

"Oh, but he does," Lisa insists.

Maria playfully pinches my arm, but she really hurts my skin. A red welt forms on my upper arm. "Watch it," I say.

"Oops," Maria says.

"She-man," Lisa jokes.

Maria's eyes bug out and Lisa runs away. Maria takes chase, but I know they're just playing. They run into the courtyard and disappear behind a wall of hedges. I start to walk out of the building, but then I see Mr. Gregory pushing a cart full of boxes to his room. I ask him if he needs help and he says yes.

"These are new beakers and thermometers," he says. "I'd really appreciate it if you help me shelve them, as long as you don't have to take a bus home and nobody's waiting for you."

"I'll help," a deep voice behind me says.

I turn around and see Peter. He grabs one end of the cart and helps Mr. Gregory push it into his room. Then Mr. Gregory opens the back room for us. He tells us to line up the beakers on one shelf and leave the thermometers unopened on another shelf. "I'll be right back," he says. "The secretary has some more boxes for me."

I'm alone with Peter. How exhilarating! Maybe I can partake in some harmless flirtation.

"Come on," he says when he sees that I'm standing there like a dope doing nothing. Hmm, he doesn't seem to be in a romantic state of mind.

"I'm right behind you," I squeak. I open a box and see the tops of beakers staring up at me like multiple eyes. I gingerly pick up each one and put them next to the old beakers. I love the back room because every time I'm in it I discover something new. I see pickled baby alligators, a human skull, all sorts of things in there. I even learn about Mr. Gregory, because he has a signed autograph picture of Robert Pattinson in a drawer that I open. Aha, I knew I saw him in the *Twilight* movie. Science is cool. Mr. Gregory is cool. Peter is the coolest.

"You like him?" Peter asks when he catches sight of the autograph.

"Of course," I say.

"Who is that, anyway? He looks familiar."

Has Peter been living under a rock? "He's superfamous," I say. That's the only explanation necessary.

I leave the drawer open. When I put the picture back, I see a Ferrero Rocher chocolate in the drawer. I pick it up and turn it around in my hands. Ferrero Rocher. Wafer, hazelnut, chocolate. I can eat a whole box of Ferrero Rocher on my own (I actually did this once).

"I know you like chocolate," Peter says.

"I guess Mr. Gregory does too," I say, putting the chocolate back.

"No, take it."

"Who knows how old it is. Anyway, I can't steal from him."

"He won't notice." Peter grabs the chocolate and puts it in the side pouch of my bookbag. Okay, if he's going to be pushy about it I'll eat it later, even though it feels wrong to steal.

"It's really hard to eat with these braces," I say.

"Your braces really fit you. You don't look weird with them at all."

Peter is so close to me that his arm brushes against mine. Our eyes meet and he smiles at me. No wonder Lisa is willing to fight for him. She'll fight dragons for him, climb mountains, roam deserts. I want to do these things for him too, as long as none of these activities kill me.

"Do you want to see my sketchpad?" he asks.

"Sure," I say. Of course. He's been hiding it from my prying eyes for weeks now. I wouldn't mind seeing all his drawings, and the hope that he has sketched me lingers, even though I know it was Shakira he was using as a model.

Peter takes the sketchpad out of his bookbag and shows me the first page. It's a scene of a gondola floating on a Venetian canal. Very nice. He randomly flips the pages and shows me a replica of a perfume ad with a beautiful model. The next page is a portrait of a movie star from the forties who I can't remember the name of. He also has a sketch of a knight and maiden, which is very close to the one I gave him, but he drew it slightly different.

"And this is Shakira," Peter says.

He shows me the page and my heart aches again. He's drawn her with so much detail that the sketch looks more like a black and white photograph than a pencil drawing. It seems like I'm staring directly at her pupils. The detailing is so strong that I can imagine her luscious hair swaying with her movement.

"You're so talented," I say.

"Thank you."

"I bet you have an A."

"I do."

"I wish I could draw, too."

"And last but not least … are you ready?" he asks.

"Sure." My heart is hammering. What's he going to show me? A picture of him and Shakira together, surely. Shakira as a mermaid. Shakira in a bikini with sea froth at her feet. Maybe Lisa is right about his love for her, and the next picture will be of my best friend.

He slowly flips the page and I'm looking on in anticipation. I almost don't recognize the sketch. The dark eyes. The black hair. Long lashes. Full lips.

"Do you like it?"

"Uhhhhhh," I hum.

"What do you think?" he asks in a near whisper.

I'm confused. I can swear that the sketch portrays me,

Almira Abdul, invisible to most boys who walk this Earth (until recently with the weight loss). But the sketch looks better than me, even on a good day when I have shiny eyes, clear skin, a smile on my lips, and an indescribable glow. It's like there's a third dimension where everything has been sketched with pencil, and I look so much better in this dimension. I look hot.

"It's you, Almira," Peter says.

"Oh!" I yelp. "I didn't know you were drawing me."

"You left a portrait photo on your desk once, I think from the last picture day we had. I took it when you weren't looking. I hope you don't mind."

"That's okay."

"I used the picture as a model, but I also used my memory. It's how I see you, so pretty all the time."

"Oh."

"I like you a lot."

"Oh."

"It was great being at the gallery with you. It's like you really understand me. I try to explain art to other girls and they act like airheads in front of me, but I saw the spark in your eyes. It was cool. I've never felt like that with another girl before."

"Peter, it was all you. You showed me something different," I say.

"The point is, it was something new for me, and you seem to feel the same way I feel about you," he says. "Shakira showed me the sketch you did of me. I know you're not an expert artist, but it was awesome that you drew me."

"Yeah?"

"Shakira said you like me, and I hope it's true."

"Huh?"

"I hope you're not embarrassed. She told me in private, so it wasn't like she told everyone. The thing is, she told me that because I'd already told her I like you."

"She did? You told her that?"

"Yes. I've even kept your drawing." He shows me the end pages of his sketchpad. Clipped to the back of his pad is the alien representation I made of him days ago, with the paper crinkled since I'd balled it up. I was so mad at Shakira for giving it to him, but now I see that she played a small part in bringing the two of us together, because we're meant to be together.

"What a horrible drawing," I say. "I'm sorry I made you ugly, because you're not."

"It's okay," he says. "It's the thought that counts, and I believe we share the same thoughts."

I'm breathless, and I'm sure I'm going to pass out. Shakira opened her big mouth, and I'm glad she did, because now he knows and there are no secrets between us. Being out in the open feels unreal, but also pleasant. It also feels painful …

The pain on the inside of my cheeks from my braces is more pronounced. When he comes closer I'm flustered, and then his lips are over mine. My first kiss. His soft lips.

I want to melt. I close my eyes and part my lips slightly, relishing the kiss despite the prickling braces. He disengages from me and my eyes are swimming from the intensity of the moment. I hope he didn't feel my braces. Why did I have to get braces right before my first kiss? My parents are always trying to ruin my life, intentionally or accidentally. And is my breath okay during my fast?

"Peter," I say.

"What?" he whispers.

"Uh, umm—"

Peter grabs my face and gazes at me as if I'm a crystal ball. He makes me feel like I'm the world to him. *Kiss me again*, I think. And he does.

24

After the second kiss, which is sweeter and better than the first—practice makes perfect with anything—I don't know what to say next. We look into each other's eyes. Peter runs his fingers through my hair (thank God it's tangle-free, or else I'd be embarrassed). Other than the braces, I think I'm in good shape. I'm wearing an icy-blue satin shirt and navy-blue skirt with black boots. My hair isn't frizzy since the weather has cooled off a bit. My breath has to be okay because of the super-strong strawberry lip balm I'm wearing. I have some shimmer on my eyes and cheeks. I'm having a pretty day.

"Peter—" I say.

"What?" he asks.

"Umm." I'm tongue-tied. What am I supposed to say after this?

"Was it okay, what I just did?"

"Yeah. Of course."

Peter smiles. Were we simultaneously worrying about whether we like each other or not? Sometimes I can't figure people out. Both of us have been silently suffering for nothing.

"Peter," I say.

"What?"

Am I going to say his name like an idiot over and over again? I simply don't know how to talk to him after the kiss. Before, when we were lab partners, I could tell him whatever was on my mind (except for my crush on him), but now his kisses have stunned my brain. I should tell him that he's a good kisser or that I like him too, but my mouth feels numb. Yet someone knows what to say.

The room becomes darker as a shadow steps over the threshold. Peter turns around and we're both facing Lisa. She has tears falling across her cheeks, creating white trails against the blusher and bronzer she's wearing. She's trembling and falls to the side, leaning against the doorjamb. Her hands fumble against the wall as she balances herself upright. I want to grab her to steady her, but I know that at this point she won't want me anywhere near her.

"How could you!" Lisa gasps.

"Lisa, it's not what you think!" I say.

"You can't even date him! Your parents don't allow you to date! You can't have him and you're taking him anyway!"

"Lisa!" I yell, rushing toward her. But she's faster than me and runs out of Mr. Gregory's room. I see the hem of her pink skirt flutter away from me and then it disappears altogether.

Peter tags along behind me. "What's going on?" he asks. I look at his frowning face. How can boys be so dense? Doesn't he realize that for the past few weeks Lisa was throwing herself at him, wanting him just as badly as I wanted him?

"She likes you," I say. "And I betrayed her."

"But I don't want Lisa," he says. "I want you."

I shake my head. He doesn't understand that Lisa is my bestest friend ever and I just hurt her. As badly as I want Peter, I don't think he's worth losing Lisa over. "I have to go," I say.

"But, but—wait."

Something then dawns on me. "Hey, you were the one leaving all those stupid chocolates on my seat!" I say.

"Yes," he admits. "You once told me that chocolate was your favorite food. So I put them on your seat or had a friend do it for me."

"You almost made me cheat during my fast!"

"Almira, please, I'm sorry. I didn't mean for you to eat them now. You said you could eat after sunset, so I assumed you were holding them until then."

"Don't you know how tempting that was to me? If I

ate one of those chocolates, it would have ruined everything! You obviously have never fasted before."

"Fine! But you printed that picture for me! And you drew me. We were both thinking about each other!"

He's right. We were both trying to impress each other, give little tokens of affection, throw around hints. But I don't have time to argue or agree with him. I sprint through the school, trying to find Lisa, but she's nowhere in sight. Mr. Gregory calls for me several times from outside his room. "Almira! Almira!" I don't respond as I search through each hallway on every floor. It's after school, and there are small groups of students who hang around for football practice, the dance club, and all the other activities we have. I go into the bathrooms to see if Lisa is hiding in a stall, crying her eyes out, but she's not in any of them.

"Almira," I hear. This time it's Peter's voice. Peter wants me romantically. Mr. Gregory wants me as a helper. Mom is thinking that I'll be coming home soon. I feel like I'm being pulled in different directions, but the only direction I want to go in is toward Lisa.

I shake uncontrollably as I walk home. This has to be the worst thing that's ever happened to me. I don't know if Lisa can ever understand that it's Peter's choice of who he likes and doesn't like. If he doesn't want her, then why can't I have him? I'm not even sure if I should like him anymore, since he tried to ruin my fast by tempting me with chocolate, but that wasn't his intention. He had found something I adored and decided to use it as a trail leading to his heart, but it was so wrong to leave it every-where. *Eat me, eat me,* the chocolate beckoned, and I had to resist it. I also have to resist him if I want to keep Lisa as a best friend.

It's still out of this world that things have happened so quickly, from an unexpected kiss to unexpectedly stabbing Lisa in the back. I place one foot in front of the other in a daze—from being hungry, from being kissed, from questioning the integrity of the kiss (did he feel my stupid braces?), from wondering if I'm bestfriendless. I rarely go home alone. Lisa usually walks with me or rides with me in Mom's car. I even wish that Mom could be here so that I don't feel so lonely. I would even tolerate her singing to drive out the loneliness.

I stop by Lisa's house and her older cousin answers the door. Lisa came home, she says, but then she stepped out. She says to try the pizza place nearby. We live in a thick block of houses with parallel streets that look identi-cal in quaint suburbia, but Lisa and I happen to live on the outskirts of the neighborhood, close to a few businesses. I sprint to the pizzeria. Breathlessly I look around, but I can't find Lisa. The cashier gives me a dirty look. It doesn't mat-ter what anyone else thinks about me. It only matters what Lisa thinks. I look at the busy street in front of me. There are restaurants, cellular stores, and drugstores spanning sev-eral blocks. Lisa could be in any one of those stores. She could be at the beauty supply store to buy hand cream or at the book-store buying books on how to drop disloyal friends. I walk back and forth for a few more minutes and then go home. Lisa's line is busy, so I go on IM to search for her.

AlmiraRules: Lisa are you there?

Nothing.

AlmiraRules: Lisa, please talk to me.

There's no answer. She probably has me on her block list, so that she'll never hear from me again. Me on her block list? I never thought it would be possible, yet the day has come. What a stupid thing I've done! Yes, Peter is a dream-boat and the hottest guy who has ever paid any whit of attention to me, but he isn't the world. Okay, maybe he is. But no, I can't put him before my bestest friend, the one who I tell everything to, the one who holds me when I cry, the girl who makes me laugh because she thinks cheesecake is made from mozzarella rather than from cream cheese.

I wait for an hour with other computer windows open, checking my email and doing research for home-work, but there's still no message from Lisa in my IM box. I'm persona non grata to her. Then I see something. I rub my eyes behind my glasses, thinking it's a mirage, but it is indeed GorgeLisa on my screen.

GorgeLisa: LEAVE ME ALONE FOR THE REST OF MY LIFE!
AlmiraRules: you don't mean that. i'm sorry. the kiss meant nothing

GorgeLisa: BACKSTABBER

AlmiraRules: you know you're my best friend and that i'd never intentionally hurt you

GorgeLisa: SNAKE IN THE GRASS

GorgeLisa: you can't even date him because you're muslim and he's not. that's the stupidest thing, wanting something you can't have and you just had to stab me in the back for your own satisfaction

GorgeLisa: you know what your parents and grandfather will think, but you don't care

GorgeLisa: YOU KISSED HIM FOR NO REASON BECAUSE YOU WON'T EVER HAVE HIM

AlmiraRules: stop saying these things, i know i can't have him, but he kissed me

I burst into tears. My best friend hates my guts. She thinks I'm dirt. We'll no longer talk, IM everyday, or go out shopping together. All because of Peter, who has never IM'ed me or even really asked me out. And Lisa is being so mean, reminding me of how different I am compared to other teenagers: good Muslim girls don't date boys, especially if they're infidels. All of a sudden I feel this wall come between me and the rest of my classmates, as if I'm an alien from outer space that has nothing in common with them.

AlmiraRules: Lisa, call me

GorgeLisa: kiss him if it makes you feel better, but you've lost me forever

AlmiraRules: this is unfair. you won't even let me make things right

GorgeLisa: it can never be right

AlmiraRules: don't say that!

GorgeLisa: I PUT YOU ON CALL BLOCK. BUH-BYE

I cry harder. Peter made me feel beautiful and wanted, and now I feel ugly and hated and weird and Muslim. Other than Shakira, who looks like a beauty queen, I'm the only one in my school who's fasting and can't date boys. I momentarily wonder if Shakira is allowed to date, but it doesn't really matter. She can have any guy she wants. But I missed this one opportunity to have a boy I really like, who is interested in me as much as I am in him. The whole situation blew up in my face.

Later on that night Mom asks me what's wrong because I look sad, but I tell her nothing is wrong. I don't want to explain to her that a boy kissed me, because I don't know if she'll freak out or not. Mom doesn't seem too traditional, especially after clashing with Grandpa, but many times she's told me I'm too young for a boyfriend. Mom and Dad will find a husband for me if I want to be with some-one after high school. How stupid. I find Peter, but loving him means losing Lisa and possibly angering my family. I'm in a bind with everyone.

25

The next day at school, Lisa avoids me the entire time. She doesn't sit next to me in class, she looks away from me, she doesn't ask me for the answers to our assignments, and she steers clear of me. I'm now invisible to her. It's like we've never met, never stayed over at each other's houses, never stood up for each other, never shopped together, never laughed together. There's an identical universe where Lisa and Almira never met way back in kindergarten and never became best friends. But this universe doesn't exist. I know that it doesn't. I have to break Lisa's resistance.

I approach her several times and she ignores me. "Hi,

Lisa," I say, and she walks straight to her locker without glancing at me. Everything about her is stiff: her walk, her shoulders, and even her hair doesn't bounce like it normally does. I turned her into a statue. I hope that somewhere deep within her she has some warmth and forgiveness that she can shower on me. I sensed that it wasn't going to be easy to win back Lisa, but I didn't know it would be this difficult. I thought her face would soften up and that she'd say a few words the more I tried to reach out to her, but she isn't doing any of these things.

I see Maria between bells and ask her what I should do. "Just give her time," she says, squeezing my hand. "We all have a beef with our friends sometimes. Friendship isn't perfect." She's right, but I've never had this big a rift before with a good friend. I just have to try and rekindle our friendship.

"Wasn't the homework hard?" I ask Lisa during history class. She focuses on the teacher's forehead and pretends I didn't open my mouth. "Lisa, meet me at the library," I say in the hallway. "I have something important to say to you." I stand in front of the library thinking that Lisa and I can walk to class together and catch a few minutes of quality time, but she never shows up. The fifth time I approach her she says, "We're no longer friends."

My heart sinks to the floor. We're in the hallway between classes. I look at her, but she won't look at me and she coolly walks away, her bony shoulders gaining distance from me. We were once everything to each other, but now we're nothing. I feel so low, like the way Nicole Richie must have felt when Paris Hilton no longer wanted to have anything to do with her and they had to tape *The Simple Life* separately, rather than doing scenes together. That whole season was awkward. There were some funny scenes and I laughed, but it wasn't as enjoyable. Something was wrong. Everyone could see it. Why weren't they together during their antics? There was even sadness in Nicole's big brown eyes that belied her false happiness and flirtatiousness. But then the two made up. I wish the same for Lisa and myself.

After those harsh words, I rush to the bathroom, afraid that tears will fall. I don't want anyone to see me crying. My eyes are watery all day and my head is down, sinking to the ground.

During lunch Shakira asks if she can sit next to me in the library. I say yes. We share a table, spreading our books everywhere, and we study silently. We don't exchange one word. We aren't friends, not yet anyhow, and we're probably sitting together for the same reason. To avoid loneliness. She feels like an outcast, with no female friends but plenty of male admirers, and Lisa no longer wants me. Even though we're quiet during lunch, absorbed in doing our homework, her presence is welcome to me. My eyes meet hers a few times and there's no longer any hostility sparking off of her. She's been tamed by being blackballed and I'm mourning my lost friendship with Lisa. Docile for different reasons, we find comfort with each other.

We walk to class together afterwards. Shakira says, "I saw Peter's drawing of you."

"He showed it to me," I say.

"It wasn't an assignment, since he already drew me."

"I know."

"He likes you."

"I thought he liked you."

"I don't think he does. Anyway, he knows that I go out with Luis."

"Your parents let you date?" I ask.

"No," she says, shrugging her shoulders. "I tell them I'm out with friends and then I go and see him. My parents are strict and I have a grandfather who would go ballistic. He already nitpicks about the way I dress and the makeup I wear."

"My granddad does the same thing!"

"At least he doesn't live with me."

"Mine doesn't live with me either." That's a plus. Grandpa doesn't live with us, but at least he could have a cordial relationship with my mom.

I still don't know how to break it to my family that I've been kissed. What if Peter comes to our house? What will happen? The prospect of having a boyfriend doesn't look appealing since my family won't approve. What is the use of Peter kissing me when I can never have a legitimate relationship with him? I quiver thinking about Grandpa's reaction to that juicy bit of news.

Peter sits next to me in science. He smiles and tries

to make me laugh, but we do our lab solemnly. I'm not even in the mood for him. For Peter. My crush. The boy who bestowed a kiss on me. The man of my dreams. Lisa sits two rows behind us since we don't have assigned seats. Mr. Gregory gives both of us quizzical looks, because we always sit next to each other. Well, not anymore. All day long people have been looking from me to Lisa, from Lisa to me. They even ask me about our obvious separateness, but I dodge questions. It's nobody's business. There are already rumors swirling around. I can hear things behind my back, that Lisa caught me kissing her boyfriend, that I'm a traitor ... when Peter was never her boyfriend to begin with.

"Almira, when are you going to stop acting this way?" Peter asks me. "You're withdrawn today."

"When Lisa talks to me again I'll be better," I say.

"I'm sure she'll get over it."

"I don't know about that."

"I didn't know she liked me," Peter says. "I thought she was being friendly, and I never shared those feelings with her. I don't think I led her on."

It's strange how some people think they're not leading others on, but in fact they are, even though it's accidental. Peter isn't aware of his own powers to hypnotize girls. "I know you didn't mean any harm," I say.

"Do you want to go to the movies with me Saturday?" he asks.

"No," I say, frowning when I should be smiling. He

asks me out and it feels like nothing. I worried about being boyfriendless for the longest time, but now I'm afraid of having no best friend. It's a scary prospect. Sure I have other friends, but not a best friend.

"So what are you saying? That we can't go out?"

"Peter, don't you get it? I hurt my bestest friend in the world."

His face scrunches up. That beautiful tanned skin of his forms ridges that I've never seen before. Not only did I hurt Lisa, but now I'm hurting him. I must be cursed if I can make people feel this much pain. "Almira, I'll wait for you to come around, and I hope you do," he says. "Lisa will be fine, and we'll be fine too."

I want to throw myself into his arms and take back my words, but I don't want to touch him or look at him in front of Lisa. I want to show Lisa that I'm not into him, which is a lie.

She sits behind me like stone, her eyes unblinking as she looks at Mr. Gregory. It seems deliberate, as if she knows I'm watching her and she wants me to know that she isn't interested in my attention, and this might mean she still cares about me. If she didn't care, then her body language would be more natural. It's the same when I'm angry at my parents: I slam my bedroom door and keep my ear to the door to hear what they're saying about me. I do that because I care, because I want them to reach out to me to say that they understand my position on something. When I don't care, I'll do normal things like read a book or play around on the computer. Lisa obviously still thinks about me. Maybe her anger is a sign that she's in deep thought about our friendship. It's better than if she were to feel nothing at all. I have to turn her anger into forgiveness, but I need a strategy.

I caress Peter's sketchpad while Mr. Gregory lectures us on cloning. Peter no longer hides the sketchpad from me, now that the secret is out about him liking me. When Peter goes to the bathroom, I look through the pad. There are unicorns, boats, lions, and other figures, either roughly sketched or completely finished. My eyes keep returning to the sketch he did of me. After my third viewing of it, I make myself flip through the pad until I'm almost at the end of it. My eyes widen when I see a sketch that I really like. I tear it out gently and put it in a folder. The pad has over fifty sketches and I don't think Peter will notice that one is missing.

26

Mom makes salmon tonight and it keeps getting stuck on my braces. It's gross, so I don't finish my meal. I go to the bathroom and brush the fish out of my mouth. Then I floss, which is not easy to do with braces. I have to push the floss underneath the wire. At least only my bottom teeth have braces. I'm grateful for this one thing when everything else is going so horribly.

Peter texts me to ask me about my plans for tonight. *Busy w/fam*, I text back. He still believes that Lisa will get over what I did and that I should simply accept losing a best friend, but this isn't possible. I have to persuade Lisa to forgive me.

I'm creating an e-card to apologize to her. If I have to pass her notes in class, email her, send e-cards, and talk to her through my other friends, I will. I'm willing to do these things everyday, several times a day, if it means getting her back. I make a PowerPoint of dancing pink flowers on a black background. The background music is Akon's "Sorry, Blame It On Me."

It makes me teary-eyed to listen to the lyrics over and over again as I check for spelling mistakes. I hope that Lisa will take the time to read my e-card. I've spent an hour making it and I mean everything on it. I feel bad and horrible and want her back as my bestest friend ever. I click *send*, praying that the card will do its magic.

It's a little past eight when I hear something crash outside. I wonder if it's a raccoon, so I part the curtains in the living room. There are no wild animals, but I do see a large car in our driveway. Our trash can has been knocked down and a black garbage bag laden with trash is jutting out of it. It can only be one person, but nobody invited Grandpa. Why is he here? I certainly don't want to see him after all the terrible things he said the last time he visited. I think about what's worse: Lisa being angry with me or Grandpa criticizing me and Mom. What happened with Peter was accidental and I had no intention to hurt Lisa (even though I was dying for Peter to notice me). Grandpa, on the other hand, meant every word he said. He really thinks Mom is infidel-like and raised me to be like that, too.

"Mom, Dad," I say.

"What, Almira?" Dad drawls, his face hidden behind a newspaper.

"It's Grandpa."

Dad drops the newspaper he's reading and Mom stops doing crunches. She gets off of the floor and peers through the window. "Almira, go to your room," Mom says.

"Why?"

"Just go."

I frown. Why can't I watch them argue? Sure, last time was nasty, but I heard everything from my bedroom anyway.

Actually, I can't hear them. I hear low, solemn voices. I put my ear to the door and only hear, "Wuh, wuh, wuh, wuh." Then I put a glass on the door, a trick I once saw in a movie, and I still can't hear anything. Why so quiet, I wonder. People either get really loud or speak in low tones when they're serious.

The anticipation is killing me. I wonder if everything's okay. After a half hour, I walk out wanting to know what's going on. Dad is back to reading his newspaper and Mom continues to do crunches, her purple leotard and shorts bright against the beige carpet. I go through the kitchen to get to the dining room. Grandpa is sitting at the table eating salmon and salad. I sit down next to him and eat a few slices of cucumber.

"Everything is okay between me and your parents," Grandpa says.

"Really?" I ask.

"Yes. They are younger and different than me, and that is the way it is."

I guess that's his way of saying he apologizes or he's okay with us.

"They live among infidels, but they are not infidels," Grandpa says.

"Infidels aren't that bad, Grandpa," I say. "All my friends are infidels."

He makes clucking sounds with his tongue. "Not all of them are bad, but they are still infidels. You know where they're going."

"Um, okay. So, are you saying that infidels are all going to hell?"

"Most likely."

"Oh." They're all going to go into the fire, according to him. I think about Lisa. Even though she's mad at me and isn't talking to me at the moment, I hope that she'll go to heaven with me. And of course I want Peter in heaven, because I assume that we'll be together forever. Then there are my many other infidel friends who don't deserve to get stuck in hell; they should end up with me. I really do think that I'm going to heaven. I don't do anything really bad. It's night, I'm tired, and I'm still confused about Grandpa coming here after his falling-out with Mom. These thoughts are too heavy for me, so I stop thinking about heaven and hell.

"I need my family with me," Grandpa says.

"I'm glad you're here tonight, Grandpa," I say.

He pats my hand and says, "I am happy to be here, and no matter how you dress and act like an American, Almira, you are a good Muslim. You're fasting and you show patience and dedication for doing that."

"Thanks, Grandpa. Are you going to finish teaching me how to drive?"

"Yes."

"Good." At least some people are getting along, and have good standing between them.

"And we are all going to the mosque together this week."

"Great." It's been years since I've been to a mosque, while Grandpa goes at least once a week. I've forgotten the prayers, but if I hear them, then they'll come back to me. I never learned Arabic, but when I was a kid I memorized the prayers, even though I speak them in a heavy, American accent. Being that it's Ramadan and I'm fasting for the first time, it makes sense to visit a mosque.

"I have a present for you," he says.

I lean forward and watch his hand disappear inside his pocket. I expect to see a pair of diamond earrings, a gold pendant, or a ruby ring. Some people want to see large boxes, but I know that the best things come in small packages. Grandpa fishes through the pocket of his high-waisted plaid pants and closes his hand around the object.

"You'll like this," he says.

"What is it?" I ask.

He puts the object on the table. It's a small pot. I pick it up and read the label. Lip-gloss. Clear. Moisturizing. It's colorless lip-gloss to replace my MAC lipstick! At least Grandpa is trying to appease me and clear lip-gloss won't make me look a prostitute. "Thanks, Grandpa," I say. I turn the plastic pot around in my hands. At least it's an expensive brand and not the cheap garbage from the dollar store (Grandpa loves dollar stores). I open it and smell it: strawberry, hmmmmm. I thank him and give him a hug before he leaves.

It's unusual for Grandpa to be at our house so late since he hates to drive at night. I fix our garbage can and watch him drive off. I call him ten minutes later and he made it back safely. He's my driving instructor, but I worry more about his driving than about mine.

After I go to bed, Mom sneaks into my room. Even though I'm a teenager, she still visits me in the middle of the night to see that I'm properly tucked in, that my lights are turned off, and that I don't have a temperature burning my forehead. It makes me feel special, but at the same time I don't want her there. I'm not a child, and sometimes she wakes me up by checking on me. Her lips brush against my cheek.

"Mom, what happened with Grandpa?" I say, my voice slurred with grogginess.

"He apologized to me," she replies.

"No way."

"He did." Mom stands above me wearing a lacy camisole, upstaging me in my bunny-patterned pink pajamas.

"So he knows he was wrong?"

"The way he sounded, he seems to accept us. He probably thinks we're still wrong, but doesn't want to say it."

"Some people can't change instantly, or ever," I say.

"He's still the same man, trust me, but I think he'll bite his tongue before he says something rude to us ever again."

"That's something."

Mom turns her head to look at something. I crook my head forward to see what she's staring at. Uh-oh. I forgot to turn my computer off and a Robert Pattinson slide show is playing on my computer. Robert in a tux, slender, buff, topless, smiling, brooding. Oh no, no, no, no, no.

Mom whistles, which surprises me. Okay, it shocks me that she's a parent admiring the same guy I'm in love with. Yet it's reasonable since what woman doesn't want Robert Pattinson? Only a woman with absolutely no taste and ice water in her veins.

"I see your files are back," she says.

"Don't tell Dad," I beg.

"I won't, but you don't do a good job of hiding things."

"I'll remember to log off every night."

"What if your dad sees this? You better turn it off."

"I will, I will."

"Am I driving you and Lisa to school tomorrow?" Mom asks.

"Lisa's not talking to me."

"Why?"

I think about how I should answer her. I press my lips together, feeling my new lip-gloss on my lips. "She thinks I stole something of hers."

"Did you?"

"Technically, no."

"Then let her see that. What does she think you took?"

"Something, someone, valuable," I mumble, drifting off to sleep.

27

Grandpa arrives to take us to the mosque. He told Dad we should do something as a family for the holiday, more than eating dinner together. I can't remember too much about mosques from when I was little, but now it's many years later and I'll be able to remember things and carry the memories with me. I want it to be a positive event. Since it was Grandpa's idea, and also it's his mosque, I'm sure he'll act domineering during this excursion. Now that he and Mom are okay again, I hope he won't say or do anything else that will piss us off.

We're going to go in Grandpa's car. Yikes. There are three seats in the back of his car, which means we can all fit in. He knocks down a garbage can and I pick it up as if I'm his personal gofer (I'm the one who usually cleans up his parking messes). Mom has a duffel bag with our praying gear of mats and clothes, which she puts in the trunk. We're all dressed conservatively, with our arms and legs covered. The women all wear scarves. I tug and pull at mine since I'm not used to having my hair covered. We have to enter a mosque in modesty.

The three of us crowd into the back of Grandpa's car. Mom, Dad, and I shuffle around, elbows in ribs, until we're all comfortable and are able to buckle our seat belts. Grandma turns around and gives us a crooked smile. She has on a navy scarf, which looks black inside the car, and dark sunglasses. I'm spooked by the way she looks, as if she's ushering us into a terrible time. It's just the lack of light when we drive past trees, because she looks like her usual self in the sunlight.

"Almira, you look so pretty today," Grandma says in her heavily accented English. "When we find you a husband?"

Awkward silence follows. My mouth drops open.

Mom grunts out an artificial laugh and says, "That's light years away, really. We have so much time to discuss that."

"Almira is getting to that age," Grandma presses on.

"We can all think about that after she finishes medical school," Dad says.

I don't want to become a doctor, but okay. That means

Dad thinks I should be in my mid-twenties when I get married. That gives me plenty of time to break it to them gently that I like boys, think about them all day, and some of them even kiss me without my parents' permission, away from their presence. It's no longer the days of yore, when Muslim girls had to be chaperoned all day. And we aren't in their home countries where that can happen. I'm living free in America. And with the exception of my friends rooting for me, I'm pretty much alone in the pursuit of a relationship.

Mom pleads with Grandpa to turn on the radio, and he finally does. James Brown's "Living in America" comes on, which echoes my thoughts. Mom begins to sing in her off-key, cats-drowning-in-a-pool voice.

We arrive at a miniature mosque. Actually, the building isn't small but regular-sized, and shaped like a mosque from the Middle East. It has a dome and a minaret, but they fit the scope of the building. The mosque pictures I've seen look majestic, but the size of this mosque is just right for Coral Gables. There's swirly Arabic writing on the front door. Below the writing is the English translation: *Coral Gables Islamic Center*. It's all very modern, and very Miami.

The door has squares of glass, and behind them I see a few dozen people milling around. We go inside to join them. There are women in headscarves, teenagers with earphones dangling from their heads, and a mix of clean-shaven and heavily bearded men. Someone is ushering all of us further into the mosque. Men are moving to the right and women are going to the left. I'm moving with the wave, unsure of what I'm doing. It's like the first day of school, not knowing where all the room numbers are but following the people who share my schedule.

The women all go to a massive locker room/restroom. There are many stalls, sinks, and benches—anything a woman needs to wash up and change clothes for praying. We take turns. There's a mixture of perfume and soap scents swirling around me, the same way different languages blend together. I hear Arabic, Persian, and Urdu, as well as languages that I can't identify. Skin colors run from milky white to coffee colored. Women who've just arrived come in to catch up with those of us who are done. Several people stop to kiss Mom and Grandma's cheeks, as well as mine.

Mom and Grandma lead me to the praying center. I'm wearing a white headscarf and a beige dress. My ankles and wrists are covered. For some reason, those bony knobs are not allowed to be seen during prayer; that's what Mom told me. Mom brought mats that look Egyptian and ancient with their geometric patterns. I have my praying mat under my arm, as well as my socks which I'll put on once the mat is out. I'll be completely covered, except for my hands and face. Thank God the building is heavily air conditioned.

Loud chanting blasts through speakers that I can't locate. It's the call to prayer. It sounds like a lot of wailing, but Mom says it's in Arabic. I shiver. It sounds beautiful, the same way an opera song is incomprehensible but mesmerizing. It's time to gather.

When we get to the back of the mosque, we see the entrance of a massive room that has curved walls rather than the flatness and angles of a normal room. Everyone has left their shoes in the lobby, so we're all barefoot. Grandma explains to me that men pray in the front and women in the back. There are several rows of men unrolling their praying mats, and then us females. The men wear loose, flowing pajama-looking clothes. Some have their heads bare and others have light-colored caps called *kufis*. I'm too close to a woman in front of me, and I back away as she unrolls her mat. I unroll my mat in the same direction as everyone else's, since we all have to face Mecca when we pray. Now we're ready.

An imam in the front is going to lead the prayer. I feel nervous because I haven't prayed in ages. Fasting is hard as it is, and to add praying on top of that seems like another difficulty. I look at the dozens of people around me who are ready. They seem purposeful … and calm. The whole atmosphere becomes very calm, as if no one has any worries, no harassing classmates, no shrill bosses, nothing on the outside that can interfere with the moment. Sunlight streams in from the large windows, warming us through the heavy air conditioning. My nerves settle down. I'll get through this. Mom and Grandma are nearby to help me if I make any mistakes.

The imam recites the prayers, and none of us utter a word. When praying by myself, I say the prayers out loud or in a whisper. But in a mosque, only one voice is needed at a mutual gathering. My anxiety leaves me, because all we have to do in group prayer is listen to the imam and make the proper movements. Whatever I had forgotten is remembered again. The first thing I remember is *Allahu Akbar*, God is Great. The imam emphatically says it when the prayer calls for the phrase. The movements also come back to me, even though I lag a second or two behind everyone else. Still, I get on my knees, place my forehead to the floor, stand up, place my hands across my stomach ... everyone is moving the same way, from the short children to the tall adults.

Afterwards, some people stay behind to read the Koran. Others put on their shoes and leave. The sun shines brightly while it's low in the sky. It will be sunset soon. Time to eat. Grandpa finds us and says, "One of the men talked about how he owns a restaurant close to here. Most of us will be going."

Mom and Dad agree to go. The parking lot is getting crowded. We hung out too long talking to old friends, and then the people who were reading the Koran flood the lot. I look at the sun. It's taking forever to set. Because I'm hungry, the momentary traffic makes time slow down. Grandpa drives the short distance of three blocks to a restaurant claiming in neon that it's the *Best Turkish Grill in South Florida*.

Inside, there's an alcove of adjoining tables that have been reserved for us. Everyone who came earlier, and who isn't from the mosque, sits on the outskirts near the windows. We sit down. Grandpa explains that everyone will pay a flat fee since we're all going to eat the same thing. There's no time for waiters and waitresses to ask us what we want. Some of them, in their white aprons and black shoes, circle around us and fill our water glasses. I'm not the only one thirstily eyeing the water. The smell of food has my stomach tied in knots.

"When can we eat?" I whisper to Mom.

"Soon," she says. She's still wearing a headscarf and so am I, since we're still with the mosque crowd.

"Mom, how come we don't do this more often?"

She looks surprised. It's shocking, since I've never asked to go to the mosque before. I used to think it was a chore, but it's cool praying together and doing something with my family afterwards. And the food smells delicious. It's awesome that we're ending an evening of prayer by going to a restaurant serving authentic Middle Eastern food. Mom's food tastes too American. She cuts corners, using tomato sauce, mashed potato mix, and all the other time-saving ingredients that housewives all over the country use. The waiters are bringing our food to us. Bowls of heaping kofta, steaming rice, and vegetables are brought to the center of our tables. The imam is here and he stands up to say something. He wears an elegant suit that goes well with his cap and his weathered, brown face. He speaks a mix of English and Arabic.

"*Massa el kheer.* I would like to congratulate all of you on your patience and strength as you fast during this glorious month ... " He tells us anecdotes about past Ramadans and Eids and his time in the United States; then he ends with a short prayer (I can tell it's a prayer since he's praising God, *Allahu Akbar*). Then we can officially eat.

Hands, forks, and spoons empty the dishes. I scoop food on my plate, passing the serving dishes to Mom and Dad. None of us are rude or beastly. It isn't like we're elbowing each other or eating like boors, but the food disappears rapidly. The other people—the non-Muslims—stare. I don't blame them. I'm staring, too, as I eat. People spoon the remaining food onto their plates. Waitresses bustle to give us more water. I drink my glass in three slurps since I'm so thirsty. There isn't much talking. Just eating and more eating.

More food is brought out for seconds, but this time we aren't in a rush to take it. I slink down in my seat when I'm full. My scarf inches down my back and becomes looser around my neck. I rest my feet against a table leg. This evening is much better than I thought it would be. It's nice to pray and eat together. It's better than surfing the net and IM'ing all night. It's also making me aware of everything I'm learning about my religion and myself during this fast.

Fasting makes you think about what it takes to do it.

Not many people can do it. You have to learn to become a very patient person, which is hard to do. Sometimes I'm impatient when a person doesn't text message me back. I stare at my phone, wondering when this person is going to text me when I texted her five minutes ago. It seems frivolous, but that's just how it is. My friend Raul had his cell phone confiscated ten minutes before lunchtime because he was text messaging under his desk and the teacher caught him. Why couldn't he have waited ten measly minutes to do that? Because of our impatience, our age, this fast world we live in.

Even my parents and Grandpa talk about how fast the world is. Dad says he used a pay phone when he was young and sometimes he had to wait in a line to use it. I've never touched a pay phone in my life. Grandpa told me stories about when he lived in Syria and had to wait weeks for airmail to be sent to him. This was decades before email. Dad had a typewriter in high school and it took forever to type and correct papers with Wite-Out, but Microsoft Office made everything easier. There are so many examples of things made easier and faster, compared to my parents' and grandparents' time.

So these days, we want things now. Fasting tells us we have to wait. Here I am, living in a world that's quick as lightning, and I have to wait to eat. Fasting also teaches me to be humble. It makes me wonder about all the starving people in the world. I starve during the day, with my stomach rumbling, and some people go through that for days, weeks, and months. The same goes for water, because there are thirsty people in this world, too. Fasting makes me think about myself and others. It's a sacrifice. Don't eat for your religion. I show God that I can temporarily live without the very things—food and water—that make me live in the first place.

"More water, miss?" a waiter asks.

"Yes, please," I say.

I notice a huge stain on the front of my long-sleeved shirt, and smaller stains on my skirt. Grandpa sits across from me and notices them, too. Normally he'd criticize me for my sloppiness. Instead, he smiles at me and says that the food was irresistible. It was.

28

AlmiraRules: we're running the final laps of ramadan
ShakiBaby: for real

AlmiraRules: soon we'll be able to eat anytime we want

ShakiBaby: starbucks whenever i want

AlmiraRules: but i don't feel like pigging out the way i used to

ShakiBaby: you look great and that dress you wore the other day hung on you perfectly except that, i mean nothing

AlmiraRules: what?

ShakiBaby: nothing

AlmiraRules: you were going to say something bad

ShakiBaby: ok, just that the fabric was bunching around your stomach and was making it look like you have a gut

AlmiraRules: shakira i thought we've spoken about this already!

ShakiBaby: it's not your fault, the belt was loose and there was too much fabric because of the weight loss

AlmiraRules: so i looked like a pregnant woman

ShakiBaby: forget i said anything

AlmiraRules: i'll try!

ShakiBaby: change the subject plz

AlmiraRules: i'm going to get lisa back

ShakiBaby: how?

AlmiraRules: i'll convince her that peter really wants her, not me

ShakiBaby: but he doesn't

AlmiraRules: he must like her a little bit, i mean they used to hang out a lot as friends

ShakiBaby: he likes her as a friend, but he loves you

AlmiraRules: i wouldn't say that he loves me at this point. he texts me every night to see what i'm doing, but we haven't gone on an official date, and i don't think we can with the way things stand with lisa. he keeps saying that she'll come around, but he doesn't understand things. i need to try to hook peter up with lisa so that she's no longer mad at me

ShakiBaby: that's not going to work if the sparks aren't there. don't you know anything about relationships?

AlmiraRules: not really

ShakiBaby: i've been around the block and i can tell you

AlmiraRules: tell me. how many blocks have you been around at your age?

ShakiBaby: shut up. i've been in your situation and a friend and i liked the same boy and he wanted me. my friend had to get over it and we had a rough patch and didn't talk for a whole year. i broke up with the guy in two months, but at least i got to see what a cool guy he was

AlmiraRules: in two months?

ShakiBaby: shut up. so yeah i lost a friend for awhile, but you can't let anyone tell you who to love or not love

AlmiraRules: but was it worth losing your friend?

ShakiBaby: no

AlmiraRules: I WANT LISA BACK

ShakiBaby: fine, you just go do what you have to do

AlmiraRules: i can hear my dad's car coming up the driveway

ShakiBaby: my grandmother is in the other room and i have to keep looking over my shoulder. she's so nosy and doesn't understand im

AlmiraRules: the sun's almost set. mom's making fava beans and rice

ShakiBaby: my mom is making kibbeh and falafel

AlmiraRules: cool, my mouth is watering

ShakiBaby: gotta go eat
AlmiraRules: bye
ShakiBaby: bye and good luck with Lisa

I look through my bookbag, going through the contents over and over again, making sure I have the right folders and books for classes the next day. Mom is calling me for dinner, yet I don't hear her. I sense her voice, but it isn't registering through my brain. The scent of her cooking wafts underneath my door and to my nose, but I'm still thinking about everything I've lost and gained lately.

"Almira! Dinner!"

I have to make things right.

"Almira, where are you?"

There's no way I can lose Lisa forever.

"Where is that girl?" Dad yells from the dining room.

My stomach growls and I slowly get up. Going to the dining room makes me feel a sense of being outside of myself. I can't tell my parents about the Peter-Lisa situation. They couldn't cope with the fact that a boy had kissed me or that I want a boyfriend. They're going to set me up with someone to marry. But I want to be a regular American teenager.

"Didn't you hear me?" Mom asks. "We had to start without you."

I look at the dining table. Mom and Dad are done with half the food. I sit down so that I can catch up with them. I use a ladle to serve myself chickpea soup, and

Mom hands me a plate of fava beans and rice. After dinner, Dad unbuttons his pants and even Mom leans back to rub her growing stomach.

"How's school?" Dad asks.

"Great," I say in a monotone voice.

"Can you floss around your braces?"

"Yes, Dad."

"Did you figure out those equations for math class? You said they were pretty tough."

"Yes."

"How's Lisa? She hasn't come here in a while."

Mom and I exchange looks. "You should invite her to dinner some time," Mom says.

"I will," I say. If she ever says yes. My chest starts to burn and I have to fight off tears. The tears fly back into my eyes as if my tear ducts go into reverse. I've been moping ever since Lisa stopped talking to me.

Mom and Dad don't notice my lackluster tone of voice. It doesn't matter, because it's best that they don't know about the goings-on in my life. I finally have some drama and I can't share it with them. Straight A's, yes. Winning a science fair ribbon, yes. Going to the mall with friends, yes. Getting my hair done, yes. Having a boyfriend, absolutely not.

29

In the morning I pack my bookbag, making sure that I have the sketch (the one I took when Peter wasn't looking) in a folder. I believe the sketch will create a miracle and make things all better again. Shakira once said that having someone sketch her is magical, as if she's being worshipped, and when Peter showed me my sketch I felt loved. A sketch is powerful. No wonder the world is full of art. Mona Lisa would be a nobody if no one ever painted her.

I walk to school and the first person I see is Peter. He's with his art friends, all with portfolios in their arms, and I try to walk by without saying anything, but he stops me by placing a hand on my arm and steering me to a secluded tree. The tree is old and gnarled, and sunlight shoots rays between the leaves. This would feel so romantic if Lisa's pain wasn't on replay in my head. What am I thinking? This *is* romantic. My heart flutters as we look into each other's eyes.

Peter holds my hand, and I don't pull away. He must sense my hesitation, because he's not being pushy.

"How are you?" he asks.

"I'm okay," I lie.

"Did you straighten things out with Lisa, about, you know?"

"No, not yet."

"If you need help or time to figure things out, I'm here for you."

"Sure."

He's being sweet and patient—how many guys really have those qualities ?—and I'm trying to ward him off. I wonder when he'll change the subject, and he finally does.

"My friend's in college and he's having his work shown in a gallery. It's really exciting. I'm going tonight. The press will be there. Maybe a photo of me will sneak into the paper."

"That sounds really exciting ... " It sounds like he wants me to attend with him, but I don't take the bait. This is so uncomfortable. He should be with Lisa to make our friendship all right again, and here he is squeezing my hand and talking about his life. One of his friends calls his name, and we separate.

"So, I'll see you around," he says.

"Sure." I say a quick goodbye and look for my own friends. My heart is breaking into fragments since I can't have him. I swallow the lump in my throat and straighten out my spine as I walk away. Taking a 360 turn on my heel, I'm relieved that Lisa isn't in sight. I hope she didn't catch a glimpse of my little tryst with Peter. The trees must have hidden us pretty well anyway, but I can't afford for her to think that I've betrayed her on the same morning I unleash my plan to gain back her friendship.

Shakira and I hang out on the same bench that Lisa and I usually sat on. I'm not trying to replace Lisa with Shakira, but Shakira now seems to be clinging to me, as I to her. She swishes her long, sleek hair from side to side, hitting my shoulder with her tresses. I no longer feel that she's showing off and trying to make me jealous. She's pretty, not evil, and she's curbing her tongue after we had our little talk. The other day I took off my glasses to rest my eyes and accidentally smashed my elbow into a lens, breaking it off, and I could tell that Shakira was biting her tongue. Her lips twitched. She was probably going to blurt a comment about my clumsiness, that I shouldn't have put my expensive glasses right underneath my elbow, but she was quiet. She said she felt bad about my glasses, that was all. I put the broken glasses away and took out a spare pair from my bookbag. No hurt feelings.

There's a bit of awkwardness with my friends now that Lisa and I aren't on speaking terms. Maria talks to me for a few minutes, and then she goes to wherever Lisa is to hang out with her. Our mutual friends are like that, dividing time between the two of us. And then there's some awkwardness about Shakira. At first people gave me dirty looks—*why are you hanging out with that girl?*—but the longer Shakira hangs out with me, the more my friends talk to her and see that she isn't as monstrous as everyone used to think. Maria and my other friends are polite to Shakira now that they see her associating with me. She's in good standing by being friendly with me. Just because she's pretty doesn't make her better than anyone else, and she certainly seems nicer after being humbled by her recent bad experiences with me and my friends.

I even see Shakira and Maria talking to one another in hushed tones before the bell rings. Shakira looks upset and Maria hugs her. Maria! Chonga Maria, who talks tough and acts at times like she has a black heart, is being super nice! It seems like everyone is apologizing and making up to each other. I decide that I have to be proactive to make things all right with Lisa. The moments of conciliation with Grandpa and Shakira have put me in a forgiving mood. I hope that Lisa can forgive me for loving Peter. It's really exhausting to try to win her back. I made another long, convoluted e-card that I sent earlier this morning. It seems like I spend hours a day writing drafts of notes, handwriting letters, making PowerPoints, and using Adobe to make e-cards. If this continues, I'll become a computer programmer and professional writer in no time. My eyes feel strained sitting at the computer for hours and my hands feel funny—maybe I'm getting carpal tunnel syndrome—but this situation calls for sacrifices.

I see Lisa before English class and I stop her in her tracks. I walk in front of her and won't let her get by the front door. There are ten minutes left before class starts and I want her to hear me out. Her whole face is contorted with anger. She used to look happy to see me, but now she views me as a traitor. She's wearing blush, but her cheeks become pinker as she tries to stare me down. It's like looking at a stranger. The thought that I'll never be her friend again flashes through my mind. Maybe I should let things be and let her go, but I can't. She isn't like other friends I've lost touch with since kindergarten. There were many classmates who came and went for different reasons: I was mad at them, they were mad at me, we were nothing more than study buddies, we were partnered up in a project, or they moved away. Lisa doesn't fit into any of these categories, because she's the only best friend that I've ever had. As long as there is a chance to make things right, I'll do what I have to do.

"Lisa, please listen to me," I say.

She looks at me with stony eyes heavily made up with spidery mascara. She crosses her arms defensively, warding me off. I stick my hands in my pockets and my pants start to slide off my hips, even though I'm wearing a belt.

"You've gotten really skinny," she says.

"Thanks," I say.

"Well, I have to go to the restroom."

"Wait. I want to tell you that I don't want Peter and you can have him."

Her eyes soften with tears. "But he doesn't want me, does he?" she whispers, her tears about to fall.

"He says he wants me, but I don't care," I say. "I want us to be friends."

"No, no, no!" she says, shaking her head and crying.

I find tissue in my bookbag and hand it to her. She pats her eyes, careful not to remove her makeup, but her mascara is already coming off with the tissue. "You're ruining my makeup," she says.

"But look!" I say. I take the stolen sketch out of my bookbag and wave it into her face.

"What's this?" she asks.

"Peter sketched you."

Lisa stares at the picture, becoming transfixed on the image of loveliness. Peter gave her passionate eyes, gorgeous hair, and lush lips. He's an awesome artist. "See, he really likes you," I say, trying to make myself believe in my own words.

She grabs the picture. "Peter did this?" she asks.

"Yes. Don't you see that he really likes you?"

"Where did you get this?"

"Straight from his sketchpad."

"What a beautiful picture!"

"I know!"

"This means nothing!" Lisa screeches.

"Of course it means something," I say. "He wouldn't do this for no reason."

"He draws many people. He drew Shakira. He drew Michael from math class. Does that mean he's in love with him? And he even drew Ms. Odige, and what boy in his right mind would fall in love with a teacher? This means nothing."

"Of course it does," I say, trying to convince her, trying to convince myself.

"No, it doesn't," she says.

"Lisa, Peter isn't as important to me as you are, and he will not come between us."

"No, that's not fair to you," Lisa says, hiccupping. "I know how badly you want a boyfriend. At least I've had a boyfriend before, when I dated Mannie last spring. You deserve to have Peter, you really do."

"But every time you look at the two of us, you might get sad or angry," I say.

"Almira, I know what I'm saying," she insists, tears streaming from her eyes. "You two belong together. You look cute together. And, Almira, think about your family. They don't want you to have a boyfriend or to date. Chances are slim that you'll have a boyfriend, even if you keep him a secret from them. This is your chance. You deserve that chance. You found what you wanted and I can't take that away from you."

I'm shocked by her words. She's giving him up so that I can be happy. This reminds me of the story about King Solomon. Two women claim that a baby is theirs and he says that he'll split the child in half with his sword. The real mother says no, please don't harm the child, the other woman can have him. That woman is the real mother, because she doesn't want any harm to come to the child, whereas the false mother can't care less if the child is cut up or not. There are differences between that story and mine. There is no baby, sword, or king, but I had been willing to relinquish Peter for our friendship. Lisa then realized that I'm Peter's true love, and I can have him. She no longer minds. We don't have to cut Peter in half.

Besides the biblical tie-in, Lisa seems to understand my plight. She's right. With the way I keep things from my parents, Peter might be my one and only boyfriend, my one and only chance to have a high school love interest. I like him and he likes me back. We've briefly talked about my parents and Grandpa, and Peter seems to understand my situation. He's handsome, smart, artistic, and sensitive. We're perfect together.

Lisa hugs me. "I had to make up with you," she says into my hair. "I'm planning your sixteenth birthday party. It's supposed to be a surprise."

"Well, it's no longer a surprise," I say.

"I guess it isn't, now that I opened my big mouth," she says, laughing.

We go to class arm in arm. Lisa puts her sketch away.

She says that she'll frame it later, because it's the nicest representation of her there is. I write in my journal about how wonderful it is to have a best friend again:

> *My best friend was mad at me for a while. I did something that she didn't like. It was an accident and I hurt her without meaning to. But now we're ok again. She's back to being my bestest friend. So many things have happened this month. I lost a lot of weight. I fasted. I finished learning how to drive. I have braces, which suck, but my teeth will look great in a year. I'll be turning sixteen soon. The boy I like likes me back. This period of time is the highlight of my life, I'm sure of it. This has been the bestest month and the bestest Ramadan ever.*

Ms. Odige reads a poem to us; then she grades our journals while we answer questions from the textbook. She writes her comments at the bottom. *Bestest is not a word. Use "best" to indicate something that is ultimate.*

I shake my head in disagreement when I read this. She doesn't get it. There's what you think is the best, but then you find something that supersedes your preconception of that, and that's what makes something the bestest. My bestest friend. The bestest time of my life. The bestest Ramadan ever. The bestest boyfriend, if Peter and I ever go out together on a real date. Sometimes adults don't get it, but that's okay. I'm sure Ms. Odige was my age at one time and referred to things as being the bestest, before she went to college and had the English police drill grammar rules into her head.

Lisa passes notes to me whenever we can't talk in class. Just like old times. In middle school we folded our letters into triangles, but now we're older and fold them in simple rectangles and squares.

I think Gabriel likes me and he asked me out today, she writes during math class.

He's cute, I write back.

He has the longest lashes I ever saw on a boy.

And he wouldn't stop staring at you yesterday.

I know!

She's moving on. From the time she caught Peter kissing me to the time we made up, she's been checking out other guys. I'm relieved. I no longer feel like a backstabbing piece of garbage that's lower than snail slime. I even tell Peter that Lisa's forgiven me, and a large I-told-you-so grin breaks across his face. He was far more confident in our relationship than I was, but only because I had more to lose with Lisa in the picture.

Peter hugs me before science class, and Lisa doesn't wince or turn away. She's handling things with the utmost maturity. I don't know if I'd be as graceful if I was in her shoes. I hope I would be. I'm turning sixteen and leaving childhood behind to become more of an adult, which means being able to turn the other cheek, move on, act less childish, and think more optimistically. Lisa is onto her next conquest with Gabriel, and I'm looking at having a real boyfriend in my life.

I'm having trouble with my homework, Lisa writes to me toward the end of class.

Why are you doing it now? I write back.

Gabriel wants to meet me at his friend's house for a barbecue tonight, she scribbles.

What's the problem?

What does Shakespearean mean?

What do you think?!

What?

You're kidding.

No, I'm not!

I sigh and write down the answer.

30

Lisa is chatting and giggling with other boys, finding a new person to love, a new interest to *mollify*—that's Ms. Odige's word of the day—her boy craziness. She has a glow about her that had gone away when she was mad at me. Her glow is back. It's more than just the bronzer and iridescent blush she wears. She's happy being my friend again and dating Gabriel. So I'm free to be with Peter.

Peter and Lisa sat next to each other in science the other day and there was no awkwardness. They talk like they used to talk before, but now Lisa doesn't have that sparkle in her eye when she gazes at him. That's a relief to me. Once you completely realize that you can't have something, you stop wanting it, I suppose. Of course I still want Robert Pattinson, even though he's always linked with Kristen Stewart, but that's more of a fantasy than anything. Yet maybe if I turn eighteen and he's in the Gables to shoot a movie, we'll bump into each other, he'll ask me out for coffee, and one thing will lead into another ... in my dreams.

On Saturday, Peter, Maria, and Lisa come over to my house. I ask my parents if it's okay to see a movie with some friends. I want to slowly warm them up to the idea that I'm seeing a boy, and a group date seems less threatening than seeing Peter alone. Mom and Dad don't act strange at all when they see Peter. That's cool. Grandpa isn't here, so I don't have to deal with him yet over the Peter issue. I see him drive by in the opposite direction of Maria's car, and I turn my head away so that he won't see me. I left the house just when he was about to visit. That's a close call, but I feel terrible that I still have to be afraid of him. The fear of the old country, the ancient ways, and his stodginess stays in my head.

During the movie, which is a lame romantic comedy that none of us are enjoying, Peter holds my hand. When Lisa and Maria go to the restroom, we kiss. Ah, to have a boyfriend to kiss anytime I want.

Peter comes back to my house, and this time it's just the two of us. I explain that Lisa and Maria went home already since they live farther up the block than Peter and me. Mom and Dad don't act stiff at all. When Peter leaves, Dad turns to me and says, "He has a good set of teeth."

"He does, doesn't he?" I say. If there's one thing Dad loves, it's definitely teeth. "Is Grandpa around?"

"No, he came here right after you left and only stayed for a bit."

Good. My double life is going fine. Actually no, it isn't. First off, I feel guilty. There's a trail of acid running down the middle of my chest. My mind is abuzz with thoughts that I'm doing something bad. How can I keep this from my parents? This is a major thing. I look over at Mom, who's doing crunches in a corner. I used to think that I could tell her everything: I came to her when I needed a training bra, then for a real bra, and then for pads when I got my first period. I can't share this with her, because of her culture, their culture. Having Peter in my life is one of the best things that's ever happened to me, and I can only reveal this joy to my friends. My parents—not to mention Grandpa—would flip out and not understand. But Dad seems to be okay with how I hung out with Peter tonight. I think this too soon, because his face becomes stern and he starts to act weird.

"Where does Peter live?" he asks.

"Nearby," I say.

"He was with you girls when you watched the movie?"

"Yes."

"Is he going out with one of your friends?"

"No." Should I have said yes, since maybe that's what he wants to hear?

"He didn't try to put his arms around you?"

"No," I lie. And we did much more than that.

"Good, because I don't want any boy getting fresh with my little girl."

But I'm not a little girl anymore. I'm a big girl and a young woman. Someday Dad will have to face the fact that I have womanly wants and desires, but this moment isn't the right time to tell him these things. He obviously isn't ready for me to reveal the truth, nor am I ready to tell it. That will be for another day. I picture that day: I'll probably feel scared and hesitant, and his reaction will be explosive. I can't imagine that the truth will come out any-time soon.

I want to test my dad some more. He met Peter, but what if there had been more?

Dad has a newspaper in his lap and the TV is on mute. I sit down across from him on a chair. "Dad, Peter's a really nice boy," I say. "What if he *had* put his arms around me? What would you do?"

He frowns, wrinkling the newspaper between both hands. "If he stuck around longer, then I would let him know what I think of that," he says through clenched teeth. "And as for you, you could forget about going out with friends for a very long time."

I gasp. Mom stops doing crunches and sits up to put in her two cents. "You're too young to date," she says.

"Maybe when you're in college it'll be okay to date, as long as it never gets too far."

Dad turns on her with fury. My spine is as straight as an ironing board and I jump in my seat when he raises his voice. "Almira cannot date, period," he says. "That is what Americans like to do, going from one person to another. We can find a few nice boys for her to choose from."

"Gee, how nice," Mom says. "Why don't we just let your father in on the action and he can pick someone out for her."

"It won't be like that for Almira. She can have choices, but it has to be with our blessing."

I roll my eyes. I don't want to pick from my father's choices, but from my own. And I certainly don't want to do it Grandpa's way: he always mentions the old country, the matchmakers, the meddling parents and grandparents. I keep my secret like a small rock inside the core of me, covering it up with layers of muscle and skin. I can feel the hard lump of it, which is my burden to carry, and it'll stay buried.

"If Almira wants to act like her friends, she'll be punished," Dad tells Mom. "Don't you want this family to look good? Remember how Mina's daughter got mixed up with that American boy, and everyone found out. It was a scandal." Mina is a family friend and her college-age daughter dated and married someone from her university. I remember how Grandpa clucked over that scandal for days until it simmered down. The same would happen to me if

I'm found out: people will talk about me and the whole family will feel ashamed. Shame is like a family virus— if you do something wrong, all your relatives become infected.

Dad turns to me and narrows his eyes. "Forget about the TV, computer, going out with friends, all that would be gone," he threatens. I'm disappointed. I know my parents are pretty lenient; they let me go out at night as long as I'm not alone, and they don't care that I go to the mall or stay over at friends' houses. But they're only somewhere in the middle—they're more modern than Grandpa, but I'm all the way out there on the other end of the spectrum. I want to live in the current decade, in the free world.

Dad speaks some more about how he'll limit my movements if I were to ever date a boy. If they find out about Peter, then all my freedoms will be taken away. They'll make assumptions that I'm dirty—a prostitute— and that I lost my virginity. I'm doing the right thing by hiding this from them.

The phone rings. It's past ten o'clock and late for people to call, but I go ahead and pick it up. "*Habibti*," the raspy voice says.

"Grandpa?" I say.

"Yes."

"Is anything wrong?"

"No. Can't I check up on my granddaughter?"

"Uh, I suppose."

"We're going out to drive early tomorrow, so be ready by seven."

"Okay," I say.

"And, one more thing," he says. "What was it? I am becoming forgetful."

"I'll drive on our way there since I need as much practice as possible."

"No, there's something else. Oh, yes. Who was that boy I saw you driving with tonight?"

I emit a long sigh and feed him the same lies I told my parents.

31

The next day, Grandpa gives me my last driving lesson. He's cranky and bossy as usual. I sneeze at one point and feel the tires veer toward a curb, but I straighten the car out immediately. Grandpa looks really mad, yet he lets it slide. He yells at a woman who cuts me off—*prostitute!*—and I grip the steering wheel tightly, willing myself not to crash. The rest of the lesson goes smoothly. I'm going to take the driving test after my sixteenth birthday. I'm fully ready to celebrate my sixteenth birthday, which is at Lisa's place on Monday.

Lisa makes sure that the timing is right and that the invitations have the start time right before sunset, so that

I won't starve at my own party. I break fast by blowing out the candles on top of a large, square chocolate cake that I eat a slice of immediately. Dozens of my friends are there, there's a DJ, and I dance with Peter. It's the bestest party that's ever been thrown in my honor.

Lisa's house is festooned with flowers and party banners. Maria approaches me with a slice of cake in her hand. Her harsh red lips, wavy black hair, and sharply drawn eyebrows contradict the warm smile she gives me. "Here's some more cake," she says.

"Thanks," I say.

"Your dress is pretty. You look good, baby girl."

"Thanks."

"Look at Lisa being a hot mama over there with Gabriel."

"Tell me about it. She looks like she's having the most fun."

"And Shakira makes such a cute couple with Luis," she says.

"And I saw you hugging her the other day," I say. "I didn't know you could be such a softie."

"I'm not a softie," Maria says. She lightly punches me in the arm, and my tricep tingles with pain. "I'm sorry for tempting you when you were fasting, but I thought you couldn't do it. I wanted to see if you were for real or not."

"I'm for real, and I did it!" I say.

"You're pretty strong," Maria says with a smile. "I wouldn't last ten minutes without eating. Go ahead and eat that cake, and it's better than anything that comes in a plastic wrapper."

"It sure beats the Twinkies you're addicted to," I say. I look at the cake in my hand. I stab it with a fork and eat it. The end of Ramadan is this week and I know it'll feel great to eat all day again. No more obsessing about food. No more obsessing about whether or not I'm boyfriend-less. No more wondering if Lisa will be mad at me for loving Peter when she's gotten over it. Lisa dances with Gabriel. She drapes her body over his as she dances. Yes, she definitely doesn't want Peter anymore. What a relief.

I dance with Peter. We make sure to be nowhere near Maria, who's bumping and grinding against a boy she just met, her arms and legs everywhere. She accidentally hit me in the eye earlier, and I'll probably wake up with a bruise on my upper cheek. People will ask me where I got the black eye from and I'll say, "You know that Maria."

"Maria's pretty wild," Peter says.

"I've known her forever," I say. "She's always been like that."

"She's feisty."

"That's one word for her."

"Do your parents like me?" he asks.

"So far, but they don't know you're my boyfriend," I say in his ear.

"Will you ever tell them?"

"I don't think so. I feel really bad about keeping this

from them, but I think I have to. They have girls my age stoned in their country for having a boyfriend."

"Wow!"

"I know! Like, they really throw stones at them and kill them."

"Okay, then don't tell them, because I don't want you to get stoned," he says.

"Okay," I say. Yeah, who wants to get stoned? Not me. I don't think it's in my parents to hurt me, but Grandpa might have a totally different reaction, a really bad one. He definitely can never ever know that I have a secret boyfriend. I'll sneak out with Peter whenever I can, while I show my parents a goody-two-shoes façade that will be impenetrable. I can keep this secret. I don't want to be barraged with shame because of something that's totally against my upbringing.

We stop dancing and Peter leads me over to the table that holds all of my presents. "Can I give this to you?" he asks, handing me a wrapped present.

He doesn't need to ask. I love presents. I open the small box and inside is a slender ring that has a ruby-centered flower. It's loose on my ring finger. Yay, even my fingers are skinnier. It fits perfectly on my index finger instead. Then he hands me another box. I open it, tearing into the ribbon and tape, and it's a Ferrero Rocher gift box. It's like he's given me a box of gold coins. The foil wrapping glistens under the strobe lights.

"It's nighttime, so don't get mad at me," Peter says.

"I love it," I say. Now that we know how much we like each other, he can give me chocolate out in the open.

I vow not to eat all of the chocolates in one sitting. After fasting for a month, my appetite isn't what it used to be and I have a greater appreciation of food. I realize that food is more about tasting good than eating large amounts until my stomach feels like bursting. Dad, who's always been trim, eats desserts very slowly, never taking seconds. He says that it's the taste that counts, so he doesn't have to eat a lot. He's right.

I tear one of the chocolates open and nibble on it, tasting how delicious it is. My favorite part is the middle, where the nuts are. It's like yum, yum, then yummy. When I get home, I know that Mom will ask me who gave me which presents, and I can't tell her that the chocolates are from a boy I really like. She was kind enough to accept my desktop and screensavers, but this isn't something she's going to be okay with. It's one thing to slobber over men on my computer screen, but to have a real-life boy to hug and kiss is totally different. And Dad had been mean about erasing Robert Pattinson from my computer. If he knew about Peter, he'd try to erase him from my life just as easily. Instead of clickety click, it would be *you're grounded, you can't look at boys, you can't touch boys, you can't do anything.*

32

Grandpa is turning me into a nervous wreck the night before my driving test. He comes over for dinner and keeps grilling me. He rubs his white beard with one hand and drums against the dining table with the other as he lectures me on driving basics.

"Don't coast through stop signs," he says. "Make a full stop."

"I know that, Grandpa," I say.

"Always watch out for speed limit signs."

"I know."

Grandpa rubs his beard some more and my head spins with anxiety. I had to cancel a date with Peter because

Grandpa wants to go over the driving booklet with me again. He flips through the pages, quizzing me and showing me pictures of right and wrong things to do. The book is full of large X's over things to avoid. Grandpa shows me an illustration of a car making a sharp sideways turn to skip over several lanes. The picture has a large red X over it. "Don't do that," he says.

"I know, Grandpa," I say. *Do you know I have a secret boyfriend that I can't tell you about and you're keeping me away from him tonight because you want to make me a nervous wreck who'll probably fail the driving test because you keep going over the same things over and over again as if I'm some dummy who can't do anything right, and that includes disobeying you because I have a secret boyfriend?*

I could be sipping on a strawberry smoothie, holding Peter's hand as we walk through the mall, but I'm sitting here being interrogated by Grandpa. He once mentioned to me that his father was some top official in Syria. They probably had torture chambers there where they pulled out people's fingernails and burned them with cigarettes. Grandpa might not torture me physically, but he's really good at hitting people's emotions. At least he's trying to improve ever since he apologized to Mom. He seems less pestering, which isn't saying much because he's had an overbearing personality ever since I can remember.

I'm relieved when the sun goes down and Mom serves dinner. Grandpa is busy gnawing chicken off the bone and I pick at my food. I wonder what Peter is doing at this moment since we can't go to the mall as we planned. He's probably eating dinner with his family, and they don't have to fast all day like we do, and he probably tells his mom about me since it's no big deal if he dates. I look over at Grandpa chewing his food. I look at his hands, which have stringy blue veins and faint liver spots. I wonder if he'd pick up a stone with one of his hands and throw it at me. Or maybe he'd slap me immediately, because my secret is so shameful. Would he really do that to his own granddaughter because he feels I deserve some sort of punishment for having a boyfriend? I'm sitting underneath an air conditioning vent and I shiver, not just from the cold but from these violent and guilty thoughts.

• • •

The next day, Mom picks me up from school and takes me to the DMV. I already took the written test and the drug and alcohol course for my learner's permit, so now I just need the driving test. Even though I felt uneasy last night and all day during school, I'm not nervous as I park, back up, stop at red lights, and turn corners. Taking the test makes my adrenaline run high, and I even ignore the BO of the tester—Mom's car stank as soon as he got in. There's an air freshener on the sun visor and, when he isn't looking, I tap on it to spray the car with a vanilla scent.

So despite Grandpa's anxiety-inducing quiz and the tester's strong odor, I pass and I'm an official driver, an official sixteen-year-old, an official girlfriend. Everything is official now. I wait in line to get my picture taken. Then, when I put my license in my wallet, I feel like such an adult. I keep taking it out, even though the picture is sort of dorky. My eyes are opened wide and I look too deer-caught-in-headlights. It says *Safe Driver* on the bottom of my license. I show Mom and she tells me that her license says the same thing. Whatever, so she doesn't know that this is a big deal for me. She's being her cool self as she drives us home, her shoulders shimmying to Van Halen's "Jump."

I'm jumpy as I listen to the song. Things seem so final now that I've survived an adventurous month, yet things are also just beginning. I'll drive more than ever before, whereas I used to drive only for practice. Lisa's relationship with me doesn't feel continuous after our spat; it's like there was a break and now we're starting all over again, the same way one rewinds a clock. And Peter and I are still so new, even though I feel like I've known him longer than I really have.

Eid, the end of Ramadan, is coming up this week. I'm planning on taking the day off of school for the holiday. Shakira wants us to go to South Beach, which is a hop, skip, and jump away from Coral Gables. Sure, we'll both wake up with our respective families to pray and eat breakfast, but the rest of Eid is about rejoicing the purification we experienced during our fast. Not only does my body feel right, but my spirit does, too. I feel light and happy. For our South Beach excursion I plan on wearing a cute pink dress, with a pink bathing suit underneath if the water is calm enough to swim in. This will be a Miami Eid for me, after all.

· · ·

I open my email in the morning. Sometimes that's the first thing I do in the morning: walk to the computer like a zombie and compulsively check my email, as if someone could possibly send me an urgent email between eleven at night and five in the morning. But my friends use their computers in the morning just like I do. I receive emails dated at five, five thirty, six o'clock, right before people have to leave for school. It can be a how-are-you message or a request for last-minute homework assistance. Dad once told me that he couldn't believe that kids these days email and text each other in the morning, as if we're so important and busy. But I do consider myself important and busy.

Twenty-three messages are in my inbox.

> *hi, beautiful, congrats that you went through your first*
> *Ramadan*
> *you're so strong to go through this cuz i couldn't*
> *you overachiever! good for you*

My heart gushes with emotion and I become teary-eyed. I had no idea that so many people, both friends and relatives, were cheering me on and thought so highly of me. I'm so down half the time, always pushing myself for more—grades, being skinny, competing in various school contests—that I don't realize all the good qualities I possess. I go on Facebook and update my status: *i did it guys, fasted for Ramadan. doing a happy dance!* Within minutes five people like my status. My phone's beeping with various text messages. Because I'm not in school today, my friends are texting from their bookbags, in their laps away from the eyes of teachers, and in bathrooms. The text messages echo the emails. And my friends miss me since I'm not with them in class. I drag myself away from the computer and my phone when I see that it's close to nine o'clock. Shakira is coming and I finish dressing to go out with her.

She honks outside. She's borrowing her Mom's Hummer and I step inside. It's like stepping up a ladder, the vehicle is so high. She's wearing a see-through tunic and I can see a turquoise bikini underneath. I used to think that her school clothes maybe hid some imperfections like bulges and stretch marks, but she has a perfect body. I think I look okay in my pink dress. I pinch my waist. I still have a bit of flab, but I can't complain. I look and feel good after fasting.

Mom waves at me from the living room window and I wave back. Shakira starts driving, and she drives kind of scary. She just got her license, same as me, not too long ago. She brakes sharply and tailgates. I grab onto my seat belt to brace myself in case something happens. Once we're on the highway, away from traffic lights, the drive isn't as terrifying. We drive over the causeway to Miami Beach feeling so awesome. We're taking the day off, and our parents even called our school to excuse our absences.

Shakira parks and the car shakes when she hits the curb. "Sorry," she says.

My legs wobble as I get out of the Hummer. I survived Ramadan and I survived Shakira's driving. She parks a few blocks from the beach. We have a scenic view of art deco buildings and hotels as we walk toward the sand. Shirtless men stop and whistle. Shakira smiles over her shoulder.

"You have a lot of admirers," I say.

"You do, too," she says, pinching my arm. And it's true. Some college-age guys are eyeing me, which makes me nervous. I've only recently gotten into boys, Peter being the first, so I don't know a lot about them. I smile and look away, since I'm taken.

We walk further along until we see sand spilling over concrete, then there's a wooden fence, and then we see the water. I'm breathless with this view of crashing waves. I even notice the awe in Shakira's face as she appreciates the ocean. We walk to the water and lay out some towels a few yards from where the waves crash. She takes off her tunic and I slip off my dress. It's winter, but warm. A breeze lifts our hair. We take turns rubbing sunblock on each other's backs and then rest on our sides to face each other.

"Do you ever wonder what your life would be like if you grew up in the Middle East?" I ask. "Sometimes I think about what would have happened if my mom's and dad's parents never came here. They all came for the same reason, for the freedom, for the opportunities, because of different wars or threats of war going on. Can you really picture it if they never came here? We'd be living over there. We would have no boyfriends. We couldn't wear our short skirts. The town gossips and family friends would bully us into obeying them."

"That's so weird," Shakira says. "Sometimes I wonder what I'd be like if I grew up there. I would have a different personality, different goals, different everything. It's strange how the environment shapes you. I email my cousins over there all the time, and they really think and act differently than I do. I try to imagine that I would be the same as I am now, but the truth is I would be different."

"But I'm glad that they came here. I like the way I live, even though my family can be strict."

"I know what you mean."

"And look at us, half naked on Eid."

Shakira giggles at the thought, especially since she's wearing considerably less fabric than I am. Her bikini is two triangles and a strip of cloth.

"Do you ever talk about Luis with your mom?" I ask.

"No," Shakira says. Her face is calm, but I can't read her eyes since she's wearing bug-eyed sunglasses. "I feel guilty and sometimes I want to say something, but I know she won't understand."

"I feel the same way."

Shakira turns her head upwards to face the sky. "We

have secret lives that we have to deal with. We'll be trail-blazers. Our children won't have to live through all this secrecy, or sneakcracy."

"I like the sound of that," I say. I envision my future kids—I already picked out the names Sebastian, Wolf-gang, and Ophelia—and how I'll never make them feel ashamed or embarrassed about having normal teenage urges.

A group of guys walk by and wink at us. I hear some innuendo and flirtatious remarks that hang in the wind. Shakira snaps the shoulder strap of my suit. "Look how sexy you are now," she says. "Look at us, on the beach, cutting class, having hot guys check us out. And we did it. I didn't cheat at all when I fasted."

"Me neither. I didn't think I could go through this Ramadan."

A year ago, when Grandpa caught me with choco-late wafer crumbs all over my lips, I felt something in me wither ... maybe dignity. How could I have told my family I was going to fast, and then cheat? I had been so psyched on fasting, researching Ramadan online and lis-tening to my parents talk about the new moon signaling the start of the holiday, and then it was a huge letdown that I couldn't last a few hours without food. They probably thought I was going to carry on a charade, lying to them about fasting, if Grandpa hadn't caught me red-handed. I let everyone down. But now, with the end of this current Ramadan, having successfully fasted every day, I can clearly see that I'm patient, dedicated, and persevering.

Shakira and I flip over so that our backs will get tanned. I don't want to get tan lines, so I pull my straps down, something the former Almira would never do. I want to keep my new tight little body. Looking down at my bathing suit, I can't believe how narrow my hips look. I vow that I'll start exercising with Mom, which will be hard since muscles that I've never used before will ache, but I imagine that we'll bond doing yoga and aerobics together. I'm no longer resentful of Mom's body now that I realize that we have the same body structure. I was never big-boned, but I used to be a big eater, munching on chips and tacos all day long. I also know that the next time Ramadan rolls around, I can fast much easier now that I've gotten used to it.

So now I have the body I want, and I'm girlfriend and best-friend material. I have what it takes to navigate dangerous Miami streets. My braces will come off in eleven months. Life doesn't seem as complicated as it once did— now that I see that good things, whether they come by hard or easy, can come my way.

I still wish I could share my romantic relationship with Mom as easily as I tell her I love a nail-polish color or that we should go get some Frappuccinos together. The blue-green water hits the sand while my mind wanders. I picture Mom and me in a coffee place, chatting easily. Our lattes sit in front of us. Her pretty face and flowing conversation fill me with warmth. I open my mouth to blurt my secret, but nothing comes out. I'm speechless during this mother-daughter coffee moment.

I guiltily close up when I imagine different scenarios of how to reveal this big secret to my parents. I don't know how to break it to them … but I hope that someday, I can tell them everything and they will understand.

About the Author

Medeia Sharif is a Kurdish-American author who was born in New York City, and she presently calls beautiful Miami Beach her home. She received her master's degree in Psychology from Florida Atlantic University. Not only does she write, but she's a high school English teacher. *Bestest. Ramadan. Ever.* is her first novel. Visit her online at http://www.sharifwrites.com.